NO ESCAPE

FROM A KILLER

A MEN OF THE BADGE NOVEL

RILEY
McKISSACK

No Escape from a Killer

ABOUT THE AUTHOR

Riley McKissack is an award-winning journalist. Cornered gunmen, cop killers, a bomb going off in a domestic terrorism incident, Riley's covered them all. Riley spent years chasing stories involving every type of bad guy and cop imaginable, including FBI, Homeland Security, homicide detectives and arson investigators.

Riley sponged up the drama, tension and danger on SWAT operations, hostage negotiations, drug busts and countless other dangerous situations.

That passion and drama spills out onto the pages of Riley's novels, along with the personal stories behind the men and women who stand between danger and the people they love.

Riley can be found at:
https://facebook.com/riley.mckissack
http://rileymckissack.com
https://twitter .com/RileyMckissack

JOIN THE RILEY MCKISSACK NEWSLETTER
http://www.rileymckissack.com/contact

CHAPTER ONE

Death could be just one careless moment away. A curling finger of mist trailed along the collarbone of the town of Hawk's Peak. From his perch on the mountain, he could easily spy on her.

Like a hawk looking down on an unaware little rodent. Nearby, a hawk circled on a wind current, screeching with that lovely, predatory cry that warned every animal around that a killer was in the air.

Emmy, as she called herself these days, was beginning to relax, with a sense of safety that could be the key to her death. She'd begun to ease back on her watchfulness.

That might be all it took. One lapsed moment of awareness of her surroundings.

A crisp mountain breeze blew through the open window of his dirt-colored SUV, a relief from the Georgia summer heat and humidity.

He'd sweated enough the last few days of summer to earn the money he'd get when she was dead. Wood smoke tinged the air, inciting his blood lust. For some crazy reason, fall always made him want to kill.

A burst of exhilaration pumped energy into his body. He was tired of waiting.

It was time to shake things up. He'd like to kill her now, but he could wait a bit more. He'd waited so long already, following, poking, and prodding her closer to insanity. Instead, she'd just fled again. But he always found her. She couldn't escape, wouldn't be able to outsmart him.

It would look better to the insurance adjusters and the cops if she killed herself. How much more could she take?

She needed another rattling, another dose of fear.

He rolled up the tinted windows and put his car into gear, sidling it quietly down the dirt road that led to the town square. Sliding along silently, as lethal as a hawk to a chipmunk.

The brisk air tossed Emmy Reynard's brunette hair wildly about as she crossed the town square of Hawk's Peak, named for the mountain that towered over it, which was named for the hawks that circled the mountain, soaring high into the air, their predatory screeches both beautiful and terrifying.

The town of Hawk's Peak felt comfortable and familiar to Emmy the first time she'd circled its square, the resemblance to the small town where she'd spent summers with her grandparents had tugged at her heart with a sense of home.

She'd pulled over and gotten hired on as a summer employee who might stay through the fall for the leaf-watching season when crowds of asphalt-and-concrete-exhausted people evacuated Atlanta and headed for the mountains and the rural ambiance of boiled peanuts, wood smoke, and fields of drying corn stalks and harvest orange pumpkins.

The town's square was made up of four sidewalks of stores that could have been used for a Hollywood backdrop of a southern movie. The type of town that every southerner remembered fondly in some way, as their childhood home or, as in Emmy's case, somewhere they visited relatives.

The brisk air brushed her face, evoking the exhilarating emotion that said, *fall at last*—every southerner's call to action and adventure. Fall, the time when humidity loosened its grip on the south.

Spicy wood smoke curled in the air, swirling above like the hawks, promising more beautiful, autumn North Georgia mountain days to come. Emmy inhaled deeply and smiled.

Was she finally free of her past? Did she have a future that she controlled?

Hope spiked through her.

Then, quickly, as if to taunt her, a dark feeling crept across her skin, an animal awareness of being watched. You'll never be free, it mocked.

She held her breath, stilling her breathing so she could hear every sound around her, instinctively contracting her stomach to make herself a smaller target, wrapping her arms around herself, protecting her vital organs.

Her nerves tensed, feeling someone coming for her. Striking her with a bullet from an anonymous gun? He could be perched on that mountain like a hawk in the breeze, ready to strike her the way the hawks dove from the sky like a lightning bolt upon an unaware squirrel or chipmunk.

That wasn't his style, but maybe he'd just want it done now, after this long year of chasing her from place to place.

Was that him she felt out there?

She stopped at the statue of the Confederate soldier in the middle of the roundabout, using its heavy stone base as a protective barrier.

She scanned the mountain that towered over the tiny town. Was someone watching her? Or was it merely her habit of fear that caused her heart to race, sending blood pulsing through her body, accompanied by her new constant companion, adrenalin?

She lowered her eyes to the plaque below the statue, as if reading all about the town's historic past, then carefully slid her gaze around to the side.

Her eyes scanned every inch of the square, with its comforting storefronts that screamed *Mayberry R.F.D., In the Heat of the Night*, or any other southern small town TV show or movie, then her gaze stopped at the corner pharmacy.

Mrs. McCloud, part of the senior husband-wife team who owned and ran the pharmacy, was sweeping the sidewalk in front of the pharmacy but stopped and lifted one hand to wave. "Hello, dear," Mrs. McCloud yelled in her high, sweet, old lady voice.

Emmy forced a smile as she drew in several deep breaths, taking a moment, letting her heart rate slow and willing her pulse to stop screaming blood through her veins. No one was watching her except the harmless Mrs. McCloud.

The stooped, round woman had an extensive collection of wrinkles on her still pretty face. Her gray hair was always well kept, as if an army of pink foam curlers marshaled it into order every night. A soft red lipstick outlined her smile.

She was the perfect grandmother. Like Emmy's grandma had been.

Man, Emmy still missed her, yearned for her warm, loving ways. Her embrace had been soft and squishy, and Emmy could sink straight through to her grandma's heart.

"You opening the store today?" Mrs. McCloud trilled.

"Yes ma'am, opening for Callie. It works out better now that her kids have started school." Emmy walked across the street, grateful for the presence of another human on the lonely, early morning street.

Mrs. McCloud smiled at Emmy, kind, caring, as if Emmy had been in town longer than just one steamy, hot summer. "Callie's lucky to have you, dear."

The compliment warmed Emmy, grateful to hear someone say she was a blessing. Before she could thank Mrs. McCloud, a car motor approaching the other side of the roundabout purred in the early morning quiet. She and Mrs. McCloud both swiveled their heads at the same moment. A dusty, light brown SUV came into view around a corner.

"Tinted windows," Mrs. McCloud noted. "They're from out of town."

"You know that by the windows?" Emmy trained her eyes on the windshield, straining to see the driver.

"No, sweetie. Nobody round here has windows that dark." Mrs. McCloud craned her neck, squinting her eyes. "The sheriff don't stand for it."

The SUV took a hard right at the opposite corner of the square, without signaling, heading away from them.

A shiver squirmed through Emmy, tickling along her nerve endings. The driver had veered away so suddenly, almost as if to avoid them, like they hadn't expected people on the square this early.

Could those be the eyes she'd felt watching her?

Was that him, circling closer, like the Red-tailed Hawks near her house, hovering high in the air, ready to streak earthward like a dagger onto its innocent prey?

As if in answer, a hawk yelled out the screech that they were known by. Threatening, warning, dangerous.

"You're shivering, dear. This early fall weather's caught you without a sweater." Mrs. McCloud touched the chill bumps on Emmy's arm.

A convulsive shiver shuddered through Emmy, carrying the cold straight to her bones. She wrapped her arms around herself, steeling herself against the fear. Her gun was in her purse. She wouldn't go down without a fight.

"I'll be okay, Mrs. McCloud, soon as I get into the store. I better hurry and open up, 'cause people will be wanting their coffee."

"Call me Margie, dear." Compassion lined the old woman's face, the empathy as clear to read as the wrinkles that spoke of the years she'd lived in the mountain town. The town where Emmy had hoped to find respite from her running.

Emmy touched Mrs. McCloud's arm, feeling the reassuring warmth of the sweet, old lady's presence.

She waved quickly and hurried away, wondering if her emotions were as easily read on her face as on Mrs. McCloud's.

The reassuring brick walls of The Corner Store beckoned to her, with their thickness providing defense against a bullet. Or so she hoped.

As Emmy walked, she looked back in the direction

the SUV with the tinted windows had traveled. Had it circled back around? She listened for the warning sound of an engine.

Though, he could have parked somewhere and sighted on her with a rifle from somewhere above the square.

She fumbled with the keys, dropping them and stooping quickly to retrieve them, looking over her shoulder as her breathing accelerated. Finally, she found the right key, jammed it into the lock and opened the door of The Corner Store.

She shut the door and inhaled deeply. The scent of yesterday's fire in the pot-bellied stove reassured her that she was now protected from an anonymous bullet.

He'd have to come in that door, announcing himself with the ring of the front door bell, giving her a chance to pull out her gun to defend herself.

She pulled her pistol from her purse and stuffed it into the back of her pants, tugging the waistband up and her shirt down to cover it. Then, she started her day, the way she'd started many days since arriving to the little town.

The deli and general store sat on one corner of the town square, down from the pharmacy. Just knowing the McClouds were already out and about gave her a sense of security.

She flipped on the lights and tried to distract herself from her fear with the daily rituals of opening the store. She started a pot of coffee, the strong smell circling her with a homey familiarity. The caffeine seekers would soon be here, wanting their morning Joe.

She checked the wooden built-in shelves, painted a crisp white and stretching from floor to ceiling, for anything out of place that needed straightening or restocking. Then, she went to the little pot-bellied stove that looked like it had been there since the store was built.

Striking a match, she ignited the little flame that would burn until closing time, when it would be allowed to slowly cool and go out. The fire caught on the paper and tinder that had been laid by Callie before she'd left the evening before and a cheery flame jumped up to surround the split kindling.

Soon it would be burning brightly, a place for the locals to warm their hands, gossip, drink coffee and remember things they needed but wouldn't have bought if they'd just run in and out quickly.

The fire gave a sense of community to the store, something Emmy savored daily. A sense of community she craved and didn't want to give up.

Please let me stay, let me finally be safe, she prayed silently.

A little bell over the door jangled like an alarm. She jumped and jerked around.

"Hey there, girlie." Mr. McCloud lifted a grizzled, age-spotted hand in greeting as he shuffled in the door. "See you got the coffee going."

"Would I let you down?" She tried to stretch a normal smile across her face, instead feeling like The Joker with an artificial-feeling, strange grimace.

Mr. McCloud looked at her for a moment with his usual kind expression, then turned and took his personal mug down from the wall. He put it underneath the stream of coffee, sneaking a cup while it was still brewing. His normal morning routine.

He hadn't donned his white pharmacy jacket yet. His

crisp khaki slacks and his ironed cotton plaid shirt were as neat as the store he kept. Salt of the earth. A man his family could count on.

She'd bet he'd never lifted a hand even in threat to Mrs. McCloud. The old woman would have whacked him with her broom if he had. Not that he would have.

"You get enough sleep last night, girlie?" He glanced over his shoulder while he waited for his mug to fill.

Though he was way too old to protect anyone, he made her feel safe, with his fatherly façade, kind and concerned.

"Yep." She smiled a more normal smile now, the fear receding. Did he know about her many sleep-deprived nights?

Glancing in the little mirror on the wall behind the counter, she pulled her hair back into a ponytail and quickly checked for dark circles under her eyes.

Last night she'd slept deeply, only to be awakened by nightmares early in the morning. The dreams were back.

Those same dreams came whenever she'd begun to feel safe, as if warning her not to get too comfortable, to be ready at any time to flee, to go with whatever little money she'd managed to save in her brief respite from running.

How much did her subconscious know? Did it protect her from what it felt she couldn't handle?

Were her restless nerves her mind's way of warning her to flee now, to run for her life?

She fixed a smile on her face and turned back toward Mr. McCloud.

He shuffled toward the counter, placing fifty cents

on it, the cost for regulars who used their own mugs. Then he looked at her for a long moment.

"Everyone's real happy you've come to town, missy." He watched for a reaction, something in his tone seemed to know she was poised, ready to bolt.

"Thanks." She put on her best just-a-girl-looking-for-a-summer-job smile.

"You gonna stay around till after the leaf peepers stop coming up from the city?"

Her boss, Callie, had practically begged Emmy not to leave until things died down, until the summer and fall busy seasons had passed.

A hint of worry played on Mr. McCloud's face, the wrinkles deepening as he narrowed his eyes at her.

Emmy's heart clenched as if it would stop beating, as if it were waiting for her answer, hoping she'd finally found a safe haven.

Then, the bell jangled again and they both looked. A large body filled the doorframe. Luke Bradenton.

Emmy's heart pulsed quickly into high gear, sending blood racing throughout her body, filling her cheeks with a flush.

Mr. McCloud turned back to her, a knowing smile quickly flitting across his face.

"Hey, Ira." The deep, masculine timbre in Luke Bradenton's voice infused the store's small space with a pheromone-laced kick.

Every female cell in her body yelled she'd been without a man too long. True, if just a few words from this man could have this strong of an effect on her.

His good ole boy clothes, jeans, boots and a well-worn, faded blue cotton T-shirt, seemed almost a disguise to make him look like just any other guy.

But, it wasn't just the body underneath those clothes that denied that. Luke Bradenton, *the widow man*, as Callie referred to him, exuded a maleness that called out to every estrogen impulse in Emmy's body.

A slow burn started in her chest, spreading up her neck to her face.

He'd begun regularly appearing just after she'd switched to the morning shift. She wanted to pretend she hadn't started looking for him, anticipating his appearance, checking the clock if he didn't show.

But heck, you oughta be honest with yourself at least, since you're not being honest with anyone else.

Luke ambled to the pot-bellied stove, warming his hands. Those well-worn jeans, with a small rip at the knee, cradled a fit body.

His sandy blond hair was shaggy now, getting longer all the time, a throwback look to the hippy seventies. Her grandpa had shown her photos of those times. Luke's beard was growing in pretty well, too.

As if the guy thought he could hide his good looks behind a lot of hair. That wasn't working.

"How's the fishing gonna be today, Ira?" he said casually to Mr. McCloud.

"Well, Luke, depends on what you're fishing for." Mr. McCloud shot Emmy a knowing smile. She kept her face as impassive as she could manage with all that blood pulsing beneath her skin.

"Trout," Luke answered. Then he took his turn at the coffee pot, filling the travel mug he always brought with him. Then he approached the cash register and pulled his wallet out of his back pocket. "I need some ice, too." He smiled at Emmy, handing her a five.

Just a normal smile.

But, their fingers touched as she took the money. And, for just a second, she saw a flash in his eyes, an awareness that felt an awful lot like what she could remember from so very long ago as attraction in a man's eyes, that draw between a man and a woman. A rubber band push-pull, sawing back and forth between them, a tension that threatened to throw her off balance.

The kind of attraction that frightened her.

So many years ago, it would have filled her with joyful anticipation.

Back when she'd thought the male-female attraction was a good thing, innocent, a safe thing.

A lifetime ago.

Now, it seemed as though she'd had a lifetime of looking over her shoulder. Of wondering if she would have to pay with her life.

All because of that male-female attraction. Because she'd fallen in love with the wrong man.

A dangerous, cunning man who would do whatever it took to make her pay for wanting to leave him.

CHAPTER TWO

She knew she was dreaming, but couldn't wake herself up. So, she had to endure it like she'd endured it so many times before in the last year:

Max Weber grabbed her collar, twisting it till she could barely breathe. He yanked her close to his face, so she could read his anger, his murderous intent.

"I've done killed one troublesome woman and got away with it. I can kill you, too." He leered down into her face.

He'd do it.

He'd do it and nobody would ever doubt him. Women would console him at the funeral and get on the list to take Emily's place, coming to the house with food in the days following her death.

Cops knew all the tricks to killing. And getting away with it, apparently.

That poor woman who'd slept with Max, then threatened to tell Emily about the affair, according to rumors afterward, had died inside a burning building. Had her heart exploded long before the fire or smoke reached her, from the pain of knowing the man she'd thought loved her had tied her up and left her to die in a burning building?

A desperate need for air took precedence over anything else right now for Emily—surviving the next few moments.

"I can't breathe," she squeaked.

Max merely grinned and twisted her shirt tighter. "Where's your granddaddy?"

Where Max would never find him.

She grasped her shirt neck with both hands, pulling at the cloth that cinched her air pipe nearly shut. Would strangling someone with their own shirt disguise that it had been a murder? Max would know.

He yanked her up onto her tiptoes with the shirt. They stood in the living room of the assisted living facility where her grandpa had stayed for the past two years.

Max had insisted her grandpa couldn't live with them, that they weren't qualified to care for him. Of course, he'd only dropped that shoe after they were married, after the honeymoon.

She'd moved her grandfather into this facility so the man who'd always been there for her would be close to her and Max's home. Then, moved him out again so Max would never find him.

She'd returned to the facility for more of her grandfather's belongings. And Max had tracked her down here.

"You even think about leaving me, girl, and I will kill something you love."

She looked up into his eyes, and suddenly she knew what he meant. "Charlie," she squeaked. "You hurt Charlie!" Her little dog. She'd left him all alone in that house.

The hand clenching her shirt tightened again.

"I know what you were planning. And somebody, or something you love," he grinned malevolently, *"will pay for your actions."*

She had to get home and see what this monster had done to Charlie. Poor little dog. He loved her so much.

Suddenly, she sat up in bed.

"You're awake!" she said loudly to herself. "You're awake! It's just a dream. Nothing is happening to you right now." But, she rubbed her throat, and felt as if she still were choking and gasping for air. Her windpipe felt almost as if it had been crushed. Air couldn't seem to pass into her lungs.

She looked frantically around, checking the shadows for Max. Though she'd escaped that day, Max had won to some degree.

Because of how many of her nights he returned to strangle and terrorize her.

Suddenly, her blood cooled into a thick gelatinous cold mass. And she remembered the poor little mutt who'd loved her more than she deserved. She said a silent prayer for his little soul.

For the little guy who shouldn't have had to pay the price for Emily's misstep.

She'd known if Charlie wasn't at home Max would have instantly guessed something was up.

All she'd wanted to do was get her grandpa's final stuff out of the facility and to his new place. Then, she was going back to get the dog and take off forever.

BZZT. BZZT.

Her cell phone practically skittered around on the bedside table. It lit up. What more could it do to get her attention?

Nothing good could come from a call at this time of the morning. It was still dark outside.

She glanced at the face of the phone as she yanked it up.

"Grampa. Are you okay?"

"Are *you* okay?" his deep voice rumbled back at her.

She laughed weakly. "I'm okay."

"Well, if you're okay, then I'm okay, and everything's right in the world."

He was the best grandpa anybody could ever dream of. If only he would live forever.

But, he wouldn't live forever and she was losing time with him.

"I've got to get you up here where I'm living now, Grampa. You would love it."

"Hmmm," he rumbled back with a negative tint. "You don't have no business being anywhere near Georgia. You're far away, aren't ya, girl?"

Lie to her Grampa? She'd never done it.

"Nope, Grampa. I'm pretty close actually, if you consider in the state close." He hadn't asked that precise question since she'd been back in Georgia and she'd always pranced around his vague questions. But, lying to him?

No.

He didn't say anything. The man could say far more with no words than anyone she'd ever known. They read each other's thoughts. Always had.

"I woke up worried about ya, girl. Couldn't sleep." He laughed. "And, if I can't sleep, why should you?"

His deep, rumbling laugh came through the phone,

warming her, chasing away the horror of her dream. "I was actually having a bad dream. Glad you called," she murmured.

"Aaah." He waited.

"Grampa, I think I could bring you up here where I'm living at some point."

Nothing.

"But first, I need to find out what happened to Max. Really find out."

"Mmmmm." No real words, just that sound, that sound that said, *Be careful, girl. Be careful.*

"It's not fair that he gets away with this, Grampa. Keeping you and me apart."

"If he is alive, then you better believe he's dangerous, Emmy. Why do you think he would do something like disappear, fake his own death?"

"I don't know, Grampa. But you can bet he's got a plan. He always has a plan. And we may never know what it is, till it's too late."

Her grandpa just harrumphed quietly. Then, he cleared his throat. "Do you think it had something to do with those life insurance policies he took out on both of you? Or how he changed his will?"

"They were large life insurance policies," she conceded. "If either he or I died, there'd be a pile of money to console the other."

"And that will," her grandpa said what Emmy was thinking.

Why had Max drawn up that new version of his will? The one where Max's brother would get anything Max owned if Emmy was out of the picture. He'd always despised his little brother's need for drugs. Said

17

if he left him any money, it would just hasten his death by drug abuse.

Silence drifted along the cell phone towers, bouncing through the night with the lonely sound of nothingness.

Whispering the regrets of the last year with all the lost time between her and her Grampa.

"Grampa, I miss you." The words forced tears to her eyes, from the tear ducts that had begun dying from lack of use. Because if she'd learned anything this last year, it was that tears were a waste of time and useless against true evil.

True evil just laughed at tears, thrived on it, as proof that it was winning.

Evil wouldn't win.

She pushed back the tears. "I love you, Grampa. I'm going to see you soon. I'm going to figure this out. Sneak down at night into Atlanta, creep around to his old haunts and see what I can find out."

Nothingness bounced along the mountain cell phone towers again.

Finally, her grandpa sighed. "I won't try and talk you out of it. Couldn't nobody ever talk you out of something once you'd decided it was the only thing to do."

Why deny the truth? She was hardheaded. Always had been. Max had thought he could wring it from her with criticism and hardness.

But, she wasn't a little child or a puppy. And it was time to stop acting like it. Time to bite back? Head down to Atlanta and look around?

Find the spot where Max, the bully dog, was hiding his bone.

There'd be a woman. There was always a woman with Max.

Emmy would find the woman who thought it was a good idea to shelter him, who believed his lies and smooth talking.

CHAPTER THREE

Sunlight exploded on the river, each watery ripple reflecting back sparkling prisms of sunshine, like crystals sprinkled across the surface of the Chattahoochee River.

Luke waded through the river, watching and waiting for the perfect moment, the exact right opportunity.

He could see the trout swimming through the ripples, taunting him, just beyond his reach, determined not to be drawn in.

A force to be reckoned with, wise to the point of knowing when to dodge and when to run. He'd dealt with that kind before. He didn't always win.

But, he was going to win this time.

That damn fish didn't know who he was dealing with. Luke cast out his line once more, playing it like a delicate morsel the trout should want.

The North Georgia mountain water ran as clear as water from a faucet, with colored polished pebbles lining the bottom of the river. Above them, the outline of the old fish shimmered, perfectly visible, as if it were framed and upon a wall.

Or on a dinner plate.

Though Luke would only catch and release this guy. An ancient fish like that couldn't be dinner.

"Damn," he cursed out loud when the fish swam on upstream, looking for more naïve victims from whom he could steal bait.

"Shouldn't let a fish make you cuss." The light, feminine voice came from the bank.

He swung around. Emmy. A quick punch of excitement shot through him and his pulse double-timed. "Hello!" he called back to her.

He might not have the fish but he'd caught something better, a bit of luck.

He waded toward the bank, taking in her shorts that left a lot of tanned, toned leg visible. For once, her hair was down, brushing across her shoulders, silky, freshly washed from the look of it.

What would that copper-burnished hair smell like if he nosed into it? Like the lavender scent that had wafted by him once when she'd passed near him to help another customer?

"You hunting for fish?" he said in his most casual, I'm-not-fascinated-with-your-long-legs manner.

"Only fish I like is battered, with fries and some ketchup. Never liked meeting my dinner before I eat it."

He grinned. "A common attitude, I've found."

She smiled, and then her clear green eyes flickered with something else, closing down, on guard. The road was some distance away. They were all alone, since hardly anyone ever came by here at this time of day.

He knew because he'd checked out this stretch of river several times before today.

Emmy started backing away, and he stopped,

keeping the riverbank and several feet of water between them. It would take time getting up that steep bank, time for her to run.

She measured the distance, seeming to come to the same conclusion because she stopped backing up.

"Whatta you doing out here, if you're not fishing?" he asked as if he didn't know, know that often she walked along this bit of riverbank, had seen her as he drove along the river road looking for new places to fish.

She looked at him for a moment, then nodded. "Just walking. Love the Hooch. It's so beautiful."

"Yeah, the Chattahoochee doesn't look anything like this in Atlanta."

She stilled, her eyes fixing on his face.

"That's where I live," he added. Damn, he'd almost spooked her, mentioning Atlanta as if he knew that's where she was from.

"Really? You've been in the area a while now. I thought you'd relocated here."

He decided to spit out the truth, or close to the truth. If Callie hadn't already told her. "It's been a while since my wife died. Decided it was time to get away, get out of the house we'd shared for so long. I needed some fresh horizons, a different landscape."

Her face softened. Women always got that look when conversation veered toward his dead wife.

This was the first person he'd told directly. Everyone who knew him already knew about Mazie's long battle with leukemia. Usually, he avoided the subject, his throat closing up, choking off words like dying, leukemia, dead. But, for some reason, he'd wanted to tell Emmy.

It was crazy but he'd wanted to tell her something about himself.

He knew so much about her.

"I'm staying at my Uncle Joe's place, a cabin on the river about five miles upstream," he tried to steer the subject away from death.

She looked at him, not asking why he was all the way down here on the river.

"My uncle told me about this little hole just a bit downstream of that bridge up there." He tilted his head toward the bridge close to where he'd parked his Jeep. "Told me about this monster trout that nobody can catch."

She laughed slightly. "I guess he was right."

He nodded in concession. "The trout lives to tell another story about humans he's outsmarted."

She smiled and there was that sparkly, lively something in her eyes again that made him want to keep talking, say anything just to keep her around. Keep her looking at him.

"Did you grow up in the mountains, Emily?"

Her eyes rounded. "It's Emmy." Her voice sounded weak and breathless.

"Sorry. I just assumed Emmy was short for Emily." The cop part of him had hoped she'd stumble, reveal incriminating information. The male side of him hoped everything had a logical explanation.

"You're right. It is Emily. But I never liked that name. People I'm closest to have always called me Emmy."

That said a whole lot about her husband and the world she'd lived in with him.

Cause everybody who knew her through her

23

husband had called her Emily. The news accounts had called her Emily.

No matter what first name she might prefer, what last name she might use now, he still knew she'd shared a last name with a man whose name decorated a tombstone down in Atlanta.

A dead cop's tombstone, for whose murder no one had been charged and whose body had never been found. Though Max's no-account brother had thrown a funeral, attended by his brother's no-account friends. Cops had shown up and given another cop a proper send off.

Standing alongside guys like Max's brother, Carl, who on any other day, they're rather have been arresting.

Taps, a motorcycle escort with a long line of blue lights. Behind a casket the cop association had bought the family. A casket that carried nothing but a few mementoes and medals awarded to Max.

Carl had wanted the whole shebang for his brother.

Because, it was intimated, this five-foot, four-inch woman had dragged Max's six-foot, two-inch body somewhere off into the woods and hidden it.

Okay, if you believed that. If anyone had done it, it would have been some of Carl Weber's buddies. For whatever reason.

Maybe that recently revised will and the large insurance policy?

Yeah, this compact beauty in front of him had a familiar face.

She was Emily Weber, AKA Emmy Renard.

Her hair was a different color, a coppery brown now, with highlights of new penny. Before, it had been a showy blonde.

But he'd recognized her. Not at first. It had bugged him, wondering where he'd seen her. Then, like a slap in the face, it had flashed full in his memory.

The blonde on the arm of the now-dead cop. She'd gone missing the same day the crime scene had been discovered.

Some of the bloodiest crime scene photos he could recall. Splatters on the walls. His cop cousin, Forrester, had brought some by the hospital to show Luke, since he'd been on the way to a meeting with the insurance agent, to check the details of the policy.

How such a little woman could have done that much damage to a man had been all he Forrester had talked about.

There'd been some talk that she might have been killed as well.

But, there'd been only one blood type at the scene of the original crime in the house, that of the husband. Confirmed by a DNA match from hair found in his comb.

His wife could have been taken to another location and killed. At least that was the original theory.

But the location of the wife, dead or alive, had been the key question as time dragged on. Money had been pulled from the bank account the day the crime scene was called in by Max's brother.

Forrester said Emmy had taken it. But that it wasn't much. Luke could have guessed that from the looks of the ramshackle house she was renting.

Luke had only secondhand information, since he'd been on leave, spending every moment at his wife's hospital bed during a particularly rough episode.

When he had gone back to work, it had been in

undercover support. So he'd had very little to do with the murder case of Max Weber.

Most of Luke's thoughts had centered on his wife—how she was doing, if another bout of leukemia was on the horizon, searching for cures, treatments. It had been all-consuming. And exhausting.

He really hadn't given a damn who'd killed Max Weber. The guy had had it coming for years.

If it hadn't been about one woman, it would have been about another. The guy was a pussy hound. And everyone in the department knew it, watched their women when he was around, and kept him away from their sisters.

He'd lived like a dog and, it sounded like, died like one.

"You catch anything yet?" Emmy peered down into the water at a line that was attached to the bank.

"Yep, a couple." He walked closer, lifting the line to show off three beauties he'd nabbed earlier. "You could come for dinner if you like."

Why the hell had he said that? Was it how she looked in those shorts? Or those eyes, intensely green?

Those river-colored eyes rounded with alarm at his invitation, fastening on him as if it were illegal where she came from for men and women to get together.

She narrowed her eyes, her mouth tightening. "Thanks," she answered. But, her expression looked as if he'd cut her off in traffic. "I can't. Got a lot going on."

She nodded several times as if that were that.

"Another time then," he said, for some reason not wanting to give it up. It wasn't the way she looked, the instant pulse acceleration she inspired.

It wasn't.

He merely wanted to get to know her better, draw her out, get her to let her guard down. Then, maybe she'd divulge some information about Max's death.

It wasn't that quick impulse to touch her he'd begun feeling every time he was around her, the urge sneaking up on him slowly, then coming on quicker and stronger each time he was near her.

She started backing away slowly and his hands itched to reach out and take hold of her, to not let her leave.

Those tanned, toned legs just called out to his hands, to touch them. But, he'd probably combust into a ball of flame at first contact.

Damn, man, shut it down. Quit letching on the poor woman.

Sick as it was, seeing her had become the highlight of his day. Outside of the store, alone with her here on the river, the sensation was heightened.

He hadn't noticed any other woman since his wife had died. Lots of widowers would have been seriously involved with a woman by now.

But, he couldn't lose the woman he'd loved and expected to spend his life with, then, when she died, just say, "Next."

Lately, though, he was starting to get an inkling of what people meant about moving on. Lately, he'd begun waking up without the persistent gray Jell-O covering everything, stretching before his eyes toward the horizon.

Since he'd met Emmy at the store, he'd begun getting up earlier and earlier, hardly able to wait until it was time to go down to the store and see if she was working the opening shift that day.

He felt alive again, as if he'd finally crawled out of the grave where he'd buried his wife. The day they'd lowered her into the ground, his world had stopped.

Now, it had begun spinning again. Faster and faster, everything centering on the moments he spent with Emmy Renard, aka Emily Weber.

Someone had made life worth living again.

But, damn, did it have to be with a woman who might have killed her last husband and done such a bang up job of hiding the body that she'd never been charged.

Just damn.

CHAPTER FOUR

Emmy hurried along the riverside trail toward her rented, ramshackle little house, aching to be inside its walls, the first place in the last year that had felt like home, actually felt safe. She touched the back of her shorts' waistband for her pistol.

The reassuring steel of the gun felt empowering, almost an extension of her body after her hours of practice with it.

Gun ranges had become her second home for a while. She'd become a deadly shot.

Walking into the shooting area, guys were flirting with her, joking, checking her out.

Walking out, not so much. A couple of guys had even decidedly avoided eye contact with her as she left.

The owner of one gun range had commented that Emmy went into a zone when she started shooting. "I gotta wonder who you're aiming at, with that look you get on your face," he'd said in a half joking manner, his mouth twitching a bit as he tried to smile.

"A man," she'd said simply, then pivoted and walked away.

"I kinda figured that," the owner had muttered behind her.

She'd thrown a cold smile over her shoulder just before the door swung closed behind her. She didn't need any man sniffing around her.

As she continued down the river path toward her home, a nervous sensation washed across her skin. Eyes watching? Dread eased past the defiance she'd felt moments ago, with her hand on her pistol.

Was he out there, watching and refusing to reveal himself?

Just this morning, when she'd spoken to her grandpa on the phone, she'd been so bold, planning to go down to Atlanta and ferret out Max.

Now, wondering was he stalking her, again the terror pushed in on her.

Her breathing felt unnatural as the blood pulsed out of her heart, gathered in her ears and began buzzing.

The whirring in her body made it hard to hear anything around her, but she concentrated on the woods just beyond her vision, watching for movement, until finally she reached her driveway.

Glancing back, she dashed inside and turned the deadbolt that she'd installed herself, making sure no one else had a key to enter her house.

She positioned her No-Kick-Ins device, touted to keep a raging bull from getting through your door.

She walked to the tightly curtained window, stood to the side and flicked the curtain aside just a tiny bit. Scanning the front yard and the driveway leading into the property, she saw no one. That didn't mean he wasn't out there.

The area beyond her yard was a tangled growth of strangling vines, overgrown bushes and ancient trees swirling together into a leafy morass that hikers had been known to disappear into and never be found again, as if they'd been swallowed whole by the forest.

Deep gulping breaths resounded in her ears like an animal sneaking up behind her. She pulled the pistol from her waistband and twirled quickly.

Pointing in a wide circle, searching for whoever had violated her home, her supposedly secure space, she readied herself for attack.

Her vision began to gray, her breathing became a panting, a huffing noise that sounded bizarre even to her own ears.

The soundtrack to a panic attack. She'd almost passed out during her first few panic attacks.

Now, she knew to breathe in and breathe out slowly and steadily so she wouldn't pass out just as he aimed for a killing shot.

Counting to three on the exhale, she then inhaled on a three count until finally the room came into clear focus.

Now that her breathing wasn't loud in her ears, a car's engine solidified as it came closer to the house. Had her sixth sense realized the car was coming even before she could fully detect its approach?

She turned to the window and moved the curtain an inch, waiting. He wouldn't come in a car, in the light of day. He'd creep in the night like something primordial slinking toward the house, something from out of the mire of a swamp.

Something horrifying.

He wouldn't drive up in an SUV like the one finally emerging from the woods.

Callie's SUV.

"Thank God," she murmured, blowing out the long

puff of air she'd been holding. Her body relaxed with the realization that it didn't need to fight or flee, and her legs went wobbly.

Callie. She could use a little bit of Callie, with her down to earth normality.

Her boss's tires sprayed gravel as she whirled in the driveway, coming to a stop underneath a tree, to the side as if she didn't want to block traffic. Like Emmy got a whole lot of visitors. Callie jumped out of her car and headed toward Emmy's front door.

Callie's dark, glossy hair shimmered in the daylight, with an opal blue streak discreetly tucked underneath but flashing now in the bright light as she strode across the driveway. Her cut-off jeans shorts were high on her thigh, nearly short enough to prove she was a girl, and her cowboy boots came to mid calf.

Irreverent, sassy and ready for anything, Callie was the original goodtime girl, in the purest sense of the word, someone you called to kick your party off right.

"Emmy," she called, her voice light and clear, not worrying about anyone noticing her. She didn't try to keep a low profile, wasn't afraid to draw attention.

Emmy stuck her pistol back into her waistband and made sure her shirt covered it. Then, she removed the No-Kick-Ins device from the door, turned the deadbolt, unlocked the doorknob lock, removed the safety chain, and opened the door.

Callie stared at her, her eyes wide. "How many locks you got on that thing?" She laughed lightly.

Emmy glanced at the door. "A couple." She didn't tell her about the chair she jammed up under the knob before bedtime and her little No-Kick-Ins device, or the one for the back door.

And little alarm devices she pasted on the windows and doors of every place she moved into.

"What's wrong with you, you look so pale?" Callie touched her arm. "You look like one of my kids after they've had a nightmare."

Emmy ignored the question and stepped outside into the sun. "Who's minding the store?"

"It's Sunday, remember?"

"Oh, yeah." Hawk's Peak still maintained old-time, southern traditions, with most everything closing down like a ghost town on Sundays.

"That's kind of neat how everybody takes the day off."

"It's the Lord's day," Callie said, with an impish smile. "The official day of fried chicken and peach cobbler."

Emmy felt her blood pressure lowering. Callie was just so normal that it was hard with her around to worry about the boogey man. Also known as her *dead* husband.

"Saw the widow man fishing down on your piece of the river." Callie raised an eyebrow. "What say we walk up the trail a bit?" She hitched her head in Luke's direction.

"I already did." Emmy felt her face heating.

"Oooh, what's that tomato-red color crawling up your neck?" Callie stepped closer, angling her head and looking pointedly at Emmy's cheeks and neck. "I do believe that's the color of attraction, the first blush of love."

She smiled wickedly at Emmy. "I guess you got first dibs on him?"

"No." Emmy tried to look indignantly at Callie but didn't think she was really pulling it off.

"Uh huh." Callie smiled knowingly. "Mrs. McCloud told me there was some sparking going on 'tween y'all two. Her words, not mine."

Callie hooked her thumbs into the waistband of her jean cutoffs and leaned back onto the heels of her cowboy boots, the better to inspect Emmy's face. "I'm starting to think she's right."

What to do now? If she denied it, Callie would say she was protesting too much. If she didn't deny it, then she'd say it must be true.

So, she just narrowed her eyes at Callie "Is he why you stopped over here, to have an excuse to walk up his way?"

Callie burst out laughing. "I ain't looking for my next baby daddy. Those two babies I got are keeping me busy enough."

"Where are they? Mike have them?"

"Yep." Callie nodded. "Thank heavens for a good ex. Took them out to his folk's place for fried chicken and cobbler. At least somebody's keeping the tradition alive for them." She lifted her face and raised her hands to the sky. "But, I got something better than cobbler, a baby-free day. Too good to be true."

She twirled and walked over to plop down on the wooden bench that fronted up to a faded wooden picnic table. Then, she turned sideways to raise her feet onto the bench and lean back, supporting her weight on her arms, turning her face up to the sun.

Always friendly, always upfront about what she was thinking, Callie had felt like family from the moment Emmy had met her.

She was a fireball of energy, careening around town with her two kids, keeping up with her children's needs, a dog, the store and all the local gossip. Laughing, telling stories, and it seemed, always noticing what Emmy might need, inviting her out to supper with her kids, when all Emmy had to look forward to after the store closed was dinner alone.

Callie was refreshing and fun, after a year with no good times at all and lots of lonesomeness.

"This fall weather feels great." Emmy sat across from Callie on the bench on the other side of the picnic table.

"Cool, but you can still get a suntan. Probably get a better one if we walked up the river to sit in the sun near that fishing spot of the widow man." Callie slanted Emmy a sideways look.

"You're not gonna give this up, are you?" Emmy laughed, feeling her mood lighten with each moment in Callie's presence. "Okay, he's cute, I guess, if you like that kind." She'd give her that much.

"The hunky, want-to-take-him-now type?"

Emmy laughed. "Yeah, that type."

"So, whatcha doing today if you're not hanging out with the widow man? Want to come on over to my place? I made up this *hunking* pot of spaghetti sauce. We could heat up some pasta and talk about the hot man."

Emmy looked around at the darks woods that had seemed so threatening a moment ago. With Callie here, all that had disappeared.

They were just two girlfriends joking around, like normal people.

"Yeah, let me get my purse." With a nod of the head, Emmy walked back in the house and grabbed her purse, tucking her gun into its depths. She turned the key, locking the deadbolt, then hopped into Callie's dust-colored SUV, so dirty it was hard to tell where mud left off and the vehicle's tan color took over.

Callie gunned the engine with a laugh, swung it around and headed out the driveway, spraying gravel, back to the road that ran along the river, passing Luke just as he was walking to his Jeep.

Callie slowed her SUV, stopping level with the back of his car.

"Oh no, you didn't," Emmy said low to Callie.

"Hey, Fisherman Luke, you catch anything?" Callie yelled across the road.

He turned to give them a friendly grin, taking in Emmy sitting on the other side of Callie with a lift of his head that sparked a little explosion inside her stomach and sent sparkles shooting through her veins.

"Matter of fact, I did." He held up a string of trout, each enough for one person's meal.

"Whatcha gonna do with all those, Fisherman Luke?"

Oh damn, Callie was angling for an invite to dinner.

He raised an eyebrow with interest, like a trout eyeing the bait. "I could cook 'em up if y'all'd come on out to my place."

"Do you need anything else for supper? We'll stop by the Corner Store and pick up stuff. It may be closed but I know the owner," Callie said about her own store.

He smiled, tilted his head side to side for a second as if going over his pantry stock. "Nothing, I guess. I got everything yesterday. Knew you'd be closed."

"I like a man who's prepared." She cocked an eyebrow. "Who's always *ready*."

Luke half-laughed at Callie's ribald attempt at humor.

Callie laughed good-naturedly, tilting her head as if she knew her comment had been lame. "We'll follow you up to your uncle's place."

"Okay, but you'll have to give me a minute to pick up the underwear off the living room floor 'fore y'all come in."

"Yours? Or some tourist chick's panties?" Callie grinned. Comments like that often got people to spill good info. The way Callie framed her comments always sounded like a joke, but still kinda close to the truth.

Luke just laughed, shaking his head, and continued loading up fishing poles and his tackle box into the back of his Jeep.

Callie and Luke joked like people who'd known each other since they were teenagers. Or since Callie had been a teenager at least. Callie was twenty-five.

Whereas, Luke looked to be in his early thirties. A man but with the *young* still written all over him, a lusty undertone to his demeanor. As if he were old enough to know what to do and still young enough to do it all night.

Emmy felt the heat starting somewhere lower than her beltline and heading toward her brain, as if it might boil away all the common sense and self-restraint she practiced so hard. As if just looking at that man might heat her brain past the point of all decency before the night was through.

He sported worn jeans and rubber boots that he now kicked off, leaving him standing on the side of the road in his bare feet.

Damn, who knew bare feet could be so sexy. The sight of the bare flesh of even his feet caused a lusty reaction in Emmy.

Callie had told her about the crush she'd had on him at one point when she was a teenager, even though he'd made it clear she was way too young for him. "He's just so protective and manly," she'd said in a swooning voice. "Gotta love a big old sexy man that wants to protect every women he meets."

Callie pulled up to a spot on the other shoulder of the road to wait for Luke to get into his car. "Girl, he is hot." Callie shook her hand like she'd just burned it. "You better nab him quick. 'Cause them widow men don't last long."

Emmy laughed. "Widow men don't last long? Like he's on sale or something."

"They're flying off the shelf." Callie emphasized the comment with a waggle of her head. "He's a guy who can commit. Been married, probably wants to be married again. Sooner rather than later. It's been long enough. He's over the initial shock. And since his wife had leukemia, he saw it coming, the long goodbye and all that."

Would that be any easier, seeing it coming? Dreading the death of the marriage. Instead of having to plot to get out of a marriage like she had to do.

It was irrelevant how quickly the widow man Luke would be off the market. Because, technically, she was still married. Or was she? Maybe legally she was a widow, too.

But, she knew in reality she wasn't. Max wasn't dead. He was out there, just waiting. Waiting for her to get comfortable. Like she'd done recently?

He'd waited until her attention was diverted. Like it tended to do whenever Luke was around?

CHAPTER FIVE

Cabin wasn't an appropriate word for Luke's uncle's vacation house. Two sprawling floors with a large, open first floor greeted them as they entered. A kitchen fronted off the living room.

The only thing *cabin* about it was the wood beamed ceiling.

A huge picture window framed the Indian mound across the road, for which the valley was named, beyond the mound, mountains danced away to the horizon, smoky and blue in the approaching dusk.

"So beautiful." Emmy stared out, cradling the glass of beer Luke had put into her hands. She hadn't taken a sip, not needing alcohol to interfere with her determination not to end up in Luke's bed.

Though that image was all that kept playing through her head. She and Luke using a bed for anything but sleeping, their bodies getting to know each other. Getting to know each other well.

Also, there was a dangerous impulse to divulge information to him that was already becoming a problem for her. Every morning when he dropped in for coffee and ice, he took a few moments to make conversation, always leaving her wanting more time with him.

"It's a beautiful view, isn't it?" Luke appeared behind her, closer than she expected, closer than was smart, because her entire body responded to the nearness.

The man had been fishing all day, but still smelled good, earthy, healthy. Lusty. With a scent that drew her to him. She wanted to nuzzle into his neck to get a good whiff, to analyze his pheromones for the answer to the age-old question—were they a good match?

Biologically, she was pretty certain. If the circumstances had been different, it was pretty clear she'd have wanted him. Bad.

Well, she *wanted* him now. But that was *bad*.

She looked around for Callie.

"Callie demanded to cook the fish," he said in a husky voice, whiskey-toned voice that made her want to renounce all AA vows to keep off alcohol until she knew for certain Max was dead or in a grave.

"She said trout's one of her specialties," he added.

Emmy tamped down a smile. That girl was totally playing matchmaker. A night off from cooking for her kids and what did she do, but take over the cooking so Luke and Emmy would have time alone.

"She's a great girl," Emmy said. "I heard she had a thing for you back when she was illegal. She's free now and of age."

He laughed out loud with a sound that ran right down Emmy's spine, underneath her clothes and bounced off every estrogen-laced part of her body. "I wouldn't have known what to do with her if I'd gotten her. She was a wild and crazy girl. She's settled down now, being the good mama."

He raised an eyebrow. "I don't think I could pass the entrance exam now."

Had he meant that double entendre? *Entrance*?

Or was that just where her mind went? Callie's ribald humor was rubbing off on her. And Luke's nearness induced sexual thoughts as well.

She looked around the living room, searching for a distraction. Family photos sat everywhere. There was a large photo with a grown man and two little boys, each holding fish, identical grins on their faces.

She walked over, picking it up to look more closely.

"Is one of these you?" The resemblance between all three was uncanny.

"Yeah." He walked over and looked down at the photo. A softness spread over his tanned, bearded face and he smiled. "That was my first fish."

"Let me guess," she said, holding up a hand as she looked carefully at the two little boys. "That's you." She pointed at the little sandy blond little boy with an identical grin to one she'd seen many times from him at the store.

He laughed. "Yeah, and that's my cousin, Forrester. He's like a brother to me. That's Uncle Joe, taught me and Forrester to fish. Taught us a lot of things. Forrester's dad wasn't always available to him, so his mama's brother became like a dad to us. We both owe him a lot."

His eyes became distant, with a warm misty expression that told her he'd gone back in time. He was that little boy, happy, triumphant, man over fish.

"You think that old trout you saw today remembers you? Remembers you and your cousin?"

He looked down into her eyes meeting them, holding them, with a connection that was unmistakable, and that she felt in every cell of her body.

Every time he looked at her, it felt like they'd known each other forever, with a connection as old as the rivers, as old as the rocks that had been polished into smooth pebbles on the river bottom.

She felt that she, like that old trout, remembered him from another time, when she was more innocent and trusting. And believed in the love between a man and a woman.

That the love wouldn't turn ugly as soon as she depended on him, opened up to him, made herself vulnerable to him.

Maybe she, like the old trout, had been around too long. Knew the secrets of men, their dangerous habits.

Though a current ran between her and Luke, it was part of a fast-moving river that held dangerous depths, into which a person could slip into and drown.

Luke touched her arm and she jumped, like she'd been stuck with a cattle prod, feeling the electricity of the connection as if she stood in water.

"It's okay." His voice rumbled low in his chest, spilling out from deep inside where his heart beat.

Was it okay? Could it ever be *okay* again?

God, she wished it so. Was just hanging on, with the belief that someday it all would be *okay*?

After it was *okay*, she'd dare to wish that someone like Luke could love someone like her.

That she could look up into his gentle blue eyes and not wait expectantly for the worse.

What was the point of living if that was all you could expect?

"What's okay?" she asked and looked into his eyes, those blue eyes that could seduce her into telling him things, things that...well, things she could never tell anyone.

"Everything. Everything's going to be okay." His voice seduced her with its timbre, its tone, the way he eased out his words.

He took his time with his words. As if he'd take his time with you. Not hurrying. Just easing you into an area where both of you could share the pleasure.

Darned if her mind didn't always go there with him. Here in his house, it was even harder not to imagine going upstairs with him.

"Drat." Callie's voice broke the moment. She stood in the doorway, waving her cell phone around.

Emmy's eyes met hers. Callie's expression stilled and then her eyes widened.

Emmy stepped back, and Luke looked away.

He cleared his throat but the words still came out huskily, as if difficult to push out. "Burned the fish? Not my pretty trout?" he exclaimed as if he had a relationship with the fish, too.

Callie laughed and Emmy followed suit, attempting for normal, trying not to look as if she'd just been imagining doing bad things with Luke. Bad things that would be oh so good?

"My kids need me." Callie lifted her phone again, as if it were a court subpoena that couldn't be denied.

Emmy narrowed her eyes but Callie pushed on with her excuses.

"Mike was planning on keeping them at their

grandpa and grandma's for the night. But this is their first night away from Mama since we split up and now they wanna come home."

She pivoted and picked up her purse, stowing the phone away deep inside. So Emmy couldn't check for that non-existent text message or phone call?

The girl was so transparent. "Can you give Emmy a ride home?" Callie tossed the words over her shoulder as if no matter the answer, she was leaving.

"I'll walk you out." Emmy followed Callie out the door, hurrying to catch her at the bottom of the stairs with a hand on her elbow to slow her down.

"Everything's done," Callie said breezily. "The fish are ready to take off the grill. I moved the pan to the back so they'd keep warm. A bit of lemon and they'll be great," she said with a sparkle in her eye.

"Girl." Emmy pinched her elbow. "Don't do this to me."

Callie whirled to look her full in the face, all joking gone from her expression. "I'm doing you a favor, missy. And Mr. Widow Man in there, too." She pointed toward the house. "You both need this. Whether or not it goes anywhere is up to you. But, I think you got a shot with that guy and you would be *insaaaane*." Her voice traveled several octaves higher on the last word.

"Insane," she repeated. "To not go for it."

She turned toward her car, throwing Emmy a sharp look back over her shoulder as she got in. "Insane." She pointed one red fingernail at Emmy. "I give you one week, then I'm going in if you haven't. Fair warning, missy."

She put the SUV in gear and backed up with a spurt of gravel. "One week," she called out.

44

Emmy watched the dust disappear before she turned toward the house.

Luke appeared in the doorway, his blue eyes piercing, even from a distance. They carried a heat like a flame that had gone blue with intensity.

———————

Luke watched her from the doorway, confusion churning in his gut, along with a multitude of mixed emotions. The attraction he felt toward her roiled around with the question of whether she had killed her husband. An acidic mixture of doubt scalded his stomach lining.

Losing his wife hadn't been a choice. And to think this woman might have chosen to kill her husband. Even if it had been Max.

He laughed to himself with a scathing warning that if a woman had killed one man she might kill another.

They say killing gets easier with each death.

Was Emmy a black widow, killing husbands and lovers? Killing a man only a year ago?

And, if she hadn't done it, why had she run, living under a somewhat assumed name now?

If she did do it, why?

For money? A life insurance policy and whatever life savings Max had put away? Maybe the anger of a domestic altercation?

Or just because Max was such a prick?

He'd watched news coverage from the chair beside his wife's hospital bed as she slept, if you could call that drug-induced unconsciousness sleep.

The television had been on silent, but he'd turned on the closed captioning on the bottom of the screen.

They'd found some video of Emily and Max going into the Policemen's Ball.

It had been a big year for Max, lead detective in solving several high-profile murders, making the news, becoming a cop celebrity, so the television crew had stopped Max and Emily on their way into the ball.

The image blazed forth in his mind.

Emily beside the assumed-dead cop, pretty as a princess, her hair up, a pearl drop necklace falling just above the neckline of a royal blue dress.

Looking hardly like a murderer, a woman whose husband would disappear only months later, leaving a bloody mess at the house.

The top of her pretty blonde head had come to just about shoulder level on Max. Could that size woman take down a man Max's size? A man who worked out, not only to stay fit Luke conjectured, but to meet women at the gym as well.

Emily had looked so innocent in the video of the ball, so innocent now. Something reporters and anchors had commented on. "She doesn't look like a killer," they'd say. And almost immediately afterward, someone would give a knowing laugh.

Presumed guilty, that laugh had said.

Anger burned inside of Luke at those presumed guilty expressions and laughs.

Maybe that was why she'd run, the feeling that she couldn't get a fair shake with the press and the cops on Max's side.

However, some cops' opinion about Max had changed after his mistress was killed by a serial killer-arsonist. The way Max had wailed and cried over his dead girlfriend—many had said they would never have believed he could show so much emotion.

Was that why Emmy had killed him—pure jealousy?

But, word on the street was that Max said he'd confessed all to his wife and they'd started over. He said he loved his Emily like he'd never loved another woman and was grateful for the second chance.

But, if she'd killed him like so many cops believed…

Killed the man who'd professed to have finally rediscovered the love of his life and just walked away free.

Black widow. Dark hearted, murdering woman, that's how she was known among police circles.

Though none of them said what they were all thinking—that if it were Max, perhaps he'd deserved it.

Still, there was something about someone killing a cop that fired up the vengeful nature of any cop. Because secretly, many of them suspected if they stayed on the job long enough they too might become like him, known for his philandering ways.

It was a hard job, hard on a person, hard on a marriage.

Emmy moved and her presence down at the bottom of the staircase infiltrated his consciousness and he realized she was looking up at him, waiting for a sign from him.

"Come on," he called, pasting a smile on his face. "Fish waits for no woman."

Her face broke into a smile, those lips easing back, exposing teeth—like a jackal that could tear a man's heart to shreds?

Or was that just the voice of so many cops talking in

his head, saying Max hadn't deserved what he'd gotten?

The uncertainty ate at him until he was certain that an animal was inside him, tearing at his organs. His confusion over Max's disappearance and his own duty to report that he'd found a person of interest warred with the attraction he felt for this woman.

It seemed impossible that the Emmy he knew could hurt anyone.

But, was she really Emily, the woman so many cops wanted to find? A person who could kill her husband in anger or for profit?

Which was the true person?

Her hips swayed as she climbed the stairs. And despite his vow to put her in prison if she deserved it, the little man part of him reacted.

Was that her power, how she'd murdered Max, seduced him into letting down his guard?

Max's brother, Carl, was driven nearly insane with grief for his brother.

Something Luke could relate to, after experiencing his own deep grief over his wife.

Carl painted a terrible picture of Emily. Scheming to kill her husband for the insurance money, a large sum that had finally been awarded to her in absentia. All she had to do was surface and claim the money.

Emmy's eyes turned wary as she neared him and he struggled to put on his public face, the face that had gotten him so many confessions.

That's what he was known for, getting the confession. In popular lingo, he was the *good cop*.

Emmy's face relaxed as he smiled convincingly. He held the door open for her and she preceded him into the house. Together, they walked out to the deck.

The aroma from the grill encircled them.

Emmy inhaled deeply, closing her eyes. "That smells so good."

"Nothing like food you caught yourself," he said, studying her. With her eyes closed, he felt free to look.

Porcelain skin, clear and unmarked. With faint purple around her eyelids that looked as beautiful as if a makeup artist had done her eyes. But, it didn't look as if she had any makeup on. Just natural God-given beauty.

Was it her choice to misuse it the way some cops and the press had insinuated she had?

Max's brother had told him about other men. How Emily had even flirted with him.

Or had other men flirted with her?

That was highly probable. Even he, knowing what Max's brother said about her, felt this draw, this desire to be closer, to touch her.

She opened her eyes, and their gazes caught. She'd caught him staring, might as well acknowledge it.

"You have such beautiful skin. I couldn't help staring."

A smile crept across her face. "Thanks. That's very kind of you."

Kind?

That a man felt driven to want to jump her bones?

"My mother had beautiful skin." Her voice became dreamy, her eyes distant. "I remember watching her get ready to go out with my father. Putting on lipstick."

She met his eyes again. "I wanted that. To be her, to be grown, getting ready for a date with my husband."

She stopped, her eyes narrowing, as if she hadn't meant to let the conversation take such a personal turn.

"Have you ever been married?" He took it right to the point.

She flushed, a light rose creeping up through the milky skin of her neck and cheeks.

"Let's not talk about the past." She glanced away. And didn't answer the question. "Let's talk about *now*."

"Now?"

"How long are you up here for?"

"Emm, don't know." She'd given him nothing, so she'd get the same. He reached for the pan, lifting the lid, checking the fish. "Callie did a good job. This is perfectly done." He set the pan on a coaster tile on the table. He reached for the wine, uncorking it. "A glass of wine?"

She looked at the bottle, as if really weighing the question, then finally nodded. "Maybe just half a glass."

What was she afraid of, that she'd spill everything if she got to drinking? He took a glass and filled it full, then handed it to her.

She raised an eyebrow but took the glass without comment. He poured some for himself, setting it on the table.

Then, he pulled back a chair for her. She sat, moving carefully as if she were afraid she might accidentally touch him.

So, as he pushed in the chair, he made sure his hand brushed the back of her waist. She jumped, almost imperceptibly, but he'd seen it. Her head half turned, allowing her to see him with her peripheral vision. And her eyes widened slightly.

Oh yeah, she'd reacted to his closeness.

He moved away, walking to the stove to pull off the

pan of vegetables Callie had prepared to go with the fish.

He brought it to the table. "Would you like some?" Removing the lid, he tilted it toward her.

"Looks good," she murmured.

The sound of her voice, deep in her throat, was overpowering, like wine in his veins, beating down his resistance.

She was a woman with a strong effect on men.

He'd do well to remember that until he had more information about what had happened to Max. And why.

He spooned out some of the vegetables on her plate, then his, and put the pan back onto the grill. Callie had flipped off the heat on the grill before she'd left.

If only he could control the heat between him and Emmy as easily. He'd seen this before, detectives getting sucked in by beautiful women, thinking the surface beauty went all the way through.

Not being able to separate a pretty face from the person they really were? Getting stupid over a woman?

Not him.

"Do you fish every day? Eat like this every night?" She looked at him with those green eyes, the color of deep river water, their depths hard to discern, with hidden pools where a man could stumble and suddenly find himself where the currents ran quick and could drag a man down.

He sucked in a deep lungful of air before he could speak, glancing away into the dark, away from the impact of her face. "The freezer is full." He looked back at her, meeting her eyes, feeling his lungs empty again, contracting under the power of her gaze.

"I'll leave for my uncle what I don't finish. Different family members come up here. They'll like finding the freezer full of trout."

"Are you still close to your uncle? You mentioned you spent time with him as a kid," She looked hungry, as if she were greedy for his family. Was she greedy for whatever someone else had?

"He was a second father to me. Actually more like the real thing. More emotionally accessible. And like I said, for Forrester too."

She nodded. "Parents have so much invested in their children that sometimes I don't think they can just enjoy us. They always see what needs fixing."

He tilted his head in acknowledgement. "Very opinionated and critical?"

"Exactly," she said. "My dad had that gene. Good guy, just always telling me what I should be doing, what I needed to do." She shrugged. "A bit over critical."

That said a lot about maybe why she was the way she was, taking the criticism from Max for just so long, as she'd been forced to from her father.

Then finally lashing out, killing him in a fit of rage?

"Where's your father now?" He took the lid off the trout and eased one out onto her plate, then a second onto his. "We'll finish Callie's, too. More for us."

Only when he set the pan back onto the tile and sat down did he realize she hadn't answered him. He looked at her.

She sucked in a deep breath and let it out slowly. "My parents were killed in a car accident when I was fourteen."

What did you say to that? Except, "Sorry, that's rough."

Was that why she was how she was, having lost her father so young, damaged so that no man would ever be good enough?

There he went, trying to excuse the beautiful woman's behavior. Just like all those other detectives, made stupid by a pretty woman.

She nodded. "Sorry about your wife. That's rough." Her eyes connected with his for a long moment, a long sensitive look that said she understood, understood how it felt to lose someone.

She leaned across, putting her hand over his, meeting his eyes with a compassionate expression that made him want to look into those eyes forever.

People gave him that *look* all the time, until he wanted to scream, "Hey, give me a break, I don't want to know you're thinking about my dead wife and my loss every time you see me."

But, this time… This time, he wanted to take her sympathy, let her soak off some of the pain. The pain he felt every night in bed when he tried to sleep and the pain he awoke to first thing each morning.

This time, it felt like she really did understand, could feel what he felt. And really sympathized.

She took his hand into both of hers and stared at him with those river-colored eyes.

He held onto her hand for a long moment, looking into her eyes, wondering. Wondering what it would be like between them.

CHAPTER SIX

The light from the candle glimmered across his face, caramelizing his skin into an enticing mixture. She wanted to bathe herself in it, to rub up against his skin, to feel his masculine roughness against her femininity, to bask in all that manliness.

For just one night, she wanted to feel like a woman again. Not some animal that was always looking over her shoulder.

Something about him said she would never have to be afraid of him, would never be afraid of anything while she was with him.

Was it the widower mystique? That innate femaleness that went *aaahhh* when they heard about him nursing his wife till the end, easing her into the next world. Callie had spoken longingly about his devotion to his wife, how he'd spent every moment with his wife in the hospital.

Had held her as she died.

Emmy had wanted to ask questions about him. But that would have revealed just how much she felt his presence, how much she thought about him, couldn't get her mind off him.

Just the thought of him had heated her from the

inside out, turned her into a clear crystal that everyone could look into and see how he affected her.

So, she'd just listened, had never said his name out loud because she knew her face would flush, she would stammer and everyone would see how just the mention of him made her react.

"What do you do for a living?" She looked across the candle at him.

His eyes flashed to her, direct, hard.

Shock rocked through her at how different he looked for just one moment. And an instant defensiveness warned her that she really didn't know him that well.

Maybe he had a hard side, like Max.

Then, he shook his head and laughed, his eyes softening. "No yesterdays, remember?"

Oh, darn. Busted by her own rules. She felt herself relaxing again, dismissing that instant flare in his expression. He'd resented that she hadn't given him anything. Had sensed her holding back.

The way she'd done to everyone this last year. Or was she merely dismissing the warning flags she didn't want to see where he was concerned?

"Actually, I've decided to move up here permanently," he said softly, in that voice that caressed through her veins, easing away any fears of him. "Gonna leave the past in Atlanta. Do what I did as a young guy, what made me happy then. Carpentry. I'm already looking for a house of my own, some place I can fix up, work on my skills."

He was planning to stay around.

A quick fantasy flashed through her, fully formed, of a future with him, a home he would build for them.

But, he'd said house, not home. As if he knew it

would only be a place to sleep and keep your stuff, not really a home, which was a place where you truly lived. Maybe with a wife and kids?

A house. Kind of how she'd viewed every place she'd stayed the last year. Until now. The river house felt like a home, a place where she could bring her Grampa, a place she could fill with love.

"A whole new life?" she said, meeting Luke's gaze.

"That's the plan." He nodded. "The past is past. And I'm looking to the future."

She liked the sound of it. That was what she wanted. Let everything that had happened before she'd gotten here to Hawk's Peak be like a bad memory. Or simply forget it all, if only that were possible.

If only she could stay. If only her ex-husband would let her.

Her dead husband, she amended. If only her dead husband would let her be.

They were alike, she and Luke. Both haunted by their dead spouses.

For a brief moment, the desire to tell him about Max flashed through her. But she couldn't. She could never tell anyone.

It would always be a brick wall between her and anyone she wanted to be close to. Because how could you have a real relationship if you couldn't be honest?

The anger roared through her again that Max was still running her life, still deciding what she could and couldn't do.

"I was married," she blurted out before she could hold herself back.

His eyes widened, then he shrugged. "Who hasn't at our age?"

He leaned across the table and took her hand, squeezing it. "There's always tomorrow. Tomorrow is full of everything good and new beginnings."

Hope flared inside of her that it might be true. That she might have a tomorrow that was normal. A husband she wasn't terrified of.

Kids who laughed and squealed when Daddy came home.

She wanted all of that. The happy home life that had been cut short when her parents died.

Looking into Luke's eyes, for just a brief second, she allowed herself to imagine all that with him.

Then, she glanced away, away from the powerful draw of his eyes.

Until she could tell him all that had happened, trust him with the truth, there could be nothing real between them.

Until then, there was only attraction, this heat that sizzled between them.

It could never be more important than a meaningless one-night stand, a body connection, without the true sharing between people that formed a relationship.

He squeezed her hand again. "Just for tonight, tell me about the past, tell me about your husband."

She couldn't look at him. If she did, she'd reveal the hate that blazed inside of her for Max. And the terror. All the conflicting emotions that made her want to run, yet at the same time made her want to strike out against her *dead* husband.

So much ugliness in her past. No man would be attracted to the ugliness that lived inside of her.

But, she wanted to tell him, to be honest with him. Something inside of her needed to connect with him, to let him know her and all the confusion and doubt she lived with every day.

She'd been alone so long, isolated in the bubble of her circumstances. She needed to burst that bubble, get outside of it, free herself.

"I was afraid of my husband."

His eyes hardened, his jaw tightened. "I'm sorry. Did he hit you?"

She pulled her hand away from his, because contact with him seemed to suck the truth from her. "He mostly terrorized me with words."

Words that drew a picture of what might happen to her.

"He always accused me of things. Always thought the worse of everything I did."

His eyes fastened on her, waiting, waiting for what she would give willingly. Not asking, not questioning.

"He saw me talking to someone at a party and automatically assumed I was planning a rendezvous." A grinding tension began building in her.

"Getting ready for a party was nerve-wracking, trying to decide what wouldn't set him off. If I dressed in something attractive, he called me a slut and said I wanted every guy there to lust after me. And if I didn't dress nicely enough, he'd criticize me for that, too."

"Damned if you do, damned if you don't," Luke said.

She nodded yes. And then the memories flooded back full force, with the anxiety that living with Max had induced. It was as if she was back there, a nervous wreck.

But she wanted Luke to understand, to somehow unload part of it onto him. She needed him to know her.

Had been wanting it for some time. The more they talked about trivial day-to-day stuff at the store, the more she'd wanted to share real things.

To have a real conversation.

She looked up at Luke, to understanding eyes, eyes that said he'd never done anything like that to his wife.

"And believe me, I didn't. Cheat or make plans with other men, I mean."

He nodded. "Some guys are insecure. Especially when their wife looks like you." He laughed oddly. "There's a song that says something like if you want to be happy, get yourself an ugly wife."

He raised his hands as if he knew most women would punch him for that thought. "I'm just saying. My wife," his eyes went misty, "was beautiful. And I gotta admit, sometimes I would keep my eyes on other guys around her, just in case I had to go over and put them in their place."

He laughed weakly. "A beautiful broad can make a guy go weak between the ears." He looked up at her, straight into her eyes, with a long stare. "Like you, for example."

Her breath caught in her chest, waiting for his next words, not wanting to miss a syllable.

"The first time I saw you, I went weak in the knees. That feeling traveled straight up to my brain."

She waited, slowly letting out her breath, quietly, intently watching him, her eyes fastened on his lips.

"I mean, what guy needs that much ice?"

His daily trip into the store for coffee and ice that she'd begun to hope had something to do with her, but hadn't quite let herself believe it.

She laughed, loving it, this feeling of being desired

by a man she was so attracted to. It had been so long since she'd reacted to any guy this way.

Finally, she felt she was returning to the land of the living. Like she'd been dead, killed by her ex-husband. Because, for a long time, all men had been guys who might incite a jealous rage by her ex or might have been sent by her ex to find her.

She'd spent the last year in fear. Of everything and everyone. And now felt as if she were emerging from the shadow of that darkness.

She met Luke's eyes, the eyes of the first man in so long who inspired impulses to get close, and smiled.

Really smiled.

The part about getting stupid was the truth. Because he couldn't think of anything right now except how much he wanted her.

His brain went still and he was just a man looking into the eyes of a beautiful woman. A woman who couldn't seem to look away either.

Was it so wrong?

After all he'd been through, after the pain he'd felt, the loneliness, the deadness—this longing to be held in the arms of a living woman came along.

It was like a gift sent from heaven.

He didn't want to think about anything, except the attraction between them.

His mind and body had been suffocated underneath an iceberg of grief that had smothered him since Mazie had died.

He gasped like a man finally breaking to the surface after so long under frigid waters, dragging in breaths that hurt his lungs as the over-heated air filled him.

He wanted to take everything this woman had brought back into his world—heat, passion, feeling alive when he was with her.

And after the illness and the death, he wanted to feel alive. Needed to be alive.

Standing, he stepped around the table and pulled her into his arms, and took her mouth.

Took it with a power and passion that assured him he was still alive. Dead for so long, he finally felt a return to the land of the living.

She melted into him, warming his skin, breaking up the iceberg that his heart had become and his soul had frozen under, finally bringing a life-giving heat to him.

Her hips met his as if of their own accord. He slid his hands down, pulling her into him, until his masculine impulses met her feminine acceptance.

Pulling her to the sofa, they fell together, fell and curled into each other's body. A perfect fit.

Made to give each other relief.

Was it so wrong?

To hell with what was *right*. He needed her, needed the life-giving pulse that flowed between them and made him want to fuse with her body.

That body that overflowed with life, he wanted to be inside her, to remind himself that he was still alive.

This was what life was all about, this heat between two people, this connection.

He shut his eyes and just felt, just connected with her on every level that she wanted, that he wanted.

CHAPTER SEVEN

Luke awoke and instantly knew something was different. A scent swirled around him, sweet, feminine, musky.

He inhaled deeply, savoring the pheromone-laced air, relishing it. The scent clearly said he wasn't alone. A woman lay next to him.

The first woman he'd been with since Mazie died.

This was such a relief from the constant waking up alone, with only his solitary masculine smell. What he'd come to think of as the stink of lonesomeness on his pillow.

He wanted to roll over onto Emmy, sink into her, so that she'd awaken as they were making love. Like they'd done all through the night, one or the other cuddling up to the sleeping partner, taking liberties that resulted in another lovemaking session when the other person became conscious.

But, he couldn't.

Fully awake now, he felt shell-shocked, rocked to his core. From everything that had happened in the night.

Just sex? Hell no.

It had been moving, tender, with feeling. There'd

been touching that had driven him beyond ecstasy. And an intimacy that forged a connection with Emmy.

The night had changed something inside him.

He got up, slipping out of bed quietly and into a pair of jeans, buttoning and zipping them as he walked toward the stairs.

He glanced back to see her in his bed, her hair flung across his pillow and her eyes closed, the sheet draped loosely, revealing one breast.

The milky skin beckoned to him, to come back, to take her once more.

But, daylight filtered through the windows.

And he knew more surely than anything that making love in the daylight would be different.

In the dark, they'd tasted and touched and taken freely with the anonymity that nighttime allowed.

Now, it was the next day. And his mind had gotten back in touch with his body.

And his mind was yelling, *What the hell?*

He padded quietly down the stairs and staggered into the kitchen, feeling like he'd just been through a fierce firefight, a swat standoff that ended in a gun battle or hand-to-hand combat.

What happened last night? And how could he have let it happen? He needed time to process it.

Cause a cop was still dead. And the main suspect, the person of interest, the un-indicted murderer as so many in the department referred to her, lay in his bed, with his sweat still on her skin.

Damn, he was an idiot. As big an idiot as all those other guys they jeered at, men who let their little head do the thinking.

He should have controlled himself. Until he'd

known she was innocent, he never should have slept with her.

The thing was, he did know it. Even if he couldn't prove it, something inside of him had known for a long time that she wasn't a murderer.

But his mind had kept arguing with him to prove it. Or as everyone on the force would say, disprove her guilt.

"Hey," a soft, slightly hoarse voice disrupted his attack on himself.

He looked over his shoulder, and his breath caught in his chest at the sight of her sleep-stained eyes and her mussed hair. She hadn't even stopped to comb her hair, just grabbed his robe and came down.

Like that, with no attempts to fix herself up, she was the sexiest woman imaginable.

She nuzzled up to his back, pressing herself against him, opening her robe so her naked skin pressed against his naked back.

"God," he breathed out raggedly, turning, pulling her in close, their hips meeting, as his mouth took hers once more, as if this were just a continuance of what sleep had disrupted.

His mind could warn him, but his body pushed back any objections and just reacted.

She slid her hands down his stomach, her fingers trailing fire along his skin, burning heat and want into his flesh. If he weren't already helpless to resist her, that touch would have done it.

He gasped out a shaky breath, looking down into her eyes as she undid his pants, pushing them down his hips, her hands skimming along his hips and legs.

He shuddered at her touch. He couldn't have stopped

himself if the SWAT team had been banging at the front door.

He kicked out of the pants, leaving them on the floor, and swung her up onto the counter. The robe fell away from her body, leaving her breasts and stomach exposed to him as he pushed between her knees.

She mouthed the skin along his neck, making soft little sounds deep in her throat. He slid her off the counter, so her legs wrapped around his waist and walked to the sofa. Then, he discarded that idea. He wanted a big, comfortable bed for what he planned to do to her. And the condoms were upstairs.

He headed up the stairs with her wrapped around him, urging him closer and closer to her center. He almost didn't make it to the bedroom, almost put her down on the hall rug and took her there.

But, he pushed on for the comfort of the bed, already scented with the soft smells of their joined bodies, the bed where he wouldn't have to worry about her discomfort on a hard floor when he lost control and just pushed into her, seeking what her body offered, seeking that connection of passion he knew firsthand was possible between them.

Finally, he reached the bed, falling with her, not wanting to let her go for even a second.

Rolling her onto her back, he took a moment to slip on a condom, then slid into her, into her welcoming warmth that took him so easily, so quickly, to that unthinking place where they were one being in search of the same thing, the same release.

Sliding in and out of her, he listened to her guiding murmurs, telling him what she wanted, what they both wanted.

"Yes," she reaffirmed when they found the perfect rhythm, the pace quickening steadily into that frantic dance of desire, that physical expression of their attraction.

The attraction of a man who'd found his mate, who found the woman with the connection to infinity, the amount of times they would make love unnumbered, the number of nights they would spend together uncountable.

Frantically and forcefully, he pushed into her, loving everything they shared, wanting this more than anything he could imagine.

He pulled back to watch the effect he had on her, her eyes closed, her face impassioned, unable to hide the power of the moment.

He watched as she came, her pleasure sending him over the top, until he drove into her with an unstoppable force. Then, finally, he shuddered to a halt, and then just savored the feeling of being surrounded by a soft, willing woman.

Together, they clung to the moment, to what their bodies could provide, to what only they could share.

He kept the connection, holding her hips to him, not wanting it to end.

Finally, exhausted, he fell back, and away, pulling her to his side, her leg wrapped over him, her center still close to his hip.

He closed his eyes and hoped never to start thinking again. Why couldn't this just last forever?

As the physical feelings subsided, he detected the doubts creeping up on him again, like coyotes at the edges of the clearing, looking out hungrily from the tree line.

He had to prove she wasn't guilty. He needed to prove it to the world, to set her free from suspicion, so she could return to her world, be a part of his, return to using her real name. Or his last name?

He needed to face down the ones who would want to convict her without a trial. In the court of public opinion.

Basically, everyone he'd worked with.

Energy shot through him, with the mad need to start on that mission, to find a way to free her from this cage of suspicion. He swung his legs over the bed and stood up.

Her eyes swept across his naked body with a heat that almost caused him to get back in bed. But he wanted to do this, needed to do this for her, to give her back her life.

"I'll get the coffee going," he said by way of an excuse for getting out of bed.

She sat up, looking away, hiding her face, without any telltale expressions. "I'm going to take a quick shower if that's okay."

"Sure, plenty of clean towels in the cabinet in there."

Something about the way she'd so quickly averted her face said she knew the moment was over, their time in bed done. He turned away so that the way she looked, her naked back as she pulled the sheet around her body couldn't influence him.

He headed to the kitchen, determined to get the coffee brewing, get his mind working, get the day started. He shoveled coffee into the filter, then flipped on the switch.

Before the coffee had even finished brewing, she came down dressed, her glossy brown hair combed, her face looking freshly washed.

No make up, yet beautiful still. His breath caught in his chest and he pulled her toward him, underneath his arm where she cozied up to him, wrapping her arms around his chest.

"Thank you," he said into her hair, his breath blowing little strands of hair upward so they flew around his face, with the full aroma of a healthy, alive woman wrapping around him.

"Thank you, too" she answered with a shy laugh. "Do we send thank you notes to each other now? Or is a verbal thank you enough? I've lost touch with the etiquette of morning-afters."

He smiled. "I think we're supposed to text each other if we really had a good time."

"I don't even have your number," she said with a laugh. "Where's my phone?" She pulled away slightly but he caught her, holding her in place against his body.

"Modern dating," he murmured, then leaned down to mouth the soft skin of her neck. He was beginning to see how people could overlook a lot of things for this.

The stuff that made life worth living.

She looked up, meeting his eyes. A spark ignited in hers, quickly flashing an answering reaction through his body.

Note to self—don't look her directly in the eye if you actually want to get anything done today.

He pulled away, dropping his hands from her. He had to think, had to get out of this house.

God, he needed coffee bad, the caffeine jolt might help shake him loose from the effects of her, the control she exerted over him.

If they made coffee that strong.

He pulled a mug out of the cabinet and handed it to her.

She spun it around. "Disney World souvenir, I'm thinking." She laughed, lightly. Obviously not feeling the day after second-guessing that was wracking him.

He tapped the Minnie Mouse-shaped cup. "What gave it away? One of my cousins must've got it there. It's been here as long as I can remember."

He picked up his coffee mug, left beside the coffee maker the day before.

"You always leave it there?" She looked from the mug back to him.

He nodded. "Yep. Want to make it as easy on myself as possible. I'm pretty oblivious most mornings before I've had my coffee. I have at least one before I stop by your store for ice and more coffee."

He filled her mug, avoiding looking directly into her eyes. He had to get her out of here. He needed to start working on her case, researching stuff on the Internet, accessing police files his cousin Forrester had forwarded to him before he'd officially taken leave, having his cousin send up stuff he didn't already have.

Forrester had made it almost a hobby for them, during one of Mazie's many long stays in the hospital, sending him info, case files, anything they could talk about other than Mazie not getting any better.

Emmy took a long sip of coffee, then held her mug out to look at it with interest. "So, this mug belonged to *one of your cousins*. Got so many you can't keep track of 'em?"

He smiled.

"Wow, you have a big family."

"Yep. Way big."

Something flickered across her face that looked like sadness.

"What?"

"Oh, nothing. I hate to sound like such a whiner. I don't have a big family," she said in a dramatically pitiful tone. "My husband was mean to me," she continued in the same joking tone.

He laughed slightly. She gave up lots of information on her own if you just listened.

"I always admired those big, noisy families with tons of kids running in and out. Down the street from me, there was this humongous family. I was friends with one of the girls. Used to hang out there all the time."

"So, you want your own big family then, right?"

Her eyes darted to his, then away. "That's the kiss of death in dating, no? That girl's looking for a baby daddy. Heck, I won't even be getting a day after, thank you text from you."

She pointed a finger like she was talking about somebody else and not herself.

The laughter came from deep inside him now. "Repartee. I remember this," he said. "This is what men and women do, make fun of each other, themselves and the whole situation. Very well done." He nodded at her approvingly. "I will definitely be texting later."

Her eyes met his, the laughter dying. "See that you do," she mock ordered.

She was a hell of a lot tougher than she looked. Able to take it and give it right back.

This damned situation. If he'd met her under any other circumstances, after last night, he'd have begun wondering if he'd found his baby mama. The woman he could be with for a really long time.

Maybe forever?

He turned to the coffee pot and topped off her mug, then his. How ridiculous was he?

One night and he was ready to tie the knot. He might as well be some teenaged girl. Next thing he knew, he'd be watching a *Twilight* movie on HBO. Or a *Titanic* rerun.

No. No matter how hot she was and how good at this morning-after stuff, she was still a person of interest in the disappearance of a cop.

The number one and only person of interest. And he had to do something about that.

"Oh, that's not good." She took a sip of coffee and looked at him over her mug's rim.

He didn't ask what, 'cause he knew the sudden turn of thought had shown on his face. What type of a detective was he when the suspected perp could read his face so easily?

The type that had just spent the night with one.

Damn.

But he wasn't a cop, he was a *former* cop. Some little voice inside said, *Once a cop, always a cop.* Even if you weren't on the payroll anymore.

He'd taken a six-month personal leave, to see if he wanted to make it full time. Since he hadn't made his resignation final, technically he was still a cop.

Did he have a duty to inform the detective working the case of her whereabouts? Probably. Of course, he'd known that for some time and hadn't made that call.

"You gonna give me a ride home?" She arched an eyebrow as if she'd noted his thoughts had been written on his face, then turned and headed toward the stairs.

And damned if he didn't watch her go, imagining the

body underneath those jeans. He could probably recover from that expression she'd read on his face and go upstairs for another round of mind-blowing sex.

"I'll give you a ride but that means I better get a text," he called after her.

Yeah, there'd be no more going back to bed. Things had gotten way out of hand last night. And then again this morning. He knew it, the little guy knew it and so did his brain.

They all just had to get on the same page.

Cause the little guy seemed like he wanted to lead a revolt, springing perkily alert at the extra sway that she put into her hips, possibly just for him as she went up the stairs.

Up seemed to be the direction of choice today. He looked at his pants. "Down, boy," he muttered softly, the only thing soft about himself.

Yeah, this was a hard situation.

CHAPTER EIGHT

Man, he couldn't have gotten her out of that house any faster if he'd just opened the upstairs window and asked her to jump out.

They had made love again this morning. He'd been tender and caring, like he'd been all through the night. On the second, third and fourth time they'd made love.

Made love?

Would he call it sex?

Tender caring sex. Still, just sex.

In the kitchen, over coffee, something in his demeanor had changed. He'd been ready to get her out of the house. Now, they both sat silent in his Jeep as he drove her home.

At least the river looked beautiful, flickering in and out of the trees as they cruised along the riverfront road to her house.

This was the dreaded morning after of a non-committed relationship. You and a guy had chemistry, clicked to such a degree that you found yourself waking up beside him in bed many hours later.

Picturing tomorrows and name changes. Stupid imaginings.

Because the reality of their morning after couldn't be

more awkward. If she were at her own house, he could have bailed quickly, avoiding the moment when she'd come to the conclusion that it had been a mistake on her part and a lucky break on his.

He'd gotten some. She'd gotten screwed. Making love? Hardly.

Sex was a real bear. It could mess your head up quicker than too many cups of coffee and no sleep.

Just damn.

"I'll always think of that river as the color of Emmy's eyes." His words purred across the dashboard, quietly, slipping up on her unaware.

She jerked her head around to look at him. He stared past her at the river.

"See that?" He extended a hand.

She turned to look as he slowed down and pointed to a spot where the river ran close underneath the bank, shadowed by trees and bushes.

"Where it reflects back the trees?" His eyes flashed with a slowly building heat. "Reflects back the color of your eyes."

A slow smile spread across her face. Maybe not so awkward after all. "Oh yeah, you're definitely getting a text later."

He smiled back, a real smile that said he'd meant his comment, not just sweet-talking.

She turned away, keeping her eyes on the river. She'd probably think of him, also, whenever she saw that color.

Think of him and the long night that had felt like lovemaking, not just sex. It had felt like her reward for surviving this long, lonely, scary year.

Deep inside, in her secret thoughts, was the little

hope that she and Luke were something more than just a fling, something that could last, could survive.

Even after finding out who she really was and what she'd been practically accused of?

He turned into the winding driveway that led to her house. The ride was almost over and the anticipation began. Would he try to make arrangements to see her again?

Or would he smile and drive away, leaving the river-colored eyes comment floating behind him as he made his getaway?

Dating was hell. Even if you weren't looking for something long term, only the now, the immediate, the near future.

Cause that's all it could be for them. It was a mistake to have even gotten involved in the first place. One she'd have to pay for later with heartache.

She couldn't tell him what had happened in Atlanta, that she was the person suspected of killing her husband.

And her Grampa, the whole reason she'd come back so close to Atlanta? It made it trickier to bring her Grampa up here.

She'd only spoken to her Grampa on the phone since she'd gone on the run. What would he be like in person? He seemed to have his full faculties, but who knew really.

With close contact with Luke, Grampa might slip up and reveal something.

She should have thought of that last night. But, thinking hadn't been her strong suit then.

Thinking had gone on hold. Feeling had taken over.

Today was about reality. Cold hard reality, her best friend this past year.

They pulled up in front of the house. The moment of truth was approaching, the moment they said goodbye.

Whatever happened, she'd pull up her big girl panties and deal with it. The possibilities for them seemed good, after last night and then again this morning.

Plus, just the general chemistry of the last month. They clicked, with everything that described a man and a woman with an intense attraction who had a good chance.

But, that could just be hopefulness. Stupid, stupid false hope.

He parked beside her car and put his Jeep into park. She sucked in a breath, willing it into her lungs as she waited for his next words.

"Looks like you've got a flat tire." Luke craned his head past her.

The air shot out of her chest, and she inhaled again, then turned toward her car. An off kilter lean of the car pointed her eyes right to the offending tire.

"No." Damn, did she even know how to change a tire? In theory she did, but it had never come to that actually.

Then the hair on the back of her neck stood up. A warning? Panic waited just off stage for its cue, adrenalin receiving notice that it might need to erupt to help her escape. Escape, such a pretty word for running for her life, running from the danger of a man who'd do whatever it took to avenge his hurt pride.

She stilled her breathing, trying to think. Looking toward the woods, she scanned the tree line, looking for a pair of eyes fixated on her, with a weapon pointed her way.

Maybe this was really just a flat tire. Ordinary people got flat tires.

Don't overreact, she coaxed herself. Just breathe.

Because maybe this wasn't her day to die.

Her peripheral vision caught Luke looking at her. Something flashed through his eyes.

He studied her. With an awareness of the alarm that had shot through her brain?

Could he read her so easily? Or was her panic obvious?

Breathe in. Breathe out, she coaxed herself.

"Car trouble, it's the worse," Luke's voice pulled her toward normality, with his level conversational tone.

She sucked in air, heated air that wanted her to run toward the house and start packing, told her this wasn't just an everyday occurrence. The air ballooned in her lungs into a large force inside her chest, pushing against her heart.

No!

There was no one studying her reaction from the woods. *Believe it*, she prayed.

"Life's a bitch?" she responded to Luke's prying gaze, fixed on her, studying her. She needed him to believe this was just a minor irritation.

She needed to believe it, too. Otherwise, the chase would be on again. She'd leave town. Leave the few friends she'd made here.

Run down the road like a wounded deer, looking for another hole to hide in. Somewhere to burrow down anonymously.

Where she'd be alone again.

She'd have to leave Luke behind.

"Exactly," Luke said. "It's always something."

A surprised laugh erupted from her. Her Grampa's favorite saying. Had she told Luke that catch phrase was one of her Grampa's favorites? She couldn't remember.

"Onward and upward," she said, with a smile. She scanned the woods one more time before she got out of Luke's car and went to the trunk of hers and popped it open.

The nasty, dirty spare coiled in the trunk, taunting her with how messy and tough the task would be. Had to be done. She pushed back the pile of clutter that had accumulated on top of it and inhaled, prepping to lug the heavy tire out.

Luke got out of his car and joined her. He leaned past her and pulled out the tire, easily. Then, he set it down on the ground beside her car and pulled out his own jack from the back of his Jeep. No manual anywhere. Like he'd done this countless times.

Had she been alone, she'd have been poring over the diagrams and probably calling Callie for backup phone support.

"What time do you have to be at work?" He pulled the tire wrench out of the little package his jack came in.

"I have about an hour. Just enough time for this," she pointed at the tire, "and to get dressed."

"Why don't you go ahead and do whatever you need to do. I'll change this, then run the tire into town to get it repaired. I'll drop it off tonight."

What a guy. Just how you imagined a guy ought to be. A smile crept across her face, with a warming sensation flooding through her whole body. A normal, nice guy. She had begun to think they didn't make them anymore.

But, the mythical creature stood beside her, his hands dirty from the tire. He looked down at her, waiting for her to approve his plan.

She took his shirt front and pulled him in.

Inches from her face, she stopped tugging and just looked into his eyes. "Are you for real?"

He tilted his head, angling his lips to match hers, then leaned in the few inches, sealing their lips together for a long moment that left her breathless, that left her thinking of plans for evenings for the indefinite future.

When he pulled back, she inhaled deeply. "Oh yeah, you're the real deal."

He laughed huskily, took her hips and pulled them into him. Oh yeah, he was real all right. And the sudden desire to spend more nights with him flooded through her.

More of what they'd had last night? She could only hope.

"Maybe I can cook for you tonight when you bring the tire back, to repay you," she offered.

He looked at her, with those sky blue eyes that made her feel cloudy days were far behind her.

"It's a deal, ma'am," he said in a low, husky voice that raked along her nerve endings. She shivered.

His eyes simmered with an answering heat. Then, he knelt down and began fastening the tire wrench onto the lug nuts.

She watched him for a moment, his big hands making quick work of loosening and removing them.

Damn, it was hot watching him work, doing the manly stuff. So manly like.

She laughed and turned toward the door.

Tonight seemed too far away.

———————

Walking into The Corner Store, she gave Callie the pretend evil eye.

Callie waggled her head at Emmy in a sure-of-herself manner. "I did you a favor, girl, and you know it. You owe me."

She already owed Callie more than she could ever repay her. "I'll just add it to the list."

Callie smiled for real now, as Emmy got closer. "So spill, girlfriend. How was it?"

It? As if she knew they'd had sex?

"Did you get a kiss at least?"

Emmy felt her face flushing. Damn her skin that showed every emotion.

"Oh, goodness." Callie eyes widened. "You got more than a kiss; you got some."

Emmy walked to the cooler and took out a Diet Coke. Then, she pulled out the little notebook she kept under the counter to write down whatever she took out of the store, so Callie could deduct it from her paycheck.

It seemed as if Callie only deducted about half of what Emmy consumed, though. Another way she owed her.

"I'm a damned fine matchmaker. They're gonna make a reality show for me, Hillbilly Matchmaker." Callie smiled knowingly. "I knew you two were right for each other. I got the touch."

She did a pretend strut behind the counter.

Emmy didn't ask her why she thought Luke and she would make a good match but Callie turned back from her strutting and volunteered anyway.

"You're both lost souls, needing just the right person to help you heal."

Emmy stopped, her hand poised over the notebook. That was how it had felt last night, like a balm for her soul as well as her body. Nothing had ever felt so right. Not even her husband, even at first, before he showed his true dark colors.

"You're both running from your past," Callie added.

Emmy pivoted to look her straight in the eye.

"Heck, aren't we all in some way or the other?" Callie's face was innocent but Emmy couldn't help the little surge of anxiety that flooded through her.

This was why she'd avoided friendships the last year, with their accompanying intimacy. Because when people started to really get to know you, they could read you.

That was too dangerous for her.

"Well, I got to go confront my past head on, right now." Callie picked up her purse from behind the counter. "Got to meet the ex to pick up the kids. No running from that."

She wagged her finger at Emmy. "Don't have kids. Cause then your past is always with you. In the form of your ex, that is."

Emmy smiled. "You love your little souvenirs of your past." A snip of envy snapped at her. Would she ever have that? Kids and mom duties.

"I do love my little souvenirs. But, I tell you what I don't love, seeing Mike's new girlfriend every time we have to exchange the kids. She's always with him for the hand over. I mean, really?" Callie shook her head, then pulled out her keys and twirled them around her finger.

"I bet you and Fisherman Luke would make some beautiful souvenirs. Just cause me and Mike didn't work out doesn't mean you guys wouldn't." She waggled her eyebrows.

"Oh, my gosh." Emmy ushered Callie out from behind the counter with a small push. "You are way getting ahead of yourself."

"I know." Callie tapped her head with one finger. "But, I got the sight. I can see it happening already. I need my own reality show."

"Keep imagining," Emmy said. "With that overactive imagination of yours."

Callie walked out chuckling.

"Wait," Emmy called after her. "I thought you picked up the kids last night at their grandparents'."

Callie just laughed as she pulled her hair up into a pony tail and secured it with an elastic band so the blue strip underneath showed just a bit more.

"Like I said, Hillbilly Matchmaker. Redneck Reality TV," Callie threw over her shoulder and nodded. "I like the sound of that. I got the touch." She looked back at Emmy and winked.

Luke fingered the slash on the tire. "Yeah, go ahead and put a new tire on that rim. No hope for this one."

Joe at Smith's garage eyed the damaged tire. "Guess it got driven over something bad." He walked away humming like he'd seen it all in tires.

Luke looked at the tire, sticking his finger through the opening. That didn't look like anything you wouldn't notice right away. Maybe she'd driven over something in the yard. He'd have to search the area when he got back to her place.

He went over to the Piggly Wiggly grocery store across the street from the garage and shopped for dinner while he waited.

A couple of steaks, a couple of potatoes and a bag of salad with all the makings inside. Better to take your own food to a woman's house, otherwise no telling what bird feed she might put on the table.

He didn't want to have to leave tonight and go looking for food. He wanted to settle in, have a repeat of last night.

Just admit it, that's what you want.

The cop part of him wanted to slap himself around for getting involved with her.

His guy side started making excuses.

She'd never been charged. From what she'd told him yesterday about being verbally abused by her husband, there were reasonable grounds to believe that if she did kill him, it might have been in self-defense.

Max might have gone off on her, or vice versa. If a woman was mentally abused for so long and finally snapped? There was a syndrome attached to that scenario.

Syndromes. He'd never put much stock in that defense before.

Now he'd slept with the woman, was falling for her, and was willing to look for any excuse not to believe she was a cold-blooded killer.

Led around by his Johnson? Slept with the girl and got stupid?

Yeah, that's how his cousin and all the other cops would see it.

He grabbed a bag of ice to chill the steaks while he went to the barbershop next to the Piggly Wiggly.

It might be time for a shave and a haircut, time to clean up his act a bit.

CHAPTER NINE

The wind whipped through the open windows of Emmy's car as she sped along the riverside road, heading home. Luke's text had gone straight into her veins, the words pulsing through her mind and body.

Can't wait to see you, he'd texted.

Her blood sang, *Can't wait to see you* over and over through her veins.

He'd also texted her he'd gotten some steaks and potatoes. Nice. If she could eat.

A man had changed her tire, gotten it fixed. And gone shopping for dinner.

So, this was what it felt like to be taken care of.

She careened around the last turn, calculating how much time she had before Luke would show up. Maybe enough time for a bath and to do something with her hair and makeup?

From the corner of her eye, she noticed something out of place.

A plume of smoke snaked up through the trees, just across the river, right where her house should be.

"No," she breathed the word out like a prayer. "No, no, no. Please, no."

The smoke piped into the air, like a warning, a smoke signal telling her not to go home.

But, every penny she'd managed to save was inside that house.

The smoky snake strengthened and thickened in size, its tail swiveling in joy as if its head were already devouring her money.

Emmy put her foot down on the gas pedal, accelerating as fast as the little car would go. Every time she'd run, she'd sold her old vehicle and gotten a new one. Well, not new, only different. Each time, the junk pile factor on the car increased. The old car rattled and shook as if it might explode into a thousand parts.

The sense of disaster forced her on, because she had to get there in time to get her money.

She slowed as she made the turn into the driveway, searching in her purse for her gun. Her hand grasped the reassuring steel and she tucked it into the waistband of her jeans, pulling her shirt out to cover it.

"Oh, please don't let my money burn up." A flat tire this morning. Now this. Could it possibly just be a string of bad luck?

Maybe she'd used up all her good luck by getting lucky with Luke the night before. A girl couldn't expect everything to be hunky dory simultaneously.

Of course not.

"It's always something," she heard her Grampa joking in an affected, old lady voice with a Brooklyn nasal accent, imitating Gilda Radner, his favorite from the early *Saturday Night Live days*. They'd watched old reruns together.

That Gilda Radner knew what she was talking about.

Please let this have a rational explanation. Don't let it be obvious that someone set the fire.

She could almost hear God looking down at her saying, "Girl, are you stupid?" at how much she tried to convince herself that she was safe.

"I don't want to run," she pushed out the plea.

She'd finally felt safe, like she could stay here. With her friends Callie, Mr. and Mrs. McCloud and the rest of the town.

And, then there was Luke.

A gasping cry wrenched from her lips, "Luke!"

A man so unlike the man she'd married.

Everything in her body clenched in protest at the thought of leaving him. As if, if she wanted it hard enough, she could will it to be so.

But a weak little voice whispered the truth.

Max would not stop coming, would not leave her in peace.

"Run now, little girl", God was sending her instagrams in the form of a curling stream of smoke. "Run now, forget the money," he messaged.

"Damn Max to hell!" she cried.

Was he waiting at the end of the driveway or in the woods ready to attack when she exited the car?

Her breath panted in spurts, her heartbeat thumping like driving on a flat tire, uneven and unnerving.

Her muscles clenched into knots as she rounded the final turn.

"Oh, thank you, God," she blew out on a whoosh of breath. It wasn't the entire house. Smoke was billowing from the back of the house like the whole building could go up at any moment, exploding into flames, devouring all her money.

She needed that money. Remembered what it had felt like having none. When her stomach had hurt from lack of food. She'd used every penny to put gas into her car to get as far away from Max as possible.

She wouldn't leave without that money.

The woods leaned in toward her and her house, as if warning her that evil lurked in their depths. Where was he? Greenery hid a thousand hiding places for a killer, for a devious man whose vitriol knew no bounds.

Max would relish watching her freak but he wouldn't kill her anonymously. He'd want to see the look on her face when she finally knew she'd been caught, when she realized there was no escape.

He would take no pleasure out of merely shooting her from the cover of the trees. Unless it was just a wounding shot, giving him time to approach for the close up, death shot.

Short, panting breaths wracked her body, dots starting to appear in front of her eyes.

She pulled her shirt clear of the gun so she'd have ready access. Should she run into the burning building and save her money, or should she try to salvage the house?

Visions of her Grampa visiting and fishing with her on the river settled the debate.

With one last, frantic searching glance, she bolted out of her car and ran toward the back of the house, toward the head of the snake.

The snake's head morphed into orange flames that gobbled along the handicapped ramp that she'd so loved, had pictured her Grampa using, already eating a fiery slash up the back side of the house.

She still had time to stop it.

Grabbing the hose, she turned the spigot until water spurted out in a powerful stream. Hosing down the flames raging up the side of the house first, she splashed water all along the wood siding.

The fire sizzled, hot tongues lapping, fighting, desperately trying to arch over the water. She continued to attack it with the hose and finally, finally, it gave up its hold on the fuel-rich wood.

Then Emmy turned the hose onto the ramp. The wheelchair ramp used by the elderly woman who'd previously lived in the house was a total loss. That ramp would have made the house a perfect place for Grampa.

Fury exploded inside her, with a hot heat, singeing her nerve endings. Max would pay.

Max, the monster, she corrected herself. He'd lost his right to be called a human with all he'd done.

A flashing memory of the body he'd left lying in the house almost caused her to gag.

A small one that was purposefully left as a message to her. That he could take what she loved and kill it. Like he could kill her or her Grampa.

She'd picked up the body of her beloved Charlie, taken him with her, and buried him later under a peaceful tree, not allowing the cops to bag him and throw him into a dumpster.

A wrenching cry of grief fought to escape from her lungs even now, fearing the agony and fear Max had inflicted on the little dog she'd loved and who had loved her. "It was wrong, so wrong," she shrieked at the fire that even now threatened the future she'd envisioned for herself.

There was no time to think about Charlie now, or

she'd unravel completely. She fought back the image of her little dog's final moments.

She needed to extinguish the fire and get her money from inside the house. Wetting down the entire ramp in one swath, she then concentrated on beating the flames back so the ramp couldn't serve as a bridge back to the house.

A voice came from the front of the house. She whirled, dropping the hose so that it swirled frantically, shooting water into the air in a liquid image of the panic erupting in her veins.

She yanked her gun from her waistband and pivoted toward the corner, dropping to one knee to make herself a smaller target and to steady her aim.

Then, she just waited, waited for what felt like ages, but had to have been only seconds. She waited.

Waited to see if Max would appear from around that corner. Blood racketed into her veins, adrenalin escaping out of its waiting room.

It wasn't Max's style to warn her with a yell but her body wasn't listening to logic. Her hands shook as she clasped the gun, keeping it trained on the corner.

Finally, someone ran around the side of the building, large, male.

Luke, his phone to his ear. His voice gave him away more than his looks because he appeared so different.

He ground to a halt, falling back on his heels, turning and ducking away behind the corner.

She lowered the gun, gasping for air, grayness edging in like an obscuring screen in front of her face.

"It's me! Luke!" he called from around the corner.

"Yeah," she called back. "It's okay." She kept the gun pointed toward the ground.

He stuck his head out, then slowly approached her from the side. His eyes remained fixed on her as he slowly put his hand on the gun and tried to take it from her hands.

She resisted, jerking her hand away, her body in hyper-drive, adrenalin sparking through her.

She struggled to her feet, the gun still firmly clasped in her hands. "Sorry for the lousy welcome," she choked out, her mouth dry, her words unrecognizable even to herself, not even sounding like English.

His face was taut, his jaw muscles working. Giving up the fight to take the gun, he grabbed the hose and sprayed it on the ramp. The final flickers of flame licked the wood, still hungry for her money inside.

She stepped back, tucked the gun into her waistband, put her hands on her knees and dropped her head. Her brain needed oxygen.

She sucked in air over and over again. Finally, the gray pulled back from in front of her eyes and she could fully see again.

Leaving Luke to finish with the fire, she ran to the front of the house and unlocked the door. Taking the stairs two at a time, she barreled straight to the closet. Underneath a pair of jeans, her spare pair of old tennis shoes lay hidden.

Please let it be there, please.

She stuck her hand in one shoe and hit the fold of bills that were tucked into the toe. Everything she'd managed to save. Relief flooded her.

Without that money—no gas, no food, nowhere to sleep.

A slight noise behind her sent shock waves jolting through her muscles. She jumped and jerked around.

"Not the gun again, please." Luke held up his hands in pretend horror.

Then, his eyes fixed on the money. She stuck the wad into her jeans pocket.

"Don't believe in banks, I see." He laughed darkly.

"Banks fail," she muttered.

Running might not give her time to get her money out of a bank. Also, she'd have needed to give the bank identifying information that would have revealed her true identity and maybe given Max more clues to track her.

No banks.

Standing up, she grabbed a duffel bag. Stuffing her extra shoes in, she grabbed the jeans that had covered them.

Then, she yanked the five shirts she'd managed to accumulate off their hangers and pushed them into the bag.

"What are you doing?" Luke's eyes narrowed.

"Packing up," she said tersely.

"Good idea. You're not gonna be able to stay here for a couple of days until the Fire Marshall gives you clearance."

She would never be able to stay here again. No matter how hard she'd fought to save the house or how she'd dreamed of bringing her Grampa up here.

Because Max had found her.

The sixth sense that had kept her alive the last year was screaming, *You need to leave!*

And fast.

Max had never gotten this close before. There had never been this type of contact. Just a sense that he was nearby.

She'd felt it this time but like a fool had disregarded it. Glancing up at Luke, she wanted to cry for what she might have had with him. And acknowledged he'd been a big part of the reason she'd refused to run.

That and her dream of finally seeing her Grampa again. Of bringing him to live with her.

Stupid. She should have just picked up her Grampa and taken him to Missouri or somewhere far away.

But, if she'd taken him to a home in Georgia, she could still have taken him back into Atlanta to see his regular doctors, doctors who'd cared for him for years, knew every in and out on his health.

And, there was also the plan she'd concocted to investigate Max's disappearance herself, to sneak back into Atlanta at nighttime, check around at the homes of women she'd often suspected Max of fooling around with.

Who knew him better than her? If he were still alive, she'd begun to think she might have to be the one to find him. If he hadn't left the area.

What a fool to think she could come back to Georgia.

Opening the chest of drawers, she grabbed underwear, socks and her extra bra. Then, she ran to the bathroom, gathering up everything in there, tossing it into the duffle bag.

She looked around and realized Luke was scanning the room.

Probably wondering why any female had so few things.

Well, it didn't matter what he thought anymore, because she wasn't staying around to give explanations.

She grabbed the framed photo of her and her

Grampa, wrapped it in a T-shirt, then stashed it in the duffle bag on top of the other things.

She charged down the stairs, Luke right behind her. She headed toward the kitchen, setting her duffle bag on the floor. She undid her No-Kick-Ins device from the back door and stuck it into a plastic grocery bag.

She turned to the cabinets and pulled out the food that wouldn't go bad, dropping it into another grocery bag. Then, she grabbed the duffle bag and the two plastic bags and headed to the front door, adding the second No-Kick-Ins device into her bag.

A roaring of heavy engines and a siren came from out front.

She threw open the front door. They better not block her escape.

"Emmy." Luke grabbed her by the arm and she swung on him, aiming at his chin. But, his other arm came up, blocking the blow.

"Whoa, whoa, whoa!" he yelled, not letting go of her arm. "Calm down. The firemen are here."

She pushed away from him and ran out to the driveway. They couldn't block her escape.

But, they already had. The large truck sat smack in the middle of the driveway leading out. Her escape route.

Four firemen jumped out of the fire truck and Luke called out, "It was out back!" pointing in that direction.

Two firefighters ran around back while two others turned to a hose that looked long enough to reach the top of a barn.

"I think we got it," Luke called to them. "Maybe just throw a bit more water on it. There's a garden hose out back."

The guys nodded and jogged around to join the other two.

Luke looked down at Emmy, questions in his eyes. The girl had just tried to punch him out.

How to make that normal?

"Sorry. I didn't mean to hit you." She hadn't even realized she was going to swing at him. Her nerves were stretched so thin that her arm instantly popped up in reaction.

In defense? Her body was prepped for a fight. Gearing up.

"It's okay. You're going to be all right. You're safe now," he coaxed in a soft, nurturing voice.

As much as she wanted to listen to the comforting words, to believe them…they weren't realistic.

She'd never be safe. Never. Her life might end one day just like this, a beautiful day when she least expected it.

A disturbance, a distraction, then boom, Max in her face. The only difference would be there'd be no Luke showing up.

It was going to end with her facing Max, with a showdown to the death. Only luck and her sixth sense would ensure she was the one who lived, the one who walked away from that moment.

Everything inside her screamed that the deadly confrontation was coming. Coming soon.

Trembling started in her legs, then moved on up to her arms. She sucked in a deep breath as tears erupted from her eyes. She squeezed them shut, willing back the weakness.

Luke lifted the back of his Jeep, took her duffel bag and plastic bags and set them inside, then took her by the waist, boosting her up to sit on the floor board.

She slumped onto the side of the car, grateful for something to support her, keep her from falling onto the dusty driveway. Closing her eyes for just a moment, she relaxed, reached for any calm she could pull up out of her depths.

Because panic wasn't going to provide the best reacting time. Then, another vehicle coming up the driveway told her she couldn't afford to relax for even a moment. Her eyes flashed open, and she turned toward the sound.

A blue light flickered through the trees and a sheriff's car rolled to a halt beside the fire truck.

The deputy got out of his car and looked around. "Don't look too bad," he said to Luke, then his gaze fixed on Emmy.

"No, I think it's out now." Luke nodded at the deputy.

Something about the way the deputy looked at Emmy made her nervous. He gave her an assessing look, almost as if he felt he'd seen her somewhere.

But, she'd made sure to avoid any law enforcement in the area. Averting her face the few times the sheriff had dropped into the store and pulling on the baseball cap she'd started keeping with her at all times for situations just like that.

He'd never acted suspicious. Still, she'd known he wasn't an ally. Cause if he realized who she was, he'd report it to the Atlanta police.

He'd call her husband's friends, those with no incentive to protect the woman they probably viewed as a cop killer.

Emmy eyed the space between the sheriff's car and

the tree that marked the end of her front yard. She could probably squeeze through there.

Of course, that would probably make things worse, drawing attention to herself by leaving suddenly. She should make a police report. Then, disappear as soon as the barest of legal requirements was met.

Don't draw attention—her motto the last year.

No need to raise suspicions, raise her profile any further. Not that it really mattered in the long run because she'd be gone before dark.

Luke eyed her, standing close by. Almost as if he anticipated she might leave without another word.

The guy had good people sense.

He was a dangerous man in his own way. The type of guy who would get into her head, whom she could care for. The type of guy who would break her heart eventually.

What was worse was she might break his. He didn't deserve that. After all he'd been through, losing his wife, he deserved better.

Because what normal guy would want to be involved with a woman who had as much baggage as her?

An unsolved murder of a husband, with her as the only person of interest. An ex-husband out there stalking her and any man she was involved with.

Yeah, she was a hell of a catch.

Luke was a good guy. She'd been foolish to involve him by spending time with him. Spending the night with him.

He might already be a target for Max. Did she need to tell him what was going on? Did he need to know about Max?

She felt her stomach roiling with acid. What was the right thing to do?

Damn Max and the no-win situation he'd put her into.

Damn him to hell and back.

CHAPTER TEN

Luke eyed her, keeping watch that she didn't slip away when everyone was distracted. The sheriff's deputy wasn't paying much attention to her, just roping off the back area until the Fire Marshall had a chance to investigate.

Emmy stood by the fire truck, talking to the Fire Chief, her eyes so large she looked like a forest creature, her skin glowing pale in the dusky light.

Darting glances all around, toward the woods, toward the river, then back down the driveway and back at him and all the other emergency workers, she pulsed with anxiety.

You couldn't fake that type of barely contained panic, the way she'd swung on him when he'd grabbed her.

Why was she so panicked? Just adrenalin from fighting the fire? Instinct told him it was more.

The firemen packed up their tools onto the fire truck and drove away with a wave. The deputy finished roping off the back area with yellow tape and approached Emmy with a sympathetic look in his eye. "You got somewhere to stay tonight, Miss Emmy?"

"I'll be fine." She nodded her head up and down in a rapid succession of movements.

Yeah, that type of panic couldn't even be simulated by a really good actor. She was about to lose it.

"Okay, then." The deputy, an older man, laid a meaty hand on her shoulder, giving it a bit of a squeeze before he got into his car to head out the driveway behind the fire truck.

Emmy pivoted on her heel, grabbing her belongings from the back of Luke's Jeep, and walked to her car. Her hands trembled so much that she grabbed onto the handle twice before she got a good grip.

Darting looks all around, she pulled it open.

"Emmy," he said quietly.

She started, almost jumping backward. "Whaat?" she stuttered, never making eye contact, just scanning the edges of the darkening woods surrounding the house.

She tossed her belongings into the back seat, then sat down in the driver's seat and stuck the keys into the ignition. He leaned over and put his hand over hers before she could turn it.

"Where are you going?"

"I've got a place," she said. Still no eye contact.

It wasn't that she was avoiding looking at him, but that she couldn't seem to tear her attention away from anywhere that someone could be hiding.

For the first time, he really believed her fear of her husband. Fear of a dead man?

He was apparently dead, with no reason to fear him now. This was getting surreal. Did a terrorized woman never get over it, going into an instant panic when confronted with scary stuff like a house fire?

"Where are you going?" he said more insistently.

"To stay with a friend."

It was a lie, he knew instantly.

"Who?"

She looked at him, resentment flashing in her eyes, rebellion. As if he were invading her privacy. Or being controlling like she said her husband had been? Under normal circumstances, he might have felt pushy, out of place.

But, something in his gut told him that if she left now, he'd never see her again. And that jolted him to his core, the thought of losing her forever, the finality.

"I have your tire." He jerked his head back toward his Jeep. "Pop open your trunk and I'll put it in."

She nodded, as if speaking would tax her last bit of control.

As he looked at the tire, he remembered the slash in it. Had someone been out at her place making mischief?

A slashed tire? A fire? On the same day?

He looked up, scanning the tree line. Then, he walked to the pocket of his Jeep and took out his gun, sticking it in the back of his waistband, pulling his shirt out to cover it. He returned to grab the tire, carried it to Emmy's trunk, stashed it, then closed the trunk.

Emmy turned the ignition, firing the engine. She put it in gear before he could reach her.

"Emmy!" he said loudly and sternly, in a voice he often used to get panicked individuals under control, to cut through the noise in their head.

"Come to my house for the night. We can talk this out." He stepped forward to see her face.

Her eyes flashed with multiple thoughts passing through her brain like a wildfire, quickly, uncontrollably. A dazed look in her eyes said she was barely listening to him, instead she was held in the grip of powerful emotions.

"No," she said in a breathy voice, so low he almost couldn't hear her. "It's not safe. For me or for you."

"I know you're afraid, but..." He lifted his shirt and turned sideways to show her the gun. "I can help you. Two are better than one. No matter what you're afraid of."

"I need to get away from here." Her breathing accelerated, until she was almost panting.

"Slow your breathing down, Emmy. You're going to pass out." He bent his knees until he was eye level with her and watched as she visibly slowed her respiration, taking in long measured breaths and then letting them out again, slowly.

She seemed practiced at this. Skilled at controlling panic?

This situation was taking on an unreal quality. He often found that at crime scenes. The unreal things people could do to each other required quite an imagination.

"I'll be fine," she said, her breathing more normal.

"You don't want to be out there driving around at night by yourself." He tilted his head until he could make eye contact with her. "Come to my house, Emmy. Just for the night. I'll keep you safe."

There, he was buying into her fear, acknowledging that maybe there was something for her to run from. But what?

The man she said she'd been afraid of for so long was believed dead.

Her hands gripped the steering wheel until her

knuckles turned white, working the hard plastic as if she could wring answers from it. But finally, she turned to give him a nod.

"Come with me in my car," he coaxed.

She flashed him a determined look. "No. I need my car."

Needed it in case she decided to run.

"Follow me, then," he said. She nodded.

Quickly, before she could change her mind, he walked to his car and whipped it around to head out the driveway.

Scanning the woods, as he was sure she was doing, he drove quickly through the overgrown, tangled, shadow-filled area out onto the blacktop and turned left toward his uncle's house.

Driving a circuitous route, he watched in his rearview mirrors for anyone who might follow.

This was crazy. But a cop's instinct told him just to go with this theory, the theory that someone was out to get Emmy.

———

Emmy followed Luke. If she hadn't been right behind him, she would never have known the route they were taking as they bypassed Indian Mound Road, the road that led straight to his uncle's house. Instead, they drove through the mountains and circled around, finally coming onto Indian Mound Road from the other side.

It was as if he'd accepted her fear at face value, read her panic and acted appropriately.

As if he believed her terror, believed that maybe it had a cause.

Or was he just humoring her?

103

Because why would any normal person act this way, like they were in a suspense movie, trying to evade someone following them?

Why had he interpreted her panic in this way? She chewed on the inside of her mouth, trying not to bite down on it, to draw blood.

She'd classify herself as a real head case, with all these crazy behaviors. If her fears weren't true.

She should run as fast as she could.

But, something deep inside wanted to stay with Luke, felt she might be safe with him. His strength, the steely determination in his eyes when he'd showed her the gun.

Something about the man said, trust me, I'll keep you safe.

And almost made her believe it.

If anyone could protect her against Max, her gut told her it was Luke. Strength of character shone from the man.

Finally, they turned into his driveway. She looked back, checking for anyone following. In the falling dark, it was hard to make out the road that circled past the Indian mound but she squinted anyway, searching. Searching for a car that might carry a killer.

She waited inside her car when they pulled up in the driveway. Luke was beside her in an instant. "I need to put my car where no one can see it," she choked out.

"Leave your keys in the ignition. I'll stick your car behind the house." He opened her car door, extended a hand to coax her out. "Get in the house and shut the drapes. Here's the key." He handed her his keys, indicating the one for the front door.

Tears rushed to her eyes, burning. Instantly this guy

had become her crusader, thinking like her, doing all the things she would do if she were on her own.

Alone.

But, this time, she wasn't alone. For now. Don't get used to this, she warned herself. Don't expect this to last.

She got out and gave him the keys, their hands touching briefly. Only briefly, but still the contact felt good. Better than being out there in the dark night, running to some new location, showing up in a strange town and trying to find a safe place to sleep.

She glanced back at the road, then ran toward the house, taking the front steps two at a time, unlocking the door, then shutting it quickly behind her, locking it.

Walking from window to window, she pulled the curtains shut, making sure there were no cracks someone could peek through.

A minute later, Luke came in through the back door. "My spare key." He held it up. In his other hand, he held her duffle bag and her plastic grocery bags.

She took the bag that held her No-Kick-Ins and quickly fastened one against the back door, setting a chair underneath the door knob and putting a couple of pans on top of it as an improvised alarm. Then, she went to the front door, setting up the other device, putting a small table that sat by the sofa in front of the door. Then, a thought occurred to her. She turned to Luke.

"There aren't any more keys hidden out there anywhere?" Max would instinctively know where ordinary people hid emergency keys.

She looked at him as he shook his head and their eyes met. Compassion and reassurance simmered in his eyes. Answering tears threatened to erupt from somewhere deep inside her where that knot of fear had lived for so long.

He was like a balm, soothing her, reassuring her, medicine for the terror she'd carried inside of her this last year.

He wouldn't always be there for her. But, he was there now.

Suddenly, his new look registered. With all the turmoil and panic, she hadn't commented or hardly noticed.

He was clean-shaven now, with a shorter haircut, still sexily shaggy but more of a professional look. With the beard gone, the strength of his jaw was granite hard.

"I like your shave and haircut," she said softly.

He ran his hands through his hair. "Decided it was time for a change. To come back to the land of the living." He met her eyes, his shining like sapphire stars in a dark night sky. "You brought me back," he said softly.

A squeezing in her chest made words impossible.

"And," he continued. "I'm not about to give that up for anybody. No idiot ex-husband is taking away what I've found with you."

He met her gaze with a hard, determined steely look, a look that said she could depend on him.

Going to him, she wrapped her arms around his waist, leaning into him. He enclosed her in his arms, infusing her with a sense of safety. For the first time in more than a year, she'd found someone she could trust with the whole truth, someone who understood her fear, someone to depend on and keep her safe.

Still, Max was somewhere out there in the night, and

he wouldn't stop. Wouldn't stop until he'd accomplished what he'd started.

Why would any man go so far as to fake his own death unless he was determined to kill his wife? To kill his wife and walk away unpunished, as he'd boasted so many times he could do.

"I'll kill you and nothing will happen to me. I can guarantee you that," he'd said with a cruel laugh.

He'd sacrificed so much. He wouldn't stop until he'd done what he meant to do.

Kill her.

A shiver shuddered through her, even here in Luke's arms. He pulled her closer and for just an instant, she decided to believe that she was safe.

Even if she knew it was only for an instant.

CHAPTER ELEVEN

Slowly, he drove past the house where she'd run like a little rat trying to escape a snake. Did she really think he was so dumb that a little driving around through the mountains could throw him off?

He'd been watching her for days. She'd sensed it, too, turning and searching around as if she felt his eyes on her, watching, measuring, waiting for the best chance to take her out.

But why was a cop helping her? That was a betrayal of enormous magnitude.

Unless he was just trying to get enough information, to get her to slip up. But, no. He'd let the slut sleep over the night before.

That wasn't investigation. Any judge would say that had compromised his information. You didn't sleep with someone you were planning to put away for murder.

So, he'd have to pay too. If for no other reason than he might testify against him, or search for him, wanting revenge for his new girlfriend's death.

Yeah, having a cop involved complicated things. Not to mention being such a betrayal of the brotherhood of the badge.

He circled through the night, waiting for his chance to take them out when they least expected it. At least, that was what he wanted Emily to think.

That's why he'd set the fire, slashed the tire. It was so rewarding watching her run, every time. Just when she began to feel safe, he'd strike, sending her running through the night like a crazed animal.

He didn't want to have to kill her himself. He wanted her to finally snap and commit suicide rather than waiting and wondering when the final moment would come. And how he would do it.

He wanted her to kill herself.

But, if she got too comfortable with her new cop friend, then maybe he'd have to take them both out. Make it look like a murder-suicide? Passion could do crazy stuff to people's heads.

Luke pulled her to the couch, down onto the comfy piece of furniture that was made for lounging. Together they sank into it. He pulled her underneath his arm and for long moments she curled into him, absorbing his support, his strength.

The closeness was so comforting after the long lonely year she'd spent running from place to place, just an anonymous piece of flotsam washed away when the rivers of terror flooded her mind forcing her downstream, forgotten by anyone she'd met, as soon as she left town.

She didn't want to run anymore. She wanted cuddling on a couch with a man who drove her crazy in bed, and out of bed made her feel safe and like she wasn't crazy.

A life with a friend like Callie and her older buds, the McClouds.

In this town, she finally had begun to feel like she belonged and had found a home. With all that that involved. Like friends.

Even a man she could love, who might love her?

Love her? That possibility seemed like such a long forgotten dream, something she'd wanted as a child, in another lifetime.

But, maybe it was possible for her. Her heartbeat seemed to synch with Luke's, slowing, calming her blood, until finally she felt like a normal person, not some panicked animal running from the hounds.

As if he could sense her heart rate, he waited till calmness had soothed through her body. Finally, he pulled back to look into her eyes. He patted her shoulders reassuringly with both hands and tilted his head.

"Talk to me," he said, guyness emanating from him, his voice low, deep in his throat with a heavy, masculine timbre.

"Talk to me," he murmured.

It might be a long conversation.

"What do you want to know?"

He raised an eyebrow. "This." He spread his arms out into a big circle and waved them all around. "This. What the hell is going on?"

Could she tell him? She held her breath, afraid if she released it that all her secrets would empty out into the room with it.

If she weren't right about Max having been behind this, did she really want to get people talking? The more people who knew, the more chance of word getting back to him.

But, what did it matter anyway? She was leaving tomorrow at first light. She ought to have left already.

Perhaps, just for once, she could unleash some of the horror inside herself, vent some of the pent up need to talk to another human being about all that she'd been through.

Maybe, just maybe, he would believe her. Be on her side. Help her.

Hell no. He'd probably run screaming into the night when he realized what she'd brought him into.

Luke run screaming? The image made her smile. In spite of everything, something had made her smile.

Luke's mouth spread slowly into a smile of his own. A sexy man smile that made her want to fasten her lips to his.

He was, hands down, the sexiest man alive. Not just the sexiest man she'd ever met, but the sexiest man that could possibly have ever existed on the planet.

After his shave, his jaw was smooth and inviting. She ran her hand across it, then slid her hand up through his sandy blond hair.

A whiff of aftershave drifted from him.

A flicker of want flamed in his eyes and he reached for her, pulling her in.

Fastening his lips to hers, he took her to that place of need and want that only he had the directions to. As if he had a map of her soul. An internal GPS with turn-by-turn instructions.

For long seconds, she thought of nothing but him, his mouth, his hands, his body and all the clever things each of those parts could do to her.

Needing to get closer, she wrapped her legs around him, nuzzling into his neck, body against body, notching the kiss up to a higher level, a level that threatened to explode every cell in her body.

His hands pulled her hips closer, until she could feel him in her center, forgetfulness coming with the passion, the ability to think of nothing but him.

The world was only the two of them.

Then, he pulled back, breaking the kiss, looking into her eyes with a dazed expression that she knew well, from the forgetfulness that making love with him could bring.

"Whoa, whoa whoa," he said, his voice hoarse and husky. Swinging his legs around, he rose to a sitting position, taking her with him then slid backward, away from her, putting distance between them on the couch though heat and desire still flamed in his eyes.

He sucked in a deep breath and looked away as if the thinking part of his brain was locked in battle with the passion that had washed over them.

She sank back into the couch, flushed with want. Frustration battled in her as well. But he was right.

They said a woman's acceptable level of crazy was directly proportional to her level of hotness.

This heat between them was sizzling.

But, no amount of hotness could compensate for all the crazy in her life.

Then, a cold flash washed through her, a river of reality rattling her to her core, pushing back against her hormones.

Luke deserved to know what he'd gotten himself into.

Even now, though she desperately wanted the life

affirming feelings that touching Luke sparked in her, it wasn't fair that he didn't know the truth.

She was grasping at life because, at any moment, Max could bust through that door and kill her.

And kill Luke?

He needed to know exactly what the situation entailed.

"Sit back, it's going to be a bumpy ride," she said with her best Bette Davis impression.

The old movies she'd watched with her Grampa kept popping up. They'd always joked and used expressions from his movies. Did her own generation even know what she was talking about? Luke smiled like he'd heard it before.

She got up and went to the window, standing to the side where no one could shoot her through the glass. Slowly, she moved the curtain just a bit so that she could peek outside.

"There's a security system," he said.

She whirled to look at him. "Yeah?"

"Yeah. My cousin set it up for my uncle, to make sure no one broke into the house when he wasn't here. Lots of vacation homes get targeted 'cause people know they're vacant most of the time. If anyone drives up the drive, a little beep will go off. There are motion detectors around the house, hooked up to a computer program."

He got up and walked to the desk sitting near the kitchen. Flipping open a laptop, he waited a moment for it to fully wake up, then motioned to her. "If any of these areas get entered, a beep will go off and a light will activate and take a photo."

He flipped through several screens. "See, that's us."

Emmy looked at several photos of herself getting out of the car and darting toward the house. One showed her looking straight at the camera, eyes wide and panicked, almost a mug shot, really.

Yeah, the crazy showed all over her in that one. What must Luke think?

"I need to do something about my hair," she said, trying to lighten up on her psycho factor.

He half laughed and shook his head. "Yeah, that's what it's for, to check hairdos." He met her eyes, nodding, as if he knew the joke had been a front.

Then, he tilted his head toward the window. "Anyone comes out here and we'll know it."

She smiled, trying to keep up the façade of not being completely panicked. "That's great." Max would spot the detection system, the cameras, and evade them, evade detection.

Wherever she went, there was always gonna be some risk. At least, she knew it. She owed it to Luke to tell him, tell him what he was risking, just by being near her.

A selfish little piece of her didn't want to give up what she'd found with him, wanted to pretend that just another night wouldn't hurt.

To enjoy one last night sleeping with a man and experiencing something that felt like it could grow into love. Grow into something permanent, something that felt like forever.

But, this wasn't about dating. This was about his life. He needed to know.

"My husband is chasing me."

Luke's eyes widened and he looked at her like he'd just realized she was crazy. Which she just might be—

the last year had driven her pretty close to that address.

"What do you mean?" He walked the few steps to the kitchen table, pulled out a straight-back chair, turned it around backward and straddled it. She walked to the table and pulled out another and sat down.

They said the really important things in life were usually settled around the kitchen table. Perfect, just perfect—a parody of normality while talking about this hideous aberration of domesticity that her marriage had been.

She glanced back at the silent laptop. No lights flashing, nothing beeping, no photographs popping up.

Wouldn't that be something? To actually get a photograph of a dead man.

That would at least make this conversation easier, provide some proof that she wasn't psycho.

She wasn't sure she wasn't insane, not anymore. Cause this was certainly what crazy must feel like.

CHAPTER TWELVE

Luke sat across from Emmy. He wasn't sure what he'd expected to hear but this story sure wasn't it.

Had he expected some reasonable scenario? One that would allow him to take her home to mom and dad and say, "Yeah, I know she was a person of interest in her husband's murder, but let me tell you the real deal."

She met his gaze straight on, her eyes never wavering. "For the last year, my husband has been pursuing me. He wants to kill me."

Kill her? What the...

He sucked in air, and looked away, trying to come up with a reaction.

How could he reveal how much of the situation he knew without letting her know that this had all started with him believing she was a killer who just needed to be given enough rope before she revealed enough incriminating evidence to be prosecuted for the murder of a cop?

Before his attraction had overwhelmed his intentions, allowing him to get to know her, and then to believe she wasn't the one the Atlanta Police Department believed might have killed Max.

"Why do you think your husband is after you?"

She shrugged with that puppet-like gesture that had become so much a part of her persona, as if by rote, and as if she didn't expect her answer to be believed.

Damn. If he was sitting across from her in an interview room, he'd be pushing hard now, pushing for details to trip her up.

All of her body language said liar. But his heart didn't want to hear it.

Stupid man, thinking with his Johnson, he could hear the gallery of cops in his head laughing at his idiocy.

"Why?" he prompted again. Make her say the words, come up with language that could contradict other things she'd said before.

Or not, he hoped. Damn, he wanted a believable explanation.

"The fire? The flat tire?" She stood and began to pace. "He's never gotten this close, but I've been able to feel him out there before and would run." She shivered, then wrapped her arms around herself. "This is the nearest he's ever gotten."

"When did you leave him?"

She walked to the fridge and opened it, staring blankly inside. "A year ago."

"And where's home?"

She glanced back at him, then quickly away before their eyes met. "Hawk's Peak, right now. Can I have a beer?"

"Sure."

She brought two to the table, handed him one, then twisted the top off the other and took a small sip. "I love the taste of beer, how it hydrates you." She took another small sip. "I can't afford to get drunk, though."

She placed the beer onto the table. "So, just a few sips for me, for the taste."

He twisted off the top of his and took a long gulping swallow. This was insane. Maybe a beer or two would help. Or three or four.

This woman was saying a dead man was chasing her.

He needed her to level with him.

He narrowed his eyes and looked at her, squinting as if he were trying to interpret her face. "You know, I've felt like ever since I met you that you looked familiar."

Her eyes widened and she picked up her beer, and began peeling the label off. That label must be the most interesting thing in the world because she kept her eyes fastened on it.

"Did you used to be a blonde?"

Her eyes jerked to his face, her skin losing its color.

He pointed his finger at her, shaking it. "Did you used to be on TV, a reporter or something?"

She pushed back from the table, standing, her chair falling over behind her. She began breathing in short pants and she worked the inside of her mouth, chewing on it. Trying to come up with another lie?

She was a liar. He was a liar. A pair of liars. The perfect match.

"You may have seen me on television, yes," she muttered.

"Wait, Yeah. You're that woman from Atlanta. The one whose husband was killed, a cop?"

He stared at her. As if he was shocked, as if all of this had just occurred to him.

"But, I thought your husband is dead. A dead man can't come after you."

She began wringing her hands, then put both of them to her face as her eyes filled with tears. One drop leaked down her cheek to her jaw.

He reached up to swipe it away with his thumb and she jumped and dropped her hands from her face, as startled as if he'd shocked her with an electric prod.

"You are that woman, aren't you?"

She looked at him for a long moment, wiping at her eyes before the tears could run down her cheeks, inhaling quick, shallow breaths.

"Slow down your breathing," he coaxed.

Her eyes met his for a second as she began drawing air in slowly then letting it out again. Then, she paced along the kitchen floor to the fridge and back again, before looking him directly in the eye.

"I am that woman," she said clearly and distinctly.

Finally, a breakthrough. Some honesty. Maybe, they could begin to talk about the realities of the situation.

Should he tell her he was a cop, so they could talk completely open and honest?

No. She was already too freaked out to react to that sort of news with anything less than a dramatic explosion. Things were too crazy to introduce that new information.

"Wow," he let out a burst of air, as if this all took him by surprise.

"I know," she said, with an understanding half smile. "It's huge."

He just looked at her, waiting for her to take the next step.

"I am that woman, the woman they called a *person of interest*."

He nodded. "They said you disappeared the same day as him."

"I went on the run."

"But why would you go on the run? It only made you look suspicious."

"Better than looking dead." She shook her head, as if even now she could see a crime scene photo with herself at the center as the victim. "Not a good look on anybody."

"I don't know why they always said I was a person of interest. Why didn't they say it was suspicious, my disappearance? Why didn't they wonder if I was dead somewhere too?"

"They said there was only blood from one victim," he offered. "Your husband's. Said something about animal blood, too."

She visibly flinched. Neighbors said there'd been a dog.

"They also said you'd withdrawn money from an ATM the same day. They had surveillance photos of you."

She leaned over and hit the table with her fist, sending the beer bottles jumping with a noisy rattle. "I could have been forced to do that, told they would kill my husband. I saw the news accounts, too. I made national news. Why did they just assume I was guilty? And not dead somewhere out in the woods after that?"

He didn't say because they'd gotten a second security camera video of her at another gas station in the next state. And no one else had been with her on the wide shot that had shown her getting in and out of her car.

They hadn't put that information out there.

He shook his head. "Don't know."

"Exactly." She pointed her finger accusingly toward the windows. "They just went on a witch hunt, pointed fingers at me." She paced, shaking her hands, balling them into fists, releasing them and then fisting them again, convulsively, obsessively. Occasionally, she pointed, as if she were making some silent point to herself.

"He's dead," he said. "Why would you think he's coming after you?"

She narrowed her eyes with a dark smile. "They found blood, a crime scene, not an actual body. The crime was a faked death. Max is not dead."

He sucked in a deep breath. That was the last thing he'd expected to hear.

"Faked his own murder?" Just keep feeding her words back to her.

"Yes." She nodded her head repeatedly, looking almost psychotic, glazed eyes unfocused, as if seeing her own scenario playing out inside her head.

Could he have been so wrong about her? Maybe she had gone completely round the bend. Had his lust for her convinced him she was normal?

He'd been partially dead since he'd seen his wife's casket lowered into the grave.

When he met Emmy he began to believe in life after the deathlike, catatonic state he'd experienced for so many months.

Emmy's face, her voice, had pulled him back from the darkness that had enveloped him in grief. She became the only thing he looked forward to and enjoyed. She made him feel alive.

Seeing Emmy had become what he lived for.

It had been later when his mind finally processed her face as Emily Weber, wife of the dead cop, with a reeling punch to the gut. He'd been unable to breathe.

Why had it taken him so long?

Had he known all along and just refused to see it? Or had his mind been so dead that it didn't operate correctly?

Whatever the reason, when he'd finally begun to realize who she was, his whole body had rebelled. He'd almost thrown up when he'd first put two and two together.

He'd felt like he was going to die, sink into the gray swamp all over again. From that moment on, if he were really honest with himself, he'd only wanted to prove to himself she wasn't guilty.

That there had been another reason she'd run.

Was he so blinded by lust that he couldn't see the truth?

Was she crazed with guilt, a guilt that chased her through the night?

No. Someone had slashed that tire, someone must have set that fire.

But who? He had no proof that it was someone other than Emmy herself.

Was she so psychotic she was doing these things and didn't even know it?

Was she tormenting herself as punishment?

Then, from deep inside his gut, where the real insights always arose, came a conflicting thought. If she'd run tonight, he would never have seen her again.

Except perhaps in a crime scene photograph of her dead body?

The image of Emmy lying in a pool of blood

crystallized like a drop of water on a frozen windshield. That such an image would come to him terrified him. Because often he sensed the reality of a situation long before any evidence existed to prove it.

His *female intuition* his cop buddies had jokingly named it. But, they'd respected it, used it.

Was this was one of those times?

If she'd fled after the fire, with no one to protect her, she might have ended up dead.

That thought kicked him in the teeth like nothing had since the doctor had walked into the room and told him and Mazie there was no hope.

That the doctor's prediction had been true, hadn't made it any easier to take. He'd become furious, gone into fighting mode, battling for his wife, for any treatment that might give her another few months even.

Because who knew what might happen during those few months. They'd find something out there, a scientist would make a breakthrough.

He'd sat up nights, scouring the Internet.

Fought with doctors.

Until finally, Mazie had said enough. She wouldn't take another course of treatment. She chose to go into the darkness, into the empty space beyond this world rather than suffer anymore.

Maybe he couldn't save his wife from some invisible disease, but he'd be damned if he'd give up Emmy to something that was of this world. Some man.

And like that, it clicked in his brain.

He believed Emmy.

Believed she hadn't killed her husband.

Just like that, he accepted she was the victim, running from the man who everyone thought was dead.

He'd seen it before, someone faking their death. For insurance or to escape criminal prosecution.

Why had Max done it? That was unclear. But if anyone knew how to fake a death, it was a cop.

And cops were human.

Luke could only fight cancer to a point. But a man? He'd fight him to the death.

A man? A human? Give him an opponent like that.

"How can I help you?" He looked into Emmy's eyes and placed a hand on her shoulder, willing her to accept his aid.

Willing her to believe in him, as he believed in her.

CHAPTER THIRTEEN

Emmy felt tears climbing to the surface, wanting to flood out of her with all the repressed fear, desperation and anger she'd felt for a year.

Anger for having to run like the guilty party, to run in fear for her life, to leave her old Grampa alone, wondering when he'd see his Emmy again.

She pushed the tears back. No breaking down now. She had to focus. There wasn't time for the luxury of something so self-indulgent as crying.

Finally, she had an ally. Someone who believed in her, was on her side, wanted to help her.

"Let's brainstorm," Luke said quietly, as if sensing just how close to the emotional edge she was.

The man was sensitive, insightful. Where had he been when she was young and looking for someone to fall in love with, to partner with, to spend the rest of her life with and to raise children?

But, that was the past. If there was anything she'd learned in the last year it was you couldn't change the past. You could only adapt to what the past left you.

This was now. And a lovely man like Luke Bradenton had entered her life just when she'd almost lost faith in the future, in the possibility that she could ever have a normal life again. Just when she needed him most, he'd appeared.

He'd given her a taste of normalcy, an appetizer, a little of him making her want a whole lot more.

She was going to have it, too. Max be damned.

"Come here."

He extended his hand as if to shake on it, shake on a contract to trust him. She took his hand and he pulled her in. She melted into his chest, into an embrace that was warm and comforting, nothing like the passion of the night before.

His heart beat so reassuringly there beneath her ear, strong, trustworthy, fierce. She breathed him in, everything that a woman could want.

That every little girl should expect from a man.

Suddenly, a beeping alert came from somewhere by the kitchen door and the laptop simultaneously. Her heart erupted in her chest, like a volcanic explosion of panic.

She broke away from Luke and twirled around. Where was Max? Was he at the door already?

She leaped toward her purse and pulled out her gun, then pivoted back and forth between the kitchen door and the front door. She wouldn't be an easy target.

If she went, they were going together. She'd accompany Max to the gates of hell.

Luke's eyes widened but he didn't say a word as he walked to the closet and pulled out a shotgun, along with a box of shells.

"Welcome to our house." He lifted the shotgun, a dark smile spreading cross his face. "Let the sound of this shotgun racking be the last thing he hears before he comes through any doors around here."

She met his eyes and nodded, but was unable to manage a smile of any sort.

Luke studied her for a second then went to the laptop, pressed a button on the computer and began scrolling through a series of camera shots.

She crept up beside him, looking at the laptop, unable to breathe, expecting the sudden horror of her *dead* husband's face to appear.

A terrifying image of him crawling through the woods toward them like some nightmarish creature searching for blood?

The seconds ticked by with the pulsing throbs of blood in her neck. Could someone of her age actually die of fear? How much terror could one human body withstand in a year?

Luke scrolled through various shots.

She closed her eyes, wanting a moment of warning.

Luke's hand touched her shoulder. "It's nothing," he said quietly, soothingly. She looked up at him and he motioned toward the computer screen as he set the shotgun on the floor.

A figure filled the screen of the laptop. Her eyes wouldn't focus, only seeing a gray, blurry blob. She sucked in air, blinked her eyes, chasing away the tears she hadn't even realized had filled them.

This time her eyes focused on the figure.

A deer.

She released a huge wracking sob of a breath, her legs going weak as she leaned back against the wall, sucking in air as if she were drowning, with just her face above water.

Finally, her vision cleared, and the gray pushed

away so she could see Luke's face again. She forced a wan smile.

"Normal to crazy in two seconds," she wheezed out. The attempted joke came out darkly, not really funny at all.

He half smiled.

"How is my level of crazy stacking up against my hotness?" she said.

He laughed out loud, leaned the shotgun against the wall, then held up two hands, one hand sinking, the other rising.

"Not sure which side's winning out," she said. "But, I bet it's the crazy. Maybe I need to get me some leather pants or something."

A fierce heat erupted in his gaze, with a flaming need for her. "No clothes required for what I've got in mind."

A flash of want shot through her, heating her core into a molten chasm of desire.

He pulled her to him, enfolding her in arms that felt like torches singeing her skin everywhere their skin touched. He didn't kiss her, but just held her tightly as if his body needed the contact.

All she wanted was to go upstairs and make love, connect with him, take what he offered. She could forget everything but the fire that sparked between them. So easily.

Risky sexual behavior? That didn't even begin to describe the situation.

The possible consequences could be death. For her, for Luke. If they let their desire cause them to lose sight of the danger out there.

All Max needed to win was for them to let down

their guard. To lose themselves in each other for one night, a night that could cost them their lives.

There was nothing Max would love more than to shoot her dead in bed with another man.

He'd feel justified, with every right to kill her for betrayal of their wedding vows.

That was the problem with a sociopath like him. He could justify all sorts of horrifying transgressions against others.

She pulled away, removing herself from Luke's warmth, that warmth that had begun melting the ice that had circulated through her veins for the last year, leaving her frozen, removed, apart from life.

Her body ached to be back in his arms, to have what everyone had the right to expect. Love, belonging.

Except her?

Luke reached for her, closing his large hands around her biceps. He shook his head, with a deadly anger lashing through his eyes. "That bastard is not taking this away from us. I'll fight him to his last breath rather than let him hurt what we've found."

"His last breath?" She met his eyes hoping he knew exactly what he was getting into.

"His last breath," he confirmed. "I'll be damned if I'm going to let him take you away from me."

His eyes held a convincing fierceness. Then, another scary thought occurred to her. Had she replaced one possessive man for another, one who assumed she was his for the taking?

He loosened his grip on her arms, his expression gentling as if he could read the thoughts ravaging her mind, the thoughts that screamed she could never have a normal love again, that someone like Max was what she deserved.

"You can walk away whenever you want," he purred in his deep, masculine voice that still sounded like honey pouring from his mouth. Sweet, seductive, passion infused. "Only, I intend to make you never want to do that."

A wicked smile worked its way across his face. "I plan to get inside of you, literally and figuratively, until I'm part of you, until you can't breathe well when you're away from me too long. Going to work is going to be difficult even."

She sucked in a deep, aching lungful of air that rattled painfully through her chest. "I'm already a little breathless."

He wrapped his hands around her hips, pulling her tightly against him, securing her in place.

"Not helping." She laughed huskily.

"Not wanting to." He leaned in for a quick kiss, his lips brushing against hers, with a taunting invitation before he took her mouth with a force that pulsed through her, making her liquid and needy.

Just when she thought the entire night was lost, that they could only fall into bed, only sate this want, he pulled back, met her gaze and his expression turned hard again.

"After I take care of this guy, after I make him pay for what he's done to you." His expression softened. "Then, you will decide what you want to do, who you want to get into bed with every night."

Every night? Had that expression just slipped out?

He pulled her into him, his hands securing her firmly against him, leaving no doubt that he wanted her.

"So," he said softly, whispering close to her mouth, looking down at it as if anticipating what he wanted to do to it, what he wanted to do to her.

"The future starts now." His voice was like mellow whisky, soothing her nerves but with a hidden danger with its ability to melt away her defenses.

"Let's go upstairs and start life, life as it will be from now on. A life that only entails you doing what you want. And with who you want to do it."

With a wicked smile, he tilted his head toward the stairs leading to the bedroom, a devilish question in his eyes.

She sucked in a deep breath of heated air that swirled with desire, the need for him and all the things they could do with the night.

"Yes." She met his eyes and nodded. "Definitely yes."

He crawled past the first detector, the indicator so apparent that a sixteen-year-old looking for a house to party in could have spotted it.

They weren't prepared for someone like him. Circling around a second camera, he approached the back of the house.

There was her car. The slut was definitely inside. He looked up at the second floor as a light came on, then turned off again with only a small flickering light illuminating the room.

A candle? Could they be more arrogant, advertising their actions?

She hadn't run like usual. Had she purposefully chosen another cop as a lover? Did she think that would save her?

It was definitely a complication, though not an impossible one.

He'd wait until tomorrow. If she hadn't taken off by then, he'd have to up the ante.

The bitch couldn't think she could get away with this.

Slowly, he slinked around the detectors, making sure not to set off any alarms. Then, he walked the half-mile back to his car, hidden in a small turn off behind some trees.

He could hardly wait for tomorrow. To increase his attack on Emily, Emmy as she chose to call herself now. What a ridiculous choice, so close to Emily.

Did the bitch have a death wish?

If so, he'd be happy to fulfill it for her.

CHAPTER FOURTEEN

Emmy stood by the window over the kitchen sink, sipping a cup of coffee, watching three deer grazing nonchalantly in the circular driveway.

They seemed particular, slowly choosing the tender blades, chewing slowly. One deer looked up at her, dark eyes contemplating her for a long moment before resuming grazing.

A warm, sunny glow filled the kitchen, mellowing the room, filling her with a sense of peace. Normalcy. She could get used to it.

"Morning," Luke's gravely, early morning voice came from the doorway.

She turned and took him in. What a sight to see first thing in the morning. Morning after, she corrected herself.

She'd had many sleepless nights the past year but none she'd enjoyed as much as last night.

A shadow of beard brushed his cheeks and chin. A pair of sweat pants clung loosely to his lower half, his chest bare.

He walked to her, taking the mug from her, gulping down half of its contents.

She laughed, deep in her throat, a slow, building

want making her voice husky, hard to force out. "Some coffee for you?"

He gave her back her mug and reached behind her to take his mug from the counter, his scent wafting around her, with a muskiness, a maleness that enticed her.

She stepped aside, out of the range of his pheromones, and turned away from the sight of him and stared blankly out the window.

All she wanted was to go upstairs, get back in that bed, and enclose herself in Luke's arms, his scent, his mouth, his tenderness, his masculinity.

Her shift at The Corner Store gave them some time. But the thought of The Corner Store immediately pulled her out of her lust-filled haze.

She needed to talk to Callie. And that conversation was going to be disturbing.

By leaving town now, she would be leaving Callie in the lurch. It would be a huge inconvenience to lose an employee at the height of the leaf season. A real hardship.

But it would be worse to keep the connection going. Anyone around her could be endangered.

Max could take a shot and miss. And hit God knows who.

She didn't think an anonymous shot from a distance was his style, but he might be sick of the cat and mouse game by now.

And decide to finish it.

Luke leaned up against her from behind, putting his knees into the back of hers, effectively forcing her to lose her balance and fall back into him.

He caught her, pulling her closer, so she found

herself leaning against his chest, one of his arms around her waist.

"Don't think so much," he murmured close to her ear, the sound deep and sensual, the voice he'd used in bed the night before, the voice that took her back to those moments in the middle of the night.

Her core heated and called for him. He pushed away her hair and mouthed along her neck, just below her ear.

She moaned softly, and he increased the pressure, moving up to her ear, his breath hot and close. The intimacy was so intense that she pulled away ever so slightly. Just enough room to breathe, to think.

"From now on," he murmured close to her skin. "Think out loud, talk, tell me your worries, so we can tackle them together, take them on full force. If you have thoughts about what that bastard might be out there doing, tell me, 'cause information is power."

He turned her by the waist to look him in the eye. "We're a team now."

A clutch of happiness gripped her heart. A team? As if this might go on…forever?

"Together, we're going to beat him." He nodded at her, seeming to look for confirmation she was going to work with him and not run.

Run alone into an uncertain future where she would have no one to help her, no one to have her back.

She met his gaze, felt the power and connection between them, held the moment for just a second longer, then nodded. "We're going to beat him."

"Yes, we are."

Hope filled her, buoying her with a promise for a future she'd not dared wish for most of this last year, instead only living from moment to moment, hoping to survive one day longer.

Luke's eyes met her fiercely, promising she could depend on him, that this man wouldn't let her down.

She tilted her head, focusing on his lips, moving in, anticipating the contact. Then her cell phone rattled on the counter, jostling her out of the heated space between her and Luke's lips.

She pulled in a deep, shaky breath, laughed low in her chest at Luke's expression of frustration. She shrugged and picked up the phone to check the incoming call ID. "It's Callie. I have to take this. To tell her I can't come back to the store."

"Wait." He stilled her hand from answering the phone, his face suddenly serious, intent. "Go to work. Keep on with your usual activities. We're going on the offensive, luring him in."

His eyes hardened, scarily so. As if he were ready to kill someone.

So quickly, he'd gone from soft and warm to this steel-cold man.

She liked it. It felt right that he would so quickly change at the reminder of the danger to her.

"This isn't his game anymore." His voice cut the air like a serrated knife. "We're going after him. You're going to work today."

She sucked in a breath, wanting to hide from the danger. To creep away like a mouse, running from the hawk?

But, going freely out into the open, living like normal? It went against everything she'd done the last year, against every impulse. But then what she'd been doing wasn't working. She'd just run from one crisis to the next, only a step ahead of Max.

They said the definition of crazy was doing what you'd been doing and expecting a different outcome. She wasn't crazy.

The urge to go after Max had been growing inside of her ever since she'd thought about coming back to Georgia. Since she'd returned here, she'd seemed to draw strength from the soil of her home state.

She'd wanted to go down into Atlanta and dig him out of whatever hole he might be using as home base in between trips out to look for her, to try to kill her.

She didn't know how he'd found her over and over again. But, she bet he'd had a woman somewhere in Atlanta providing a safe house.

Since he'd found her again, maybe it was time to take a stand. He'd come to her once again. Maybe it was time to take the fight to him. Not wait to do it at another place, another time. A time and place of Max's choosing, where she'd have no allies.

Slowly, she nodded. This time would be different. Callie's call had gone to voice mail, but Emmy hit the call button and Callie answered on the first ring.

"Emmy, are you okay?" Callie's voice trilled high and shrill. "You should have called me about the fire."

The fire? It seemed so long ago, as if the night she'd spent with Luke had been a year, with so many emotions.

"I'm okay, Callie. Really," she soothed in response to the genuine alarm in Callie's voice. Two people showing so much concern for her welfare in one day was overwhelming.

She'd been alone way too long.

"Mr. McCloud told me about the fire first thing this morning. Everyone's talking about it. Girl, you should have come to stay with me. You aren't staying out there at your house, are you?"

"No. I'm fine, Callie. Listen, I'm getting ready to head in now so we can talk. Okay?"

Callie paused for a long moment, then she let out a soft laugh. "You're with Luke?"

Emmy didn't say anything.

"Gotcha," she said with a sparkly laugh. "Do I need to cover your shift for you? Good excuse and all, what with the fire."

Emmy laughed. Laughed as only Callie could make her laugh. She'd never had a girlfriend as much fun as Callie.

All of her girlfriends from before her marriage had trailed away once they'd gotten a taste of Max's nastiness. He'd either hit on them, or confronted their boyfriends or husbands in some macho display of dominance.

"No, I'll be there." Maybe Luke was right to lure Max in. How else were they going to finally end this?

"See ya at work. We'll talk then." Callie laughed again with a satisfied sound, then disconnected.

A deep sucking anxiety ground through Emmy's stomach. "I don't feel good about this, Luke. I need to at least tell her what's up. She's my friend. I can't let her be a sitting duck without saying anything."

Luke looked at her for a long moment, took a sip of coffee then looked out the window. "Those deer are still there."

He was dodging her comment about telling Callie but she walked to the window and stood beside him looking out, looking out together toward any danger that might approach. "Still?"

"Yeah. They beeped earlier this morning. I saw them on the laptop. You were out cold." He laughed slightly. "Didn't get much sleep last night. My fault. We really should have been catching more shut eye so we'd be on our toes."

She shook her head, decisively. "That was one of the most restful night's sleep I've gotten since…well since the other night we were together."

He laughed and playfully stuck out his chest with pride. "Just call me Sominex. Take Luke tonight and sleep, sleep, sleep." He turned toward her.

She wrapped her arms around his waist and hugged him, her face against his warm chest, inhaling his scent, his lovely male scent. "Usually, I sleep but when I wake up I'm not rested 'cause I've been dreaming all night long."

He leaned back to look in her eyes, all humor gone. "Yeah, I hope Max," he said the name like it was an expletive, "gets no sleep for a really long time in prison, sleeping with one eye open, wondering who's sneaking up on him for a little midnight rendezvous."

She nodded. "Payback's a bitch."

He smiled darkly, then stepped back slowly as if he had to force himself away from her. He filled his mug with more coffee then walked to the table, sitting backward again on a chair in what she was beginning to realize was his favorite position.

"So, let's plan," he said.

Just then, the laptop began to beep.

She jumped, adrenaline releasing, pushing alarm throughout her body.

Together, they walked into the living room to look at the screen. The first screen showed an SUV pulling into the front driveway.

"He wouldn't be so stupid as just to drive in here," she said.

Luke smiled darkly. "It's my cousin." He tilted his head to her. "Why don't you go on up and take your shower, while I have a few words with him."

She looked down at Luke's T-shirt that reached mid-thigh on her. She'd slipped into it before coming downstairs. "Yep. Not dressed for meeting the relatives."

A loud banging on the front door said Luke's cousin was moving fast to have already gotten out of his car and up the front steps.

"I can't get in the door," a male voice yelled from just outside.

Luke went to the front door and removed her No-Kick-In device as she scurried up the stairs.

She ducked upstairs just before the front door opened and a pot crashed off a chair onto the floor.

"What the hell is all this?" a deep masculine voice echoed up the stairs.

"My own little trip wires." Luke laughed like all this was normal.

His cousin's voice lowered, but she was still able to make out his words. "What the hell's going on, Luke?"

"What do you mean?"

"What do I mean?" Irony laced his tone. "That security system I installed up here for Uncle Joe? I've got it routed to my laptop as well." He laughed harshly.

"I saw that woman you brought over here. What the hell's going on?"

The voices became more distant. Luke had led him into the kitchen. She walked down the first two stairs but couldn't hear a thing.

Luke had purposefully led him away from the stairs and to the back of the kitchen. Why was he being so secretive?

What was there really to say about a grown, unmarried guy choosing to spend the night with a woman?

Then, it hit her. His cousin might live in Atlanta. If he'd gotten a good look at her face, he might have recognized her.

No one in Hawk's Peak had said anything to indicate they'd recognized her. But, there probably hadn't been such intensive coverage up here.

In Atlanta, there'd probably been wall-to-wall, non-stop news coverage.

Dying her hair, wearing little makeup and dressing differently? She'd tried to change her appearance. But…

Was she such an idiot to think she could have come this close to Atlanta without people recognizing her, knowing who she was?

She'd wanted to try and live here so that her Grampa could move in with her.

He had some social services set up here in Georgia that would have been difficult to move out of state, would have required some identifying paperwork that would have left a trail for Max.

She'd thought bringing him to Hawk's Peak might have worked out. But, obviously she was wrong.

How had Max found her? Had someone spotted her and it had gotten back to him somehow?

No, that wasn't it. He was in hiding himself, so not in contact with his old network. Besides, he'd found her even when she'd been much further from home than this.

No cops had come knocking on her door. But Max always knew where she was.

How had he found her all those times?

CHAPTER FIFTEEN

Luke gritted his teeth as Emmy drove out of the driveway. He didn't want her out of his sight, wanted to take her to and from work, protect her every moment of the day.

But, that couldn't happen. Not if their plan was going to work.

Max needed to think they weren't on to him. Emmy needed to look like she was going to work just like normal.

Luke's cousin, Forrester, stepped in front of him, his face two inches from Luke's. "So, what the F is going on?"

Luke laughed and pushed him away with two fingers to the chest. "That not cussing thing seems to be working out for you."

Forrester grimaced, his face carrying the same message as the foulest expletive could have conveyed.

"How long since you last cussed?" Luke asked. "How long you been with Cassie again?"

"Long enough." Forrester blew out a disgusted burst of air. "But, she said I still cuss way too frequently for her. Says she doesn't know if she wants to have kids with someone who cusses like I do. Says she doesn't

143

want a bunch of little foul-mouthed kids running around the house."

And Luke knew Forrester really wanted kids with Cassie.

Forrester's mouth twisted. "You know how hard it is being around cops all day and not cussing?"

"Yes, I do." Luke had been shocked when he'd become a cop at how liberally and unselfconsciously so many cops littered their conversations with expletives.

His own wife hadn't liked it either, said she didn't want a husband who felt comfortable flinging around that type of language.

"Well, if I stopped, you can too," Luke said.

Forrester's face darkened because he knew why Luke's language had changed.

For his dead wife's sake.

He blinked several times but didn't comment on Mazie. They'd both been through the wringer during her long illness, with Forrester helping out, taking a shift at the hospital along with other family members when Luke was at work.

Luke had taken full-time leave from work only in the worst times and toward the end. When nothing could have pulled him away from Mazie's bedside.

Forrester's jaw twitched before he returned to the subject that had brought him up here. "Man, I couldn't believe it when I figured out who she is. She looked right up at the camera one time when ya'll were going in. I laughed when I saw it, thought Old Lukie found himself a girl. Then, I kept looking at that face, thinking where had I seen it before. Then, it came to me this morning. Woke me up out of a dead sleep."

Forrester lowered his voice. "She may not be blonde

anymore. But I recognized her. And, I bet you did too."

Luke's cousin shook his head. "So, fill me in on this situation with this woman. Tell me it isn't what it looks like."

"It's exactly what it looks like." Luke leaned in toward Forrester, daring his cousin to take that know-it-all tone again. "I'm sleeping with the person of interest in a cop's murder." He stared at Forrester, waiting for it to hit the fan.

"The person of interest who vanished the day her husband's blood was found all over their house?" Forrester lowered his eyebrows. "In case you're forgetting any of the details."

"I remember," Luke said, straight faced.

He shrugged, and braced himself for the disbelief that was about to stain his cousin's face when he heard Emmy's story. "I'll fill you in on the rest in the car. I think she's got about enough of a head start."

Forrester's eyebrows shot straight up. That was nothing to the looks he was going to give him when he heard everything Luke had to tell him.

And the cussing. It would set him back a bit on the cussing.

He grabbed the laptop so he could check the computer throughout the day, keep tabs on things at the cabin.

Didn't want to come home to someone already inside.

"You got your piece?" He looked at Forrester who arched an eyebrow.

"Hell yeah, I'm packing. I see there's a cop killer hanging around my uncle's place, I headed right up here with my gun." He pulled his shirt up to reveal his holster on his jeans waistband.

"I'd have brought backup but I didn't want to make you look bad." He glared at Luke.

"You've never been able to make me look bad before, so don't start thinking you will now," Luke shot back at him, giving as good as he got like he'd done his whole life.

Six months older and Forrester had always thought he could boss him around. Not that he'd ever gotten away with it.

Forrester guffawed. "I also brought my common sense. I'd 'a brought you some, if I knew where to get any extra. Cause you sure don't seem to have any, never did."

Luke chuckled. "You don't have any to spare, that's for sure." As he put his hand on the doorknob, he became very serious again. Max could be anywhere.

He'd never really liked the guy, didn't like how he'd gotten a little too close to Mazie at a few cop barbecues and picnics when they'd first started dating. Max had been on his first or second wife then. Luke couldn't keep up with the furious women that guy had left littered behind him like pieces of trash tossed out the window of a car racing down a rural highway.

He opened the door, covertly scanning the woods in case anyone had slipped through the motion detectors.

Emmy had lived like this for a whole year? Was still living this way?

Living wasn't the word for it. That was merely existing, keeping breathing one more day, one more month.

What a way to live. Looking over her shoulder,

jumping at anything that went bump in the night, thinking a falling limb outside could be her ex husband coming for her.

Max had put her through that.

There weren't enough expletives to express what he wanted to do to the guy.

Well, they were coming for Max now. He looked back at Forrester. "You couldn't have showed up at a better time, Cuz."

"My thoughts exactly. Somebody's gotta keep an eye on you." Forrester shook his head, rolling his eyes like he did the time Luke said he was gonna walk across Anna Ruby Falls at the point that the waterfall dropped off to the forest below.

"Come to think of it, you ain't never had no common sense," Forrester growled. "I don't know how you made it through life this long."

Luke chuckled, even as he kept scanning the wood line. "You've always been funny, Cuz." He slapped Forrester on the back. "Good to see ya."

Emmy walked into work, guilt gnawing at her conscience. She might have already endangered Callie just by being around her.

How to start this conversation?

How to explain the circumstances?

They had time before Callie had to pick up her kids from her ex-husband's house.

"So, another night with Fisherman Luke?" Callie grinned like she hadn't just invaded her privacy, like it was acceptable for bosses to ask employees about the men they were sleeping with.

If that's the only way she thought of Callie, as her boss. But she was much more.

She just prayed Callie would understand when she explained everything, wouldn't be angry and think she'd put her and her kids at risk.

A customer walked in, a guy Emmy had seen a couple of times. He went over to the cooler, returning with a Coke. Callie rang it up and gave him his change with a smile. She waited until he'd left before turning back to Emmy, her eyebrows arching.

"So, spill," she said. "Is he as good as I always imagined he'd be? Wait, make that, fantasized." She arched an eyebrow suggestively. "So tall, so built, with those strong forearms and those…hands."

"Emm." Callie shuddered dramatically.

Emmy laughed. Despite everything, despite the conversation they were about to have, Callie could make her laugh. Emmy walked around the counter to stand by Callie.

Emmy wrapped her arms around herself, feeling as if she were about to throw up. She didn't want to lose her friend, the friend she'd been able to joke and really laugh with for the last few months.

If she had to leave Hawk's Peak she'd be losing so much, a man who felt like home and a woman who felt like a friend, a town that felt like somewhere she could live forever.

"What?" Callie's eyes narrowed and she reached forward, taking Emmy by the biceps, squeezing. "What's going on? Don't tell me Fisherman Luke told you he really wants *me,* has always had a thing for me."

She released Emmy's arms and fluffed her hair with one hand, then tossed it back from her face so that the blue streak in her dark hair showed brightly. "Cause most guys do, you know."

Emmy looked down at the floor, summoning the strength she needed to disclose the information Callie had a right to know. Then, she raised her eyes, meeting Callie's. "I hope you don't hate me when you hear what I have to say."

Callie's mouth tightened and she looked Emmy intently in the eye before shaking her head. "I can't imagine anything you might say that would make me hate you." She shrugged. "Except that you slept with my Mike. He may be my ex and all, but if you said that, I'd have to cut you."

Emmy laughed at the lame attempt at humor. You could always count on Callie for a joke.

"That's not it, right? You're not sleeping with Fisherman Luke and my ex at the same time?" Callie twirled the blue streak around her finger.

Emmy forced a smile. The closer they got to the moment, the harder it became to think about anything but what she had to say. "No. That's not it."

"So, spill." Callie dropped the blue ringlet and her eyes reflected back the darkness that filled Emmy.

Callie walked to the front door, turned the deadbolt and flipped the sign over to Closed. Then, she walked around the counter and leaned back against it, facing Emmy.

Emmy sucked in a deep breath.

"Just say it, Emmy." Callie used her Mama tone, the one she used for her kids when she really meant it, when they'd pulled their last mischievous prank of the day.

Emmy sucked in a deep breath then let it out, visualizing all her anxiety going with it.

"My name isn't really Emmy Renard. It's Emily Weber."

Callie tilted her head and narrowed her eyes, then just shrugged. "Well, I already knew that, honey."

The floor of the store began falling away, leaving Emmy teetering precariously on the edge, struggling to maintain her balance. "You knew?"

"Sure," Callie said. "Mr. and Mrs. McCloud and me, we put it together a while ago. Me and Mr. McCloud, we kept saying who does she remind you of? One day, Mrs. McCloud overheard us and said, 'Why that's that girl from down in Atlanta whose husband showed up missing.' Just like that, like she'd known it all along."

Callie laughed. "I wonder how long she knew and if she would've said anything if she hadn't heard us talking."

Emmy felt the blood leaving her face.

"Sit down, honey." Callie pulled a chair from behind the counter and pushed Emmy into it. "You done gone all vampire on me, white as one of those Cullens in that *Twilight* movie."

Emmy looked up at Callie. "How many other people know?"

"I don't know. Nobody talks about it. Me and the McClouds figured it's your business, and if you didn't say anything then you didn't want it known. Or didn't want to talk about it." She looked at Emmy with the softest expression.

"Can't say that I blame you, that must have been horrible to have something happen to your husband like that. Hmm?"

Emmy nodded. It had been one of the worse days of her life. But, not exactly how Callie meant it.

"The thing is, Callie, my husband isn't dead."

Callie arched an eyebrow. "I heard they didn't find the body, but, honey, don't tell me you're still holding out hope he'll be found alive. After all this time?"

A hopeless romantic? Her? Hardly.

Callie and the McClouds thought she was grieving, not wanting to talk about the murder of her husband.

"You never thought I killed him?"

"Oh, no." Callie threw up her hands like someone had just accused her of the murder.

"They never arrested you. Me, I always figured you'd been taken away by force or something, then maybe got away."

She looked to Emmy for confirmation. Emmy shook her head.

"It's a horrible story, Callie. Long and involved, but the short version is my husband isn't dead."

Callie's eyes widened. "Not dead? Sounded like he'd have to be."

"I don't know how he did it, but he spread his blood around, maybe he'd been saving it or something. Taking out a little at a time?" She'd wondered about that too. "Max had a way of planning out evil."

Callie twirled her blue streak of hair tightly around one finger.

She'd seen that once when he'd waited to catch her doing something he'd told her not to do.

Eat ice cream.

Emmy told Callie about how Max had shown up at the ice cream store when she'd just sat down to enjoy a cone. Had yelled he wasn't about to have a fat pig for a wife, and did she think he was stupid enough not to know she'd been sneaking ice cream.

The teens behind the counter had looked on in horror as she'd silently gotten up and dumped her cone into the trash and walked out the door.

At that point, she'd been just trying to stay alive. Stay alive long enough to be able to run.

"The point isn't how he did it but that he did it. He faked his death."

Callie's eyes kept getting wider and wider until she looked like she had some sort of *condition*.

"He figured out I was about to leave him and faked his death. So, he could kill me and not be charged." She raised her hands and shoulders in an exaggerated shrug. "Can't charge a dead man."

She felt the blood flooding back into her face full force, along with her anger. She stood up and began pacing. "He always said the only way I'd leave him was in a body bag. He meant it."

Callie's face paled as if Emmy's anger had drawn its strength from Callie, vampire style. Callie slumped into the chair Emmy had just vacated.

"Oh lord, honey, that's terrible." She looked up at Emmy with pure pity.

"Don't look at me that way." Emmy held up her hands. "You're gonna make me cry."

Tears began to well in Callie's eyes. "It's plumb terrible."

"Don't do that. Don't do that." Emmy turned, pacing, forcing back the tears Callie's tears had called forth. "I need to be strong and the best way to do that is to be angry."

"I'd be angry, too." Callie sniffed and her tone changed to indignant. "The nerve of that man. I never heard the like. Why if my Mike had said even half of that, I'd have taken a pan up side his head. He knows it too." She pointed her finger and shook it repeatedly for emphasis.

"Who in tarnation does that man think he is?"

Emmy did laugh then. "How many down-home expressions can you fit into one conversation? I swear I can tell when you've been hanging out with some of the mountain folk from round here, 'cause you get plumb southern and start mountain talking."

Callie looked at her, then broke into laughter. They both began to laugh, in anxiety-releasing fits, not able to stop, until tears came to Emmy's eyes. She reached over to grab a paper towel from underneath the counter and swiped at her eyes.

"I need one, too. You're right, the longer I live up here, the more I start talking mountain. I'm a chameleon, taking on the characteristics of the people I'm around." Callie reached to take the paper towel Emmy passed her. "We're sick, laughing about something so horrible. But, I guess it's better to laugh than cry."

Emmy held up the paper towel. "Looks like we did both."

"Yeah, honey. But, these are good tears."

Emmy swiped away the last of the laughter tears, then looked seriously at Callie. What she was about to say, Callie wouldn't find funny at all.

But, it had to be said.

Just then, the phone rang. Callie got up and answered, "Corner Store, this is Callie."

Her face flashed completely white. "Well, where's Mike? Why ain't he taking care of the kids like he said he was? I'm gonna kill that man."

She listened for moment, then screamed suddenly, a panicked animal sound, and slammed down the phone.

"Come on!" She grabbed her purse and ran out the back door, dropping things out of her purse as she ran.

Emmy leaned over to pick them up but Callie yelled, "Come on. Forget that stuff. Somebody got one of my kids."

Got one of her kids?

A horrible stabbing knife gutted Emmy, spilling out all her most terrifying fears.

Was it possible? Had Max struck already?

Because she'd always known it would come in some unexpected form, when she least expected it.

Max would take pride in how he drove her completely past the point of sanity. Would take pride in the manner in which he killed her.

He was a homicide cop after all, had seen or knew the details about every murder that had taken place in the city of Atlanta over the last fifteen years.

Chapter Sixteen

Emmy jumped into the front passenger seat just as Callie slammed the car into reverse. It jerked backward, throwing Emmy forward into the dashboard then almost instantly back against the seat as Callie propelled the car forward with a maniacal ferocity, putting her foot down on the gas like a cop driving to a scene.

Max had driven like that with her in the car several times when he wanted to be the first homicide cop on a scene, making it his own.

Callie's face was strained, white, lines running from her neck up into her face, as if one single nerve had been drawn straight through her, controlling all actions, crouched around one intent. Reaching her kids.

Got her kid? Had she really said that?

Oh God, had Max beaten her to the punch? Had he already gone on the attack, hurting people she cared for, taking a child?

Emmy's mind rolled in slow motion but maybe it only seemed so slow in comparison to the car's speed.

Callie drove insanely, as if she were immortal and couldn't be hurt, flying around corners with barely a glance for pedestrians or other cars.

Emmy fastened her seat belt. "Slow down, Callie. Put on your seatbelt."

"To hell with seatbelts. Someone got my kid!" she shrieked, with a shrillness that shot straight into Emmy's brain, piercing, sharp, stabbing. "Call the police on your cell!" Callie yelled. "Call them."

Emmy's mind slowed even further, crawling through the possibilities, imagining Max with Callie's kids. Those innocent children with that devil? No, no, no. One word formed in her brain, no. It was unthinkable.

"Emmy! Now!" Callie yelled and Emmy looked at her, her mind clicking back into real time.

"Sorry." She pulled her phone out of her pocket and began dialing, waiting impatiently, holding her breath so she wouldn't miss the operator's answer through all the noise in her brain. It was probably only one ring but it seemed like forever. Her lungs ached for oxygen, panic ate up the air in her body, making her want to take gulping breaths.

"911. What's your emergency?" a voice said insistently as if Emmy had missed the first time she'd spoken.

"Oh," she gasped out, inhaling quickly. "This is Emmy Renard. I'm with Callie Bruner."

"Yes, dear, we already know about Callie's kids over at the vet. Do you have any more information?" the woman coaxed as if she were used to dealing with distraught people.

"Just that Callie said her child is missing."

"We've already got officers at the scene. Everybody we've got available is headed that way. Are you with Callie now?"

"Yes. We're on the way."

"Is she driving?"

"Yes."

"Not a good idea."

Emmy's head banged against the window as Callie took a hard right. "I know."

"Won't let you drive, huh?"

"Right."

"Oh well, that's how they all get, parents, when there's been a school bus fender bender or something, they show up screeching round the bend, causing real danger. Just buckle up and call us if you get any more information. Tell her to be careful, dear."

"Thank you." Emmy hung up. "The cops already know. They have every deputy and cop in the county headed over there."

She looked at Callie. "Where is there? The operator said something about the vet."

"The vet out on Highway 9." Her voice was strained, unnatural. "Near the edge of town. The kids' dog got shot, a hunter or something. They put it in the truck and hauled ass to the vet."

Her face twisted with rage. "Mike's hussy girlfriend told the kids to wait outside at the vet, said it was too scary for them. What the hell was she doing taking care of them? Where was Mike?"

"My kid, little Mike, is missing. Where is he?" Her voice broke and tears filled her eyes. Her face scrunched convulsively for a moment, then she got control again, her mouth tightening, her eyes narrowing. "His little brother said a man came and offered Little Mike a puppy and he got in the car with him and they drove awaaay." Her voice lost all control on the last word, wavering up and down, hitting several different octaves until it became hearable only by dogs.

"Pull over and I'll drive," Emmy said forcefully.

The forcefulness seemed to work because Callie straightened, gripping the steering wheel. "No. We're almost there." Strength returned to her voice and face but only momentarily. "Oh God, where is my little boy?"

Tears streamed down her face but she slowed the car minutely and took the next corner without banging Emmy against the window.

She remembered something Callie had said.

Someone had shot their dog?

That reverberated through her like the image of the little body she'd found lying in Max's blood.

Max had taken away the one good thing that had come out of their marriage, the little dog Max had given her for Christmas. She'd asked for the puppy, taken Max to see the dog she'd wanted, because Max would never have thought of such a gift.

Max was opposed to getting a dog. But, had relented in the spirit of Christmas.

She and that dog had loved each other, which made Max furious. "You love that dog more'n you love me," he'd bellowed in a fight once.

After that, she'd tried to take Charlie everywhere she went, knowing how Max's mind worked, knowing he wouldn't hesitate to hurt the little creature. But, she'd been going to her Grampa's place the last day and couldn't take the dog.

Had figured she'd be back before Max got home from work. Had he even been at work that day? Or just pretended so he could follow her and spy on her?

When she'd seen Charlie lying in all of that blood—the horror returned.

Damn Max. Damn him for killing the little dog that had loved her with such pure joy and that she'd loved in return.

Now, a dog had been shot and a child was missing. Everything inside of her screamed that Max was on the loose in the county and he'd hurt a dog and taken a child.

Little Mike, innocent and sweet. Like her dog, Charlie.

They screeched around one last corner, into a field of blue lights and running cops. Callie yanked the car to the curb and jumped out, charging like a mad woman toward her littlest boy, Ricky.

A young, blonde woman held him, the tears running down her face mixing with the tears on Ricky's cheeks. They both called out to Callie in unintelligible sounds of relief.

Callie reached for Ricky and the little guy clutched at her, wrapping his arms and legs around her like a baby monkey, clinging and crying.

Callie swayed back and forth, holding onto her youngest, their faces forming mirrored images of distress.

Finally, Ricky pulled back to look into Callie's eyes. "I tolt him not to go, Mama. But he said he was the big brother and I couldn't tell him what to do. I tolt him but he didn't listen."

He puffed up big and said, "The man asked me to get in too. But I didn't."

Callie stroked his hair, brushing it back off his tear-stained face. "You did the right thing, Ricky, not going with him. And telling him that, even if he is the big brother."

"But then, I wanted to go since he was going." He drew in a shaky breath. "But, Mike said, 'Nope, you said it weren't a good idea. You go inside with Lulu. She'll babysit you.' He said I was a baby." Ricky wailed like he'd been beat up.

Callie hugged him close, hiding her face in his hair.

Squealing brakes announced the arrival of a pickup truck that slid to a stop in the middle of the street. Big Mike, Callie's ex, jumped out, running cross the road. Callie's head snapped up and she eyed him like he was the kidnapper.

"Where's Little Mike?" Big Mike's head whirled from Callie to the young blonde. Lulu, his girlfriend, sat on the steps, mascara and tears streaming down her face. She sniffled, wiped her nose and stood up.

She raised her arms and ran the few steps toward him, but Mike held up a hand. "Where's my kid?"

"He left with somebody," her weak voice sounded like a child's.

A deputy stepped forward. "I think I've got the basics here, Mike."

Mike twirled to meet the deputy face to face. He didn't say a thing, just waited.

"Some unidentified man stopped by here about twenty minutes ago and told your older son he had a puppy he could have since your son told him his dog had just been shot."

Mike pulled his head back on his neck, his eyes rounding, registering the fact that his dog had been shot but he didn't interrupt the deputy.

"Now, no one knows who this man was." The

deputy held both hands up as Mike opened his mouth, a crazed look in his eyes. "But, your other son here gave us a description and we're putting out an all-points bulletin looking for that car."

"What the…" Mike cut off the curse that had almost exploded full force, then turned to look at his way too young girlfriend, who Callie had said was only a few years out of high school. "Where were you? Did you see this guy?"

Tears ran down the girl's face and she sniffed loudly and took a step closer to Mike. "I was inside with your dog. I didn't want the kids to be scared any more than they were." Her mouth wavered in a good imitation of Ricky's earlier when he'd been crying full force.

Mike nodded, his expression gentling. He pulled her underneath his arm, patting her distractedly on the back. Even though he was incredibly upset, he didn't turn his anger on her.

Callie's face twisted with an evil expression, tinged with jealously and self-righteous rage, as she glared at the girl.

Shock rolled through Emmy at this different Callie. Someone she'd never seen before.

Callie's opened her mouth then closed it again as she looked down at her son who still clung to her, his little head tucked under her chin, his thumb in his mouth. He pressed his face against her chest as if she held the key to his sanity, the only thing keeping him from completely losing it.

She pointed a finger at her ex as if she might stab it into his chest. "We'll talk later, mister." Her voice was level and civil, a mother's tone to a bothersome stranger, but her mouth was tight and hard, her eyes almost malevolent, something Ricky couldn't see from his position.

Fear shot across Mike's face before he got it under control. He stepped back from his girlfriend, putting space between them. Lulu looked from Mike to his ex-wife's face—and chose to say nothing.

The girl had good survival instincts.

"Did you see anything, Lulu?" The deputy asked the girlfriend in a gentle tone. "The car or the guy?"

"No." She shook her head, as if a bug had gotten tangled in her hair.

"Are you hurt?" He pointed at her shirt.

For the first time, Emmy really registered the blood on Lulu's shirt.

"No, it's from carrying the dog." She motioned back over her head at the vet's door. The emergency of the hurt dog had faded into the background with the missing kid.

Lulu had done the right thing actually, immediately taking the dog to the vet, but had been distracted in the moment from keeping an eye on the kids.

It was, after all, Hawk's Peak, and nothing ever happened in Hawk's Peak.

Until Emmy had brought evil to town?

He kept his gun trained on the old couple at the pharmacy as he ordered them about.

"Okay, you two, just put all that money in one bag and put every type of painkiller you got in the other one," he said in a level tone. He'd found it worked better if you didn't yell, kept panic out of the equation.

The old couple rushed to do what he'd said. Every

cop in town would be over at the vet's by now. This was his time to make hay. The sun was shining on him.

Painkillers, money, and the old couple. It was a heat wave.

"Okie dokie, we got it," the old pharmacist said genially, as if this was just another prescription he'd filled. He handed the two bags over. In all his years, the old guy must have been in a few situations himself.

"Out the back door now, both of you." He motioned to the couple with his head toward the way out.

"My wife, too? You don't need both of us." The old guy looked at him politely as if this was just business.

Which it was. The business of getting even with that little whore, Emily.

"It's quicker than tying her up," he answered the old pharmacist in a level tone. "I ain't gonna hurt y'all. Just need you to help me get out of town. If a cop stops us, you just smile and say I'm your nephew. And we'll go on our merry way and I'll set you out by the side of the road not too far from a convenience store or something."

"Okay." The old guy nodded like he was dealing with one of his grandkids. He hadn't gotten to be this old by being stupid, obviously.

He seemed to recognize a business exchange when he saw one. The guy who'd come into his store wanted painkillers and he didn't want to have to pay for them. Probably been robbed before.

He kinda hated the idea of having to kill the old guy; he was just so likeable. But hell, this was a business deal for him too, with a financial payoff that would exceed any other he'd gotten in his whole life.

Besides, it all was Emily's fault. Or Emmy, as she

called herself. Like that name would throw him off. She must take him for an idiot.

"Hold on," he said. "We got to make a quick little phone call. Then, we'll leave."

Emily had used disposable phones for a while, then, finally, had gotten a regular phone when she'd settled in Hawk's Peak. But, he'd gotten the new number. Amazing how much information a couple hundred dollars could buy you.

That money was only an investment for the big payoff of the insurance money. Once Emily was dead, the insurance money would be his.

He picked up the pharmacy landline. "You, ma'am, take it and say exactly what I tell you and nothing more. Ya got it?"

The little old lady nodded matter-of-factly. She was made of strong stuff. They must make little old ladies tough up here in the mountains.

Yeah, he was gonna hate to shoot her, too. But that was also Emily's fault.

CHAPTER SEVENTEEN

The usually easygoing Callie was unrecognizable. A vein throbbed in the side of her forehead, panic and distress pulsing out from her like a lighthouse beacon, piercing the sea of blue police lights that covered the block.

Her face glowed pale, her eyes big as if to take in any sign that might lead her to her lost child. She clutched her little boy to her like a life preserver, the only thing keeping her emotionally afloat, from drowning completely.

Cops and sheriff's deputies circled her and Ricky like protective dolphins watching over sailors who'd fallen overboard.

A shark was swimming in their midst, maybe already having done fatal damage.

And Emmy hadn't warned them.

She had to tell them now, give them the information they needed to find the man who'd taken Little Mike.

She turned to the sheriff, opened her mouth and a scream pierced the air.

Startled by the intensity of the shriek, Emmy wasn't sure it hadn't come from her own mouth.

Then, Callie screamed again, hollering words that

were indistinguishable. But the message on her face was clear. She ran, Ricky bouncing on her hip.

A red, tricked-out, new model Jeep pulled to the curb, a teenaged boy at the wheel. Little Mike was buckled in the front seat, holding a Golden puppy and smiling ear to ear.

His face beamed with happiness. But as his screaming mother ran toward him, fear swept across it. He pulled back, cringing away from the crazed woman charging at him, reaching for him with her free hand.

She grabbed him as he sat in the car seat, and hugged him, engulfing him in motherly mania. Big Mike ran forward, wrapping his arms around all three.

Little Ricky's face popped out above the group, smug and self-satisfied. "You are in so much trouble," he gloated at his brother. The enormity involved in a child going missing failed to register in his innocent mind.

Thank God, he hadn't been forced to learn a horrible life lesson today, the lesson of all the dangers that existed in the dark corners of certain minds.

Hopefully, he would never learn it first-hand.

The family portrait was intact, a crying mother, a father barely holding himself together, the gloating little brother, and the shocked eight-year-old who'd just wanted a puppy.

Emmy drew in a deep breath for the first time since the call had come in. A smile spread through her with a lightness like sunshine filling the dark void that had opened when she'd heard Little Mike had been taken by a *man*.

The teenaged boy who'd looked like a *man* to Callie's littlest boy stared at the family, a hangdog expression fighting with fear. He knew he was gonna get what-for once the jubilant reunion died down.

He'd innocently taken a kid for a ride. *I figured it wouldn't hurt nobody*, she could almost hear him protesting already, his eyes narrowing as his mind rocketed around for excuses that wouldn't get him punched by Big Mike or yelled at by all the cops surrounding him.

Then, Emmy remembered.

The kid might have acted small-town, innocently making a mistake.

But someone else had shot the dog.

The chasm of crazy inside of Emmy, that had begun to close, opened wide again, threatening to pull her and everyone she cared about into the depths of insanity.

They'd dodged a bullet today. Was it literal or figurative? Had Max meant the shot for the children, instead hitting the family dog?

No, she felt sure shooting the dog was a message to her, telling her Max could kill anything she loved. A direct connection to his killing Charlie.

This time, he'd only chosen a dog. Next time?

Everything began graying in front of her eyes, the blue lights fading out. She clasped onto the nearest cop car, leaning backward to steady herself. The horrifying image of a dead child floated before her eyes inside the curtain of gray.

Max was still out there, waiting for another chance, waiting to hurt someone she loved. To intimidate her? To force her to make a mistake?

She pushed away from the car, sucked in a long deep breath, and looked around. Was he nearby, laughing his rear off, thinking the teenager in the red car taking away Little Mike was perfect timing, that he couldn't have arranged it better?

Big Mike unbuckled Little Mike, still holding the golden retriever puppy, and pulled him out of the Jeep.

"Son, what have I told you about getting in cars with strangers?"

"Daddy, he ain't a stranger." The little boy's eyes glowed innocent and earnest. "He's Mrs. Boyton's son."

"Your teacher?"

"Yes, sir." Little Mike was all about the politeness now, earnest attentiveness on his face. Ticked off parents who were very upset? Was that going to translate into a spanking for him?

"He came to class to drop off Mrs. Boyton's lunch, Daddy. I met him. He ain't a stranger."

"Even so, going off like that without telling anybody." Big Mike shook his head, fear and panic still etched on his face. "You had us all worried."

He turned to the teenager, looking him up and down, his mouth tightening.

The sheriff and all the cops in earshot glowered at the teenager, raised eyebrows, hands on hips, legs akimbo. The teenager didn't need to be a schoolteacher's kid to read that tough message.

"I'mmm sorrry, sir," he stuttered out, his face turning the same color as his brand new Jeep. "Mike was really upset about his dog and we've got a litter of puppies to give away, so I didn't see no harm."

A number of deputies turned away to hide smiles. Had the teenager's action been about making Little Mike feel better or finding homes for all the extra puppies?

Big Mike looked the boy up and down, his glare lessoning a few notches. "Well, we really like your mama."

The teen's head bobbed up and down, ready to accept anything that didn't seem like Big Mike, who had twice the muscle on him, was about to pound him.

Emmy felt a smile starting to spread across her face. Small towns. This was what she'd been looking for when she'd chosen Hawk's Peak.

Chosen Hawk's Peak. Like a sharp jab to the ribs, she remembered she wasn't going to be able to stay here.

Like all the other anonymous towns she'd stopped in, this was just one more town on her run for her life.

Unless she just told everyone the truth, that she thought her dead husband was trying to kill her.

She certainly had the right audience for her statement, most of the law enforcement officers from the entire area, it looked like.

How to present it? How not to get herself arrested immediately as a possible suspect?

Before she could get her statement organized in her head, her cell phone rang.

She pulled it out of her pocket. A local area code.

"Hello?" She walked away from the crowd, holding one finger to her other ear to shut out the racket.

"Emmy, this is Margie McCloud." Her voice trembled and shook like the old woman that didn't usually show in her.

"Yes, Miss Margie? What's up?"

A shaky breath preceded words that seemed forced, rehearsed. "There's a man here. Says he's a friend of yours." She spoke as if she'd been given a script.

No. No. No.

Instantly, she knew Max had circled back around, going for the town's unprotected underbelly, the weak members, the elderly.

"Are you okay, Miss Margie?"

"Yes, I'm fine, dear." Her voice had regained its usual strength. She was bucking up. "But your friend." The word *friend* rang false. "He says not to tell anyone but just drive out of town on Highway 9 north, heading toward the lake."

She'd been looking left and the blow had come from the right. Max had deliberately distracted her and the rest of the town by shooting the dog.

Emmy's legs began to shake. She leaned a hand toward the nearest cop car to keep from falling. But there wasn't time for weakness. She stood straight again, inhaling deeply. "Has he hurt you?"

"No, dear. But you're not to tell anyone or to bring anyone. Says that's very important." She spoke levelly, as if instructing one of her grandchildren how to make cookies.

She'd detected the panic in Emmy's voice and had gone into grandmother mode.

"Me and Mr. McCloud are going to meet you out there. We'll call you with more directions when you get out that way, okay dear?"

"Yes, ma'am."

"You be careful now, dear, he has a gun."

A harsh male voice barked indiscernible words. If she'd had to testify in court, she'd have felt justified in saying it sounded like Max.

Her gut knew it was.

Then, a noise like a blow and a yelp came through

the phone line. The yelp had sounded like an older male. Mr. McCloud?

A fierce ripping anger filled Emmy at the thought that Max would hurt this sweet old couple.

Mrs. McCloud's voice came back on, a sob obscuring her first few words. "Sorry dear, you just be careful and come on out that way. Don't bring anyone with you. Don't tell the police, says he'll be sure and kill us if you do."

Mrs. and Mr. McCloud. He had them both. That's how he was controlling the old couple, making them each worry about the other.

She'd kill Max herself. He would not hurt anyone that she loved. Either he or she would be dead by the end of the day.

———

Emmy had thought about calling Luke and his cousin, or telling the police. But something had warned her that Max would know, would then just kill the McClouds and disappear again.

This was a chance to corner him, and contain or kill him.

She'd taken Callie's car to get a quicker start. Callie had looked at her funny when she'd asked to take it, but said she'd go home with Mike and the boys. Said it didn't matter if the store remained closed the rest of the day, as long as her boys were safe.

Slowly, Emmy drove up a gravel road that wound through an isolated area. The directions had been texted to her by an unknown number, as she'd gotten further out of town on Highway 9.

The road was surrounded by heavily forested

mountains, with woods that would act as a sponge, absorbing the sounds of murder, soaking up the screams of terrified people as they died, lives fading away as if they never existed.

The red clay of Georgia would hide the color of blood, the tangled, mountain terrain their bodies. She'd vanish just as Max had.

The only difference being that she really would be dead.

Along with Mr. and Mrs. McCloud.

The fierce anger that had sustained her since she'd gotten the call grew, forming a red haze across her vision as scarlet as the Georgia clay. Her insides flamed with fury that Max would hurt such innocent, good-hearted people.

They'd lived a long time before they'd encountered something truly as evil as Max. She'd brought that into their lives.

And she'd take it out.

They wouldn't die today somewhere near this stretch of lonely road. No matter what it cost her.

They had children and grandchildren, probably even great-grandchildren.

An entire McCloud clan would mourn them.

Who would really miss her?

Her Grampa would miss her, but he'd be taken care of at the assisted living facility. He'd been fine without her the last year.

But the McClouds? Too many people loved them. Including her.

She would not let that monster hurt them.

A text came through on her phone. Chills shuddered through her every time the phone lit up with a contact. The monster?

No. It was Luke.

Where are you?

Running an errand, she texted back.

Where?

I'll be back at the store in a bit. An emergency with Callie's kids. She hoped that held him for a bit. It would be easier sneaking up on Max if it was just her.

Or was she just making excuses so that she wouldn't also endanger Luke?

Luke.

When she'd finally found someone she thought she could love and trust and perhaps have a life with, this evil had found her again.

Many people lived their entire lifetime without finding something like she'd experienced with Luke.

And just when she found it, this monster had hunted her down. Again.

She'd miss Luke, all the way into the next life—if that's what it took. As she was fading from the earth, her thoughts would be of the warm, soft passion-filled hours of the nights she'd shared with Luke.

That image would make the dying easier, that she'd at least had some of that in her time on Earth.

She reached the mentioned turnoff, but parked Callie's car just short of it and got out. From the directions, she figured the cabin was straight through the woods to her left.

If she could sneak up on him, they had a chance. She, and the sweet Mr. and Mrs. McCloud.

At least they'd have a chance.

She picked her way through the undergrowth, heading toward a rendezvous with the monster.

Chapter Eighteen

The thick underbrush fought her, vines catching at her ankles, branches slapping into her face. As if Max had convinced the tangled Georgia backwoods to take his side.

She edged closer and closer, peering through the greenery, searching for the cabin that had to be there. She pushed through the undergrowth, trying to keep the gravel road in sight, as well as trying to make no identifying noise.

Suddenly, a figure arose.

Her pulse raced and blood racketed in her head. She pointed her gun.

A deer. It jumped away into the woods, as if she might be a hunter, eager to take it home on the hood of a truck.

She was a hunter all right. Just not for deer.

For a monster.

Blood pulsed through her veins, and her breath sawed at her lungs with ragged gasps. Dropping her head for a moment, she practiced slow breathing until finally she could hear again, notice the buzz of insects and the wind rustling through the treetops.

Then, she stood erect and took one more long, steady breath of the mountain air.

Her success depended on being alert, able to detect the slightest sound, the first movement of an attack.

Max would be waiting for her, so she had to be ready for him, ready to take him out at the first contact.

Slowly, silently, she edged forward. Willing the cooperation of the undergrowth, praying for no more deer surprises. That was the last thing she needed, to fire off her gun at a deer and alert Max.

A mosquito buzzed around her, landing on her neck. With a slap, she took it out.

"Don't move." The words came from just behind her.

She jerked to a halt, her hands fused to the gun. Her breath came in quick pants, and her pulse accelerated like a horse running from gunshots.

Her attention had been on looking for the first sign of the cabin and she'd forgotten to keep checking behind her.

Please help me, God, she prayed. Though prayers seemed futile. Because there couldn't be a God if he kept letting this happen to her. She didn't deserve this. No one did.

Now that she'd had a couple of seconds to process it, she realized something was off. The timbre of the voice was wrong. Turning her head slightly, she braced herself to meet Max's eyes for the first time in a year.

Then, she saw him.

It wasn't Max. She gasped. And felt weak, her knees threatening to drop her to the ground.

It was his brother. His no good, drug-using brother. The younger drug-addicted brother to a sadistic, murdering older brother. What a family.

"Carl," she breathed out. "What are you doing?"

"What do you think I'm doing?" He arched an eyebrow. "Finishing the job my brother wasn't capable of."

They were in cahoots?

Cahoots? *A Three Stooges* term for a murderous team. She almost laughed with hysteria.

That was another way she'd learned to defuse terror this last year, by talking to herself, objectifying herself and her situation as if from outside her own body.

The techniques she'd practiced this past year were working. The terror coursing through her veins wasn't completely disabling.

Her heart beat at such a rapid pace that she almost couldn't catch her breath, but she counted the breaths in and out to a three count.

Then, slowly she turned her head to get a better look at Carl.

Unwashed, brown hair lay across his forehead in a lanky, oily mess. An unkempt beard crawled across his face. His biceps were muscled underneath a dirty white T-shirt.

Max had always taken such care with his appearance. You just never knew when you might meet a new, hot babe.

Max worked out, the better to attract women. Carl did it in order to push other people around.

Max's clothing had always been clean and pressed. The physical contrast between the brothers could not have been more defined.

But there was just enough of a mean glint in Carl's eyes to assure her that he and Max shared genetic material. Carl's brown eyes were dark and malicious with the triumph of sneaking up on her. Making him look just like Max when he was in a rage.

Carl smiled. "Hey, sister-in-law."

"Hey, Carl." She tried to keep her voice level, non-antagonizing. Why poke a dangerous bear? "Where's your brother?"

"You killed him, remember? So, I guess about now, he's in hell." He laughed, sounding so much like Max on a bad day that she almost threw up.

Was he here for revenge? Was that what this was about?

Or was Max just waiting to step out, for maximum dramatic effect?

She turned her head further, looking for Max. Waiting for the snake to strike from the bushes.

Carl tilted his head, then laughed low in his throat, with a guttural sound that traveled to her stomach with a disgusting, roiling sensation that made her want to hurl.

"Drop your gun, Sis." He poked her in the side with his gun. "Now."

He liked to give orders and expected immediate compliance, just like his brother. She opened her hand and let her pistol fall to the forest floor.

Carl shoved her hard, sending her flying several feet in front of him. She caught her ankle on a root and fell, but rolled quickly to her side and raised her hands, ready for an attack.

Carl leaned over to pick up the gun, keeping his eyes and his rifle trained on her, although as he leaned over, the rifle strayed away from her.

She judged the tilt of the gun. Did she have time to get up and run?

He jerked his gaze up at her. "Ehh ehh ehh," he taunted, pulling the gun back toward her. "No escapey." He straightened. "Let me remind you that I still have the cute little pharmacist and his sweet little wife."

Her heart clutched.

"Now, as much as I'd hate it, I'd have to shoot them if you get away."

She eyed him carefully.

"Then, it'd just be your word, a woman who's already murdered once, against mine, saying I was never here in the first place."

"There must be some evidence you were here." Draw him out, get him to talk. It would give her time to think of something, more time before he killed her. Cause that was his plan, for sure.

Or to let Max kill her.

Either way, the plan was for her to end up dead.

She brushed her hands off on her jeans and straightened her legs, testing them. Nothing was hurt. If she got the chance to run, she could.

He smiled wickedly, so similarly to Max that it was apparent they were brothers if their evil natures weren't proof enough.

She'd thought they were flip sides of the same coin when she'd first met Max.

Max—the cop, the good man, fighting against everything Carl stood for—drug using, stealing to support his habit, doing whatever it took to provide him with an easy life.

Now, she knew they were the same, born from the same evil, genetic material.

"Get up." He grabbed her by the hair before she could comply, yanking her to a standing position, then he dragged her by her hair through the trees. She stumbled often because of her awkward position but his fierce hold on her hair kept her from falling.

Finally, they reached what looked like a vacant vacation cabin.

She couldn't see it very well, but as they approached, she noticed there were no tire marks on the driveway leading in.

No lights shone from inside. It looked as if no one had been to the house in months.

———————

"Grind it up real well," Carl instructed her. He added a few more pills to the cutting board.

The spoon cracked the pills, spitting pieces out everywhere. Carl followed them greedily with his eyes, like a dog that hadn't eaten in days.

Or a drug user jonesing for a hit.

Painkillers. His drug of choice, according to Max.

He leaned forward and wet a finger in his mouth, then touched it to a stray bit of powder. He put it into his mouth, sucking on it, moaning with pleasure.

"Hurry up," he growled at Emmy. "Get 'er done," he mimicked a workingman's catch phrase.

It sounded so wrong coming from him. A man who'd never held down a real job in his life, according to Max. Instead, living off selling drugs to high school kids and even some kids in the younger grades.

Yeah, selling drugs to kids had been his milieu.

Mr. McCloud eyed her from across the room, probably hoping, like she was, that all of Carl's tasting of the pills would disable him.

Maybe, he'd dose himself into a drug-induced state

of unconsciousness. Emmy ground harder, took a few more pills and added them to the pile.

"That's the attitude," Carl said slyly.

He turned and shuffled through the kitchen cabinets until he came up with a jar of applesauce. Setting down his gun, he twisted the top off the jar and emptied some applesauce into a bowl.

Carrying it over to the table, he set it down. "Now, dump that in here."

Surely, even he knew it was way too much for one person. He'd be comatose, or more likely dead. The expression on Mr. McCloud's face said the same. A glimmer of hope sneaked around his eyes.

Carl swung around, following her gaze to the pharmacist's. "What?" He waved his gun as he approached the old man. Mrs. McCloud sucked in a quick gasp.

"Is that too much, old man? Tell me the truth." He jumped at Mrs. McCloud, and she let out a squeak.

Carl bellowed out a laugh. Yeah, he was exactly like Max. "Tell the truth, old man. Is it too much?"

How good a liar was Mr. McCloud? He had to be asking himself that about now. Not good enough, 'cause even Emmy could see him warring with the part of him that wanted to let Carl eat the entire bowl and die.

But the fear for his wife won out, the fear that if he gave the wrong answer, the beast would shoot his Margie.

He let out a long, defeated breath. "It's too much," he answered honestly.

"I thought so." Carl nodded. "What would happen to me if I ate that entire bowl?"

"First, you'd fall into a deep sleep." The pharmacist tilted his head. "Eventually, your breathing would stop. It wouldn't be a real bad way to go. Die in your sleep. Most people say that's how they want to go."

"Is that how you want to go, old man?"

Mr. McCloud narrowed his eyes. "I guess that would be my preferable way. Under the circumstances." He tilted his head toward Carl's gun. "After my wife, of course. Want to see her though her days." He looked at his Margie and smiled sweetly. A smile formed in her eyes and she reached out a zip-tie bound hand and took his also bound hand.

They clasped their hands together tightly for a long moment that even Carl seemed hesitant to interrupt.

Tears pushed up from the back of Emmy's eyes, threatening to erupt full force. The love of the old couple had such a visible sweetness. But she pushed back the tears. She needed to keep her vision clear.

What was the monster going to do?

His evil was building, as obvious as the love of Ira for his Margie. She'd been able to sense when Max was working himself up, justifying whatever rage he expressed.

Just as Carl did now. What was he going to do to them? Kill her for sure. But, what about the McClouds?

How could she get them out alive?

CHAPTER NINETEEN

"That's sweet. Ain't that sweet, Emily?" Carl looked at her with a malicious glint in his eye.

He tilted his head and repeated, "I said, don'cha think they're a sweet old couple?" He stepped closer to her, menacing, relishing his power.

The mean gene had strengthened as the children were born, the second born son even meaner than the first.

A stringy, drugged out thinness emphasized his muscles. A nervous tick kept causing his right eye to flinch. Like a man who was used to getting his drugs on a regular basis and needed a hit real bad.

Though his words were kind, his expression streamed pure evil toward the McClouds. He turned his gun toward them and took a step closer.

Was this the moment? Was this her last chance to stop him before he killed the old couple?

She lunged up, grabbing the chair between them, using it almost like a spear, and stabbed the legs into his side, then into his gut as he twisted toward her.

"Emmph," he crumpled backward. Mr. McCloud jumped up and latched his bound hands around Carl's head, pulling him in a circle so that his back was to Emmy.

She grabbed the stock of the rifle. They were going to win. Good beating evil. She wanted to laugh with relief.

Just then, the gun began to fire. Mrs. McCloud jumped sideways to avoid the bullets. But Carl was stronger than she and Mr. McCloud combined.

He kept circling toward her, firing as she ran, until finally Mr. McCloud yelled, "All right, all right, we give up! Stop shooting."

The gunfire stopped and Mr. McCloud raised his hands, releasing Carl's head. Emmy had no choice. She let go of the gun.

Carl jumped backward, putting distance between them, fury contorting his face. He rubbed his neck with one hand.

"You still got some strength in you, old man, I'll give you that. Wouldn't have thought it." He laughed roughly. "Never should have untied your feet when I let y'all go to the john. Didn't think you were a threat at your age."

He smiled with pure evil. "But, that just now, that really pissed me off. Made it easier to do what I got to do."

Emmy's stomach clenched and she kept her gaze fastened on the rifle. If he lifted it to fire at them, she'd have to go into action again. Even if it proved futile.

"Sit down!" he yelled.

Both the pharmacist and his wife glanced quickly at Emmy.

"What you looking at her for? I'm in charge here. I'm the one who decides who lives and who dies."

Emmy motioned with her head for them to sit and they did.

Carl grimaced. "I'm in charge!" he yelled again, then motioned with his gun toward Emmy. "You sit down too, Sister."

Emmy and Ira might have been able to finally overpower Carl, but their weakness was their love for each other, their unwillingness to sacrifice someone they loved just to save themselves.

How different from someone like Carl, who'd kill just about anyone to get whatever petty, earthbound pleasure he wanted.

Good people couldn't even begin to hope to defeat people like Carl and Max.

She looked toward the door. When was Max going to show up?

Without a doubt, he wouldn't want to miss the fun of seeing her die.

What happens now, she wanted to ask, the anxiety, the not knowing worse than if he actually killed her, because every moment pounded more adrenaline, more despair and panic through her, until she felt her heart would explode.

But why hurry toward death? It was coming soon enough. She began breathing with measured counts, slowly in and out.

If another chance came, she had to be ready. She wasn't going out easily. She'd try to take Carl or Max with her, or at least cause them some injury that might require medical treatment, attracting attention to them.

Maybe in death, she'd get her revenge. Max had said many criminals were caught at the hospital for injuries they'd received in the commission of a crime.

"Did you mix that applesauce up real good, Emily?" Carl's voice jostled her out of her fantasy of him on death row. He leaned over to look at the applesauce and painkiller mixture.

The need for it was obvious on his face, as the drug spoke to him in a language only he could hear, his expression like that of a lover gazing at the face of his beloved. He and the drugs had shared pleasure that ordinary people couldn't imagine.

He groaned, low in his throat.

"You want it, don't you?" Emmy said in a seductive voice, the same tone as the drug would use if it could speak. The tone it used every day to thousands of people who lived for the pleasure and relief it provided from everyday pains and disappointments. "Take it."

Please, let his hunger for the drug beat out his caution. Please let him just eat the applesauce and test the limits of what a human body could endure.

He continued to stare at the drug-filled bowl for a long moment, then finally with a shudder, he jerked his gaze to Emmy, anger replacing his drug hunger.

"Start shoveling it in," he growled, jealousy tingeing his voice as if she were forcefully stealing the drug away from him.

She looked up at him, still hoping his need would overpower his intentions to kill her and the McClouds.

"Start eating it," he ordered in the tone he and Max had mastered so well. Their lord of the universe tone.

Start eating it? Like ordering a child to finish their vegetables. So easily, he ordered her to eat what was obviously a prescription for death.

She shook her head, slowly.

He shrugged, casually, nonchalantly, as if he weren't ordering her to commit suicide. "It's probably more pleasant than a bullet in the head," he drawled in a slow southern accent that would have been so beautiful on the lips of someone besides a no-morals, low-life criminal.

"This was your plan all along," she said.

"No, missy." He leaned over and laughed close to her ear. "This was *your* plan. You bounce from town to town." He gestured with the gun, like a follow-the-bouncing-ball demonstration.

"Your drug habit has made it hard to stay in one place. What with all the stealing and all to support your need."

"What will the news people say?" He waggled his head side to side, one finger at his temple, as if he were editing headlines for newspapers or writing scripts for TV news. "You were a friend to the old couple. How could you have killed them?"

Margie gasped and Ira's face paled. Their death was eminent, along with Emmy's. But, they had no options because they'd both seen just how strong he was.

"You needed the drugs and they wouldn't cooperate," Carl continued, as if unaware of the panic his words sent through the trio. If he'd allowed any of them to think the others might survive, they'd all be more inclined to cooperate.

But it was as if his need for power and control exceeded his common sense. Or his total lack of understanding of human nature.

"I'm a little unsure of the details." He tapped his finger to the side of his head. "That's okay, the police will be too. But, basically, you brought them to the cabin, killed them and then overdosed on pills. Your dependency got worse and worse, what with all the guilt you lived with after killing Max."

"Max isn't dead!" she screamed at him. Panic pulsed through her. None of her control techniques were working.

This was the moment of her death and control seemed overrated.

"He isn't dead!" she screamed again, punctuating every word with fury.

"Yeah, like you won't be dead," Carl sneered. "Just start eating or you may decide to shoot yourself in the head instead. I hear that's not all that much fun. They say you hear the bullet entering your brain, and feel your brain exploding."

He laughed again, with that horrible laugh so much like Max's. "Course no one's ever really around to describe it afterward, if you do it right."

He pointed the gun at her, then back over at the old couple. "Go ahead and start eating."

A ferocious rebellion began building in her. She wasn't going down that easily. She measured the distance between her and the gun.

Could she erupt out of the chair before he turned it back to her?

"If you cooperate," he spit out quickly, as if he'd read her thoughts. "I might let them go easier, eating the applesauce, rather than shooting them in front of each other." But for extra measure, he turned the gun back on her.

He looked at the McClouds, tilting his head toward the applesauce. "You want some?" Like he was doing them a real favor.

They both shook their head no, the panic behind their eyes barely controlled by a lifetime of experience. Though no amount of living could really prepare anyone to face down the evil inside this cabin.

A powerful, primal scream began forming inside Emmy, spiraling toward her mouth with the need to disperse the fear, terror and anxiety that roiled around in her gut. She held it back as long as she could but made the mistake of meeting Carl's eyes.

Her control faltered for just a second. She closed her eyes and imagined herself screaming, screaming like she was on an out of control roller coaster, heading toward an unfinished track, getting ready to fly into space, crashing down to her death.

She would scream and scream, closing her eyes against the sight of Carl's evil face, knowing a bullet could shut her up at any second, that knowledge only increasing her panic.

Then, she imagined the McClouds, the pain and panic her desperation would cause in them. She had to hold it together for them.

As long as she was calm, they still had a chance.

Then, for a brief second, she imagined herself getting away from Carl, beating him and Max at their own game. But, she needed weapons for that. What were her weapons?

Slowly, she opened her eyes.

Horror waited just on the other side of her closed eyelids, like a poisonous snake.

Carl stared at her, his gun still pointed at her. She slid her gaze to the left and saw the steady expressions of the McClouds. They understood exactly what she was thinking.

Because they were thinking it too.

Caught in the grips of something they had no control over, they weren't hopeless. All of them were still measuring the distance between themselves and Carl's gun.

She met Carl's eyes and he tilted his head toward the bowl.

"Eat your applesauce," he coaxed, realizing just how close to the edge he'd pushed all of them. They were all one scream away from losing control of themselves, going berserk, crazy.

Everyone knew crazy people were harder to deal with. An unpredictable element. He might not even be able to keep control of them with the gun.

"If I don't?" Why should she make it easy for him?

"Then, the newspapers will say you tortured the McClouds with a twisted violence, shooting them in the knees and other parts before killing them." He walked toward the elderly pair, looking them up and down, his gun wavering from their stomachs to their knees.

"Wait." She grabbed the spoon, scooping up a bite and shoveling it into her mouth.

"Uugh," the sound escaped from her. It was bitter. She dropped the spoon back into the bowl. Maybe one spoonful would satisfy him for a moment or two, give her, Ira and Margie a moment to regroup.

"It's an acquired taste," he agreed silkily. "Sometimes it doesn't even touch the tongue you get so anxious to get it into you."

He walked toward her, eyeing the mixture. "I'd have some but need to keep my wits abut me." He looked hungrily at the bowl. Then, quickly, his hand jerking, as if he couldn't stop himself, he grabbed the spoon and took a huge bite.

"Ahh yes, that's the stuff," he groaned. He scooped up another bite and swallowed it.

Then, stopping, he breathed in and out. Like he knew he needed to stop but didn't know if he could.

The more he ate, the less for her. She prayed he lost all control. That he would eat the entire bowl and pass out.

The effects of the painkillers were already mellowing her fear, the powdered drug entering her bloodstream quickly. The drug hummed in her veins. She could see why people broke laws to experience this feeling.

Now, her death seemed much less terrifying. Complacency in the face of your own death?

How much more relaxed could you get?

Contentment washed through her. A feeling she'd had very little contact with the last year.

It wasn't a bad way to go.

But then, the memory of her Grampa, with no one to make sure he was taken care of, impinged on her drugged cloud. He was still in control of all of his faculties. But, what if that changed?

Who would watch out for him?

The McClouds would die immediately after her. She needed to hold on for them.

And Luke? She wanted more mornings spent in his bed.

She wanted to cook him pancakes and bacon.

They hadn't even had a real breakfast together, a lazy morning-after sleep in, with breakfast when it was almost time for lunch.

She wanted that and more. She wanted it all— children of her own, Christmas mornings with deliriously happy kids.

They said your life flashed before you when you

died. But it was the life she'd never had that was flashing in front of her, taunting her with all the might-have-beens.

No! The word bellowed up from deep inside of her, coming from the place that all of her tomorrows lived. She wasn't done living or done with fighting against the evil Carl and his brother had brought into her life.

She would not submit to evil.

CHAPTER TWENTY

Mr. McCloud narrowed his eyes at her. Through the hazy blissfulness that was sweeping through her body, through the lovely nothingness that beckoned to her, she met his gaze and saw an intent expression in his eyes.

He tilted his head toward the little window over the sink. Emmy stirred the applesauce and checked that Carl wasn't watching.

Carl's focus was intently on a bit of stray powder that lay on the table. With a sigh, he licked his finger and touched it to the powder then put it into his mouth. He didn't seem affected by the pills at all, though she could swear he'd had enough to knock out a cat.

She was starting to float away into nothingness. But she had to resist.

"I need some water," she forced out, standing and weaving toward the sink.

Carl laughed at her drunkard's stagger. "You look like you been too long at the bar. It's closing tiiimme," he yodeled out.

She leaned against the counter, steadying herself, forcing herself to focus through the haze, the warm blanket that wrapped around her, tugging her toward sleep. She took a glass from the cabinet, and turned on the water, filling the glass.

She raised the glass to her lips, taking a long drink, as she gazed casually out the window.

Luke crouched near the window.

The water almost clogged her throat, but she kept herself still and continued to drink. Luke motioned to his left with his thumb.

What did that mean?

Luke mouthed the words, "My cousin."

Forrester was out there too. Good. They'd need all the help they could get to leave this cabin alive.

Relief swelled up inside of her, and she wanted to start bawling. She stopped herself, even though the drugs were affecting her, making her weak and feeble.

The drugs would not win. She fought against their effects, trying to push back the sleepiness, the lack of caring about anything, except laying down somewhere to sleep.

But it wouldn't be sleep. It'd be giving up and dying.

And she would never accept that, never go willingly, never let Carl and Max win.

She nodded to Luke, as if nodding to herself but really sending Luke a signal that she'd seen him.

He held up his fingers in a silent countdown, going from five to four, to three, to two, then holding up a single finger, then dropping it.

He pointed toward the ground, then ran.

"Get down!" she yelled, leaping toward the McClouds, covering them with her body.

"What the hell?" Carl said, just before a crashing noise at the front door took his attention off them. He swerved toward the door, pointing his gun.

Emmy jumped up, struggling through her weakness, and flung herself toward Carl, grabbing his legs, her weight dragging him to his knees.

At the same moment, a huge crash at the back door sounded like it was being kicked in.

Carl rolled over to point his gun toward that but Emmy leaped over onto his arm, her entire weight pushing the gun down.

Carl knocked her aside just as Luke kicked open the front door. There was enough distance between Carl and Emmy that Luke had a clean shot.

He fired his gun.

Carl screamed and dropped his gun, writhing in pain on the floor, gripping his wounded hand with his other hand. Just then, Forrester kicked in the back door and entered.

Luke and his cousin both trained their guns on Carl. Luke kicked Carl's gun away. Forrester flipped the groaning man over, handcuffed him then began checking him for other weapons.

Carl moaned. "My hand. My hand. Have mercy on me. My hand."

His pitiful cries might have moved Emmy's heart if just moments before he hadn't pointed a gun at Ira McCloud's kneecap and threatened to shoot.

"Save your crying for the jury," Luke spit out.

He kneeled beside Emmy, checking with his hands for injuries, looking her over. He looked so beautiful, hovering above her, his hands on her so tender. She wanted to smile, to thank him as well as Forrester.

But she was so sleepy.

"He made her take a bunch of pain pills," Mr. McCloud said, looking down at her, over Luke's shoulder. "Enough to knock out a horse. Better get an ambulance up here, real quick like."

"Emmy," Luke's voice called down into the tunnel she was sliding further and further into. She couldn't speak. But looking up, she saw the most beautiful blue eyes gazing down through the darkness.

If only.

Just before she lost the battle to stay awake, she thought, if only they'd had more time.

CHAPTER TWENTY-ONE

Emmy sat on the edge of a hospital bed, swinging her legs tentatively, checking for injuries or weakness. Luke sat across from her in a chair, studying her with those crystal blue eyes.

Dirty grime and dried sweat coated her skin. She needed a shower bad. Soreness kinked her shoulders.

"I feel like day old grits that've been sitting out in the pot all day," she said.

Luke's face crinkled into a smile.

It was good to see that look on him again. His smoothly shaven cheeks displayed those white teeth so well.

"You feel like what?" He tilted his head.

"You know." She waved her hand. "You run out the door, forget to dump the last of the grits, you come home later and there they sit." She scrunched up her mouth in disgust. "A congealed, gelatinous mass that you can grab with a fork and dump into the trash in one quivering, solid hunk."

"Not good for much of anything," she continued. "Wasted."

"Old grits ain't so bad, honey." Callie's voice came from the doorway, an impish look in her eye. "You can't catch too many food borne diseases from grits. You could probably slice the congealed grits up, heat it up with a little cheese on top and have it for lunch."

She walked in, several hangers of clothing in her hand, and a makeup case, curling iron and blow dryer in the other. She dumped them onto the bed and looked Emmy over, turning her head side to side.

"What's all that?" Emmy eyed Callie's beauty supplies.

"We're going to put a little cheese and butter on the grits, toss them in the microwave and don't think about the fact that they've been sitting out all day."

"You jumped on board with that gelatinous mass of grits analogy awfully quick." Emmy craned her head to try and get a look at herself in the mirror.

"Oh darling, you'd look just fine on an ordinary day." Callie tilted her head toward the window. "If there wasn't every type of television crew sitting outside to try and get an interview with you when you walk out of here."

Emmy pushed off the bed, then swayed, the effects of the drugs still not completely out of her system.

Luke grabbed her arm to steady her. She looked up into his eyes. An instant connection with a flicker of want glimmered back from him.

A warming started deep inside of her that would melt anybody's butter.

The guy was hot. His strong shoulders underneath that cotton shirt made her want to be wrapped in him.

And, he was a hero. He'd saved her and the McClouds' lives.

The McClouds?

"How are they, the McClouds?" She turned toward

the door, thinking to go check on them, but Luke stopped her with a squeeze to the elbow.

"They're fine. Wanted to get back to the store once the EMS guys checked them out for bumps and all. Said folks would be 'needing their prescriptions'." He paused for a second, then his voice dropped in tone when he said, "They said you saved their lives."

Saved their lives? Like she'd done something positive. When in reality, everyone in town should be angry with her. A familiar knot of guilt coiled in her stomach.

"I put their lives in danger," she forced out. Why not say it, acknowledge the truth before someone else did?

"How?" Luke squeezed her elbow and leaned in to make eye contact. The blue of his eyes sparkled with icy intensity. "How? Just by being alive? By not wanting to be killed?"

"Sugar, we all knew who you were." Callie leaned in, catching Emmy's eye.

Emmy turned toward her, seeing a gentle tenderness in Callie's eyes.

"We knew you were running from your past. No one ever figured some crazy person was stalking you." She shrugged. "Honey, that's not your fault."

Wasn't it? Somehow, she'd felt all this time that she did deserve it, that everything Max had put her through was her fault, for picking him, choosing a crazy man for a husband.

As if she'd looked around the party the night she'd met him, bypassed all the normal guys and said, "You, I pick you, crazy man." She'd felt as if she'd brought this on herself.

"You heard me? It's not your fault, sugar pie." Callie

patted her on the leg. "Any of this. I'm just sorry you had to go through it."

Emmy met Callie's eyes and tried to hold back the tears. She'd been right in her feelings about Callie, anyway. She was a woman she could be friends with for life.

"Thanks," she said with a sniffle. Callie hugged her tightly, squeezing her and rocking back and forth like with a baby. It felt good. She might not have a mother anymore but the mothering Callie gave her felt good.

Callie pulled back and waggled a finger toward the window, all business now. "Look out that window and tell me if we don't need to start doctoring up the grits. Cheese and butter, and heat you up with some lipstick and hair products. I'm telling you."

Callie went to the window and Luke joined her there.

Emmy walked between them and looked out the window. "Oh, holy mother of pearl."

Callie and Luke's head swiveled around to look at each other. "Guess she can match you Southernism for Southernism," Luke said to Callie.

She nodded. "Guess so. Let's go, Miss Grits Queen." She fluttered her hand at Luke. "You might want to make yourself scarce for a little bit. Don't want you to see how the magic happens."

"Just get it over with." Luke gripped her elbow. Through the hospital's front glass door, she could see a large contingent of Georgia's finest media representatives hovering, waiting for her to leave the protection of the hospital.

TV cameras, reporters and still cameras formed a solid phalanx at the end of the sidewalk.

"Isn't there a back entrance we can sneak out of?" Emmy glanced over her shoulder, prepared to make a run for it.

"Just go out there and give them a sound bite, let them get a little bit of video of you and they'll leave you alone. Otherwise, they'll be tracking you for days, if not weeks." He barked out a rough laugh. "Thought Carl was a stalker? You don't want to see what a news crew who's afraid of getting scooped is like."

She laughed slightly. "Sounds like you've been the subject of news crew stalking before."

He tilted his head, not quite meeting her eyes. What wasn't he telling her?

"I'm surprised they'd come all the way up here," she stalled for time.

"It was a pretty big story in Atlanta, a cop maybe killed, his wife goes missing. Anything involving a cop getting hurt, or whatnot is always big news." He laughed harshly. "Now, the brother shows up, kidnapping the wife and two other mountain folk. Oh, yeah, that's a story."

"Mmm," she murmured.

"Ready?" He squeezed her elbow.

Was she? After a year of running from the spotlight, avoiding recognition at all costs, she was about to let them put her image on television and newspaper sites everywhere?

Yes. The running was over.

She nodded.

"Let's go," Luke said encouragingly. "It's show

time." He pushed open the swinging doors leading from the main hospital entrance.

A security guard stood near the sidewalk, making sure the crews didn't come onto hospital property.

Luke stopped her about a foot before the end of the walkway, leaving a bit of space between her and the cameras and reporters with their extended microphones.

"Emily," a reporter called as if she were a block away.

"Emily," another said loudly and insistently, as if trying to catch Emmy's attention before she turned toward the first reporter's cameraman.

"Mrs. Weber," a reporter toward the outside of the group yelled.

She'd never heard her name shouted so many times in such a quick succession. Silently, she counted two breaths, in and out, until the reporters stopped yelling questions at her. She let out the last breath and smiled toward the cameras.

"I want to thank everyone who was involved in helping rescue me and the couple who were kidnapped with me." She purposefully didn't say their names. If the news people didn't already know, she wasn't going to give them that information. "It was through their efforts that we had a good outcome. Thank you."

She'd made her statement. Now, they could leave. And get on with the rest of her life.

Nodding at the group, she turned to walk around them toward Luke's waiting Jeep, which the security guard had allowed them to park by the front walk.

But thinking she could call an end to the impromptu news conference was obviously naïve. A female reporter began speaking quickly, slipping her question in before the other reporters realized Emmy's statement was over.

However, she looked at Luke instead of Emmy.

The pretty blonde leaned toward Luke, her microphone extended his way. "The McClouds said you were directly involved in the rescue. Have you always known Mrs. Weber's brother-in-law was stalking her, Detective Bradenton?"

Detective? What the hell?

He was a detective?

A jolt of coldness shot through Emmy, her body temperature dropping as if she'd fallen into the river in January. She began floating up above her body, looking down, seeing it from a great distance.

A victim was standing on the sidewalk surrounded by news crews. And beside her, giving a sound bite to the pretty reporter was a police detective?

Apparently!

A police detective. He wasn't Luke, the fisherman, the widow man.

He was Luke, the detective.

Just doing a job, ma'am.

She swiveled her head and looked up at him. Their gazes met and locked, hers filled with shock, his filled with...deception.

A thousand questions shot through her brain. Piercing, stabbing, accusing questions.

No matter the answers, one conclusion yelled out at her, like the reporters who'd shouted for recognition. One fact was indisputable.

She was the worse judge of men on the planet.

Luke turned back to the reporter and said, "No, I

didn't know he was stalking her until he took the McClouds hostage."

Had Luke, the detective, been following her the whole time too? Was he trying to get her to implicate herself in the murder, maybe reveal where she'd hidden the body?

Had sleeping with her been part of the plan or just something that happened?

Anger, shame, embarrassment. All of that filled her, with the final conclusion that she'd been such a fool.

She wasn't a criminal.

But she had criminally bad taste in men. The worst judgment. No doubt.

The hell if she was going to stay in that prison for the rest of her life.

She pivoted on her heel and walked back into the hospital, catching Callie watching the whole thing just inside the hospital front door.

Callie's eyes rounded. "What, too much for you?"

"Can you give me a ride home?" She wasn't explaining anything. If she talked about it, she would explode into a screaming ball of rage. "Get me out of here, please?" she said through tight lips, lips that needed to guard against the fierce primal scream that wanted to explode from her gut.

Callie nodded, her face filled with a thousand questions.

The hospital door swung open with a whoosh of air and Luke blasted through it as if blown in by the power of the yelling reporters outside, who continued to holler for more information.

Emmy didn't even look at him. Because she was done talking to him.

And the hell if she wanted to hear a thing he had to say.

She pivoted on her heel for the second time in a few minutes and began putting as much space as quickly as possible between herself and Luke.

The detective who'd obviously been following her for some time.

He'd better not follow her now.

CHAPTER TWENTY-TWO

Luke watched Emmy's backside as she showed it to him as quickly as humanly possible, pivoting again on her heel. She was getting pretty good at that pivoting maneuver.

She never looked back, striding across the hospital lobby as if she were a reporter chasing a sound bite. Looking every bit as determined as a news photographer trying to get the picture.

Callie hustled after her, throwing confused looks over her shoulder at Luke.

Damn. Damn. Damn.

Maybe he should have briefed Emmy on his job before they'd walked out to face the phalanx of reporters and television cameras.

Or had Callie escort her out to the media. But, he was better equipped to maneuver Emmy through the full press event, with all of its intensity, how they would try to get more information out of her than she had planned to give.

He'd been out of the loop on the media circuit for so long he hadn't expected anyone to recognize him out of context, put two and two together that the guy walking the "widow" out of the hospital was an Atlanta homicide detective.

Former detective, he corrected himself. He might never go back. Death wasn't just a puzzle to solve anymore, finding justice for the victim.

After his wife's death, death had become personal. Too personal. Every person who'd lost a loved one would tap into his own personal pain over the loss of his wife.

Yeah, he was probably a former detective for good.

People got new titles in life.

Emmy had been titled a person of interest. But Carl's involvement had put everything into a new light. Now, she was *the widow* and *almost victim.*

It seemed pretty clear that Carl had killed his brother, then tried to kill Emmy or get her to kill herself so he could collect the insurance of his dead brother. The will left a clear motive that if Emmy died, then Carl was in line to collect on the insurance policy.

Was the life insurance policy still in place on Emmy? Would Carl have collected on Emmy's death as well? Needed to check on that.

Either way, with Carl in jail, Emmy had gotten a new title. She'd gone from person of interest to heroine.

Yeah. Luke sucked in a deep breath. He'd probably gotten a few, new titles from Emmy as well.

Jerk. Liar. User. And he'd earned them.

Emmy was happy to be back at work, into a normal routine.

Normal? After the last year, she'd never expected she'd say that about her life again.

She ran the cash register while Callie stood to the

side making up an order list for when the deliveryman got to the store.

A young guy handed Emmy a dollar. She rang up his Coke and gave him back his change. He couldn't be over twenty.

"Have a good day," she said and smiled extra nice at him. He looked like he could use a little attention.

"Thank you, ma'am, I will." He gave a slow, sweet smile and walked out the door, popping the top of his drink as he went.

When the door swung to after him, Emmy looked over at Callie. "What's the deal with that guy? Comes in every day at this time like clockwork."

Callie looked up from her order forms. "That's Ronnie. I'm sorry. I'll introduce you next time. He came home from college to help out his daddy."

Emmy watched through the front window as the kid got into a beat up pickup truck and pulled out.

"How's he helping his daddy?"

"His daddy got banged up bad in a tractor accident, so Ronnie and his brother both came home to help out. Ronnie's a real smart boy, got a full scholarship down to UGA. But, that type of money couldn't help his daddy, so he dropped out of school."

"He works on the farm in the morning, helping with the cows and the crops, then he goes over to Lloyd Johnson's farm for about four hours for pay, then he showers, comes in here for a Coke and goes on down to Gainesville for a full swing shift at one of the chicken factories down there."

"Wow. How long's that supposed to last?"

Callie shrugged sadly. "Till his daddy gets better, if that ever happens."

"I'll have to smile nicer at him from now on."

Callie laughed. "Don't know how that would be possible. I think he comes in here for your smile as much as anything. Half the boys in the county come in here now a whooole lot more often."

She grinned up at Emmy. "You're good for business."

Emmy laughed half-heartedly. Seems she did most things half-heartedly these days. "Glad I can help."

Callie looked at her for a long moment. Emmy could almost see her counting to ten. That was Callie's secret coping technique. She counted to ten before she spoke sometimes when she knew she was entering forbidden territory with someone. When she really needed to control her mouth.

But it rarely worked, the control part. It usually just forestalled what she'd been planning to say, delayed the interference, the meddling.

"Spit it out," Emmy said, with a smile. "You've earned the right."

Callie looked up at her, and Emmy could almost hear the counting continuing. "Ten," Callie said with a smartass smile.

She stood up and walked closer to lean against the counter beside Emmy, looking into her eyes.

"When are you going to forgive Detective Luke?" Callie looked at her with an intensity that was rare for her. "Can't you forgive him?"

Emmy looked away and sucked in a breath on three counts then let it out.

"It's not that I don't forgive him. If he ever needed forgiving for just doing his job."

"I owe him my life and also a lifetime's debt of

gratitude for saving the McClouds. If he and his detective cousin hadn't shown up when they did, we would have all been dead. So, yes, I *forgive* him and am eternally grateful to him."

Emmy tried to smile. "If he ever needs a kidney, I'm his girl."

Callie gave an obligatory smile at the attempt at a joke, then her eyes narrowed. "But?"

Emmy pursed her lips, trying to think how to put it into terms that someone who hadn't lived her nightmare could understand.

"It's just I'm not sure if I can ever trust him." She gestured at her chest with both hands. "Trust what we had was true."

"I thought we had something so special. But when I think that maybe he was just working the case and happened to fall into bed with me…"

The pain stabbed into her as fierce as when she'd first heard Luke called detective. Would it ever subside, the wound heal, leaving just another emotional scar.

Compared to the scars Max had left, this was nothing really, a pinprick. Luke had saved her life. He could ask her for anything and she'd have to comply.

But a wholehearted trust in the two of them? The knife twisted inside of her, hurting deep down, with a pain that needed tears.

She usually tried to distract herself as much as possible from thinking about it, or she'd be a tear-stained mess all day long.

She looked at Callie for confirmation, needing her to understand, but Callie just shook her head.

"Honey, y'all are as real as it gets. The way that man looks at you." She fanned herself with one hand. "I would have given anything back in my pre-Mike years to get half of that from him, a quarter of that." She sighed melodramatically.

Then, she gave up any pretense of joking around.

"You look plumb serious," Emmy attempted a joke.

Callie shook her head. "I know you were worried about calling yourself by your mama's maiden name when you were undercover." She put a hand on her hip. "But I thought that wasn't going to be an issue for long. Thought Luke would give you a new last name, solve all that messiness of explaining to folks and all."

Emmy couldn't help but laugh just a bit. Callie always had a way of making anything she said a bit funny.

But, once again, the might-have-beens, the life she and Luke could have had, hurt just a bit more than the things that had really happened. They could have had a wonderful life, if things had been different.

The day when she really did lay on her deathbed, an old lady looking back, she knew it was the might-have-beens, the could-have-beens, and the should-have-beens that would haunt her.

She and Luke could have been so great together.

If only.

"Emmy Bradenton?" Callie said. "Sounds so right."

"Yeah," Emmy said softly. "Don't know if that's going to happen. I had one marriage built on pretenses, don't think I want another. I don't want things I can't trust in my life."

"Emm." Callie rubbed her toe over a rough spot on the old wooden floor.

Emmy studied Callie. Something had been bugging Emmy a lot.

Did she even want to bring it up? To seem ungrateful. To say something that would offend the woman to whom she owed so much?

But it was getting in the way of their friendship, the not knowing.

She inhaled deeply and jumped in. "Callie, you knew he was a detective." Emmy glanced away, not meeting Callie's eyes, drawing in another deep, steadying breath.

Then, she looked back at Callie, meeting her gaze directly, softening her tone so she'd know she wasn't angry. "Why didn't you ever say anything about it? Especially since you knew I'd been a person of interest."

Callie looked away, leaned back and picked up her forms and began studying them. Then, she shuffled them together, straightening them on the counter and clipping them back onto her clipboard.

Counting to ten? Finally she met Emmy's gaze, straight on, letting her read the truth as she spoke.

"Well, considering you'd slept together, I wasn't sure that he hadn't told you." She shrugged. "But, the reason I didn't tell you myself, about his past." She pointed a finger at Emmy, wagging it in her best schoolmarm imitation, the one she used on her kids. "Is because we all have a past, Emmy. You have one. I have one. And how much of our past we choose to tell folks is our own business."

Callie slanted a look up under her eyelashes at Emmy, as if trying to see if that was enough, if she needed more.

Emmy needed more.

"Okay," Callie blew out the word on a huff of air. "I

wasn't going to go all Hallmark card on you, but here goes." She put her hands on her hips and stared into space for a long moment.

Then, she looked directly at Emmy. "I didn't want the circumstances, the facts, the cold hard truth, to get in the way of what I knew you and Luke could have together."

"*What you knew we could have together?*" Emmy repeated back Callie's words and purposefully kept her expression blank, not condemning, not accepting, just blank.

"Yes, Emmy." Callie leaned in just a bit, her eyes narrowing, intensity glowing from them. "I saw two lost souls who maybe," she wagged a finger, "just maybe, could heal each other."

Callie had noticed she needed *healing*? Her breath caught in her chest and tears started lining up for the march to her eyes.

It was like the first time Callie had trusted her to open the store by herself, trusted her with a key to her business.

It said Callie saw into her soul, really saw who she was. And cared.

How could you be mad at something like that?

Her eyes began to burn, tears accelerating toward the surface. Another second and she'd be bawling all over the place.

She breathed in for three counts and out for three counts.

Then, when she knew she had control of herself, she looked up to meet Callie's eyes.

"Thanks," she pushed past the knot in her throat.

Callie just nodded. "He's a wounded soul, too, with his wife's death."

"But it wasn't just his wife dying," Callie breathed out shakily, tears glistening in her eyes. "It was that he couldn't save her, no matter how hard he tried, no matter how much he researched. That was a hard blow for a detective. He couldn't save her." Callie's face scrunched, a tear running down her cheek. She swiped at it like she was annoyed with herself for crying.

"He was broken hearted," Callie summed it all up, another tear streaking down her cheek and just as quickly was brushed away. "And a failed detective. A failed husband? He'd failed in his duty to protect his wife."

Emmy looked down at the counter, tracing patterns in the wooden surface, running her fingers along the knots of old wood. "You are really trying to make me cry here."

Callie looked up with a wet, shaky laugh. "Why should I be the only one?" Her eyes narrowed, swirling with emotion. "Two wounded souls." She wagged her finger at Emmy.

The noise of a car engine pulling up across the street broke the mood. "Well, speak of the detective." Callie wiped at her eyes then touched Emmy on the arm, a happy glint replacing the tears in her eyes. "Been a long time since that Jeep's come 'a calling."

A month since *the incident*, as she and Callie called it, and she hadn't seen Luke face to face alone once. He'd been good about abiding by her wishes.

"Breathe in for three and then out for three," Callie said, with a little grin. They really were getting to know each other too well.

Callie grabbed her purse and headed toward the back door.

"Hey you, get back here," Emmy called after her.

"Got's to pick up my kids," she sang, "You two need to work on your hearts. Need some alone time for that." She smiled again, this time more sweetly, then disappeared out the back door, leaving Emmy to face Detective Luke alone.

Panic out of proportion to the situation flashed through her. Her pulse accelerated and a mist of sweat spread underneath her clothes.

She couldn't catch her breath, feeling like it had been blown out of her by a hard fall.

Finally, she began to breathe but only shallow pants not carrying enough oxygen to sustain her brain for long.

Anticipation began overtaking her, knowing that any second, Luke would walk through that door. She began wanting what she couldn't have, wanting a man who'd saved her life, but as easily would have put her in prison given the chance.

If it had all been just a job for him, why did it feel so personal, such a deeply personal betrayal?

CHAPTER TWENTY-THREE

Luke got out of his Jeep and looked across the street at the *forbidden place*, The Corner Store.

For the last month, he'd shopped for groceries at the Piggly Wiggly, instead of invading Emmy's place of business.

It had been long enough, and if they were going to live in the same town, he had to face her some time.

Man up, his testosterone yelled. *She's just another girl. Get over it.*

But, she wasn't *just another girl* and it wasn't that easy. In the first days after the kidnapping, he'd called her cell, shown up at her house and left a note when she didn't come to the door.

Finally, she'd texted him she wasn't up to seeing him. Had asked for time to *process everything*.

Then, he'd stayed away.

No woman just getting over one possessive jerk and being stalked by his brother wanted to feel like she was in a repeat nightmare.

No woman had ever claimed to be afraid of him. If a woman said she didn't want to see him, then that was within her power to control.

But, he'd given her a month.

They could at least get the first meeting over with while they were alone, exchange pleasantries, get past the awkwardness, so if they encountered each other in public, with people watching, they'd already have gotten past the first hurdle.

That's all this was, just what you had to do when you lived in a small town.

The sheriff, his long time friend Grant, had been pushing him to take a job with his force and he was thinking it over.

The level of crime in these parts was nothing compared to Atlanta. But couples fought here like they did everywhere and sometimes ended the fight at the end of a gun barrel.

There were robberies and break-ins and other petty crimes. Guys got into brawls at the bar. Cops seemed to have a guaranteed job anywhere because human nature always seemed to include some trouble.

If he was on the force, he'd be sure to see Emmy.

Might as well get it over with now.

So, why did his muscles tighten as he walked across the road? Fight or flight? This was neither. Just a couple of people who'd dated, had a fling, and needed to be friendly now.

Still, his pulse accelerated and his palms began sweating. No reason for that. Except for the anticipation of seeing her and the desire to touch her.

What would it be like to see her and not be able to touch her? Hell, he'd put up with it for at least a month before he'd finally been able to put his arms around Emmy.

But now? With less hope of ever having her in his bed again?

If he were a perp, he'd jerk himself up by the collar for even thinking like that.

This was just an initial meeting to get over the awkwardness. Not a chance to restart the relationship.

He sucked in a deep breath and pushed open the door. The darkness blinded him for a second. But when his eyes adjusted, when their eyes met…a kick of excitement and desire coursed through his body.

And a lightness.

Such as he hadn't felt since…the last time he'd seen her. Lightness, buoyancy, hopefulness, all coursed through him with the dream that his life could be right again, with all the things that made life really worth living.

Love, companionship, desire.

Desire so fierce, he wanted to talk himself out of his high-minded principles that you don't pursue a woman who's asked you not to.

The guyness in him said to hell with that bull, go after the woman, the only way you're gonna get a woman is to go after her.

But, this situation was different. It wasn't about wooing. After all she'd been through, she didn't deserve to be pushed.

Still, there was the lightness and the hopefulness pulsing through him, making him want to be in her presence, if for no other reason than to know that someone like her existed in the world, that maybe he could have what they'd had again.

If he acted normal, didn't set off her alarms, maybe he could drop by and just look at her occasionally, just say hi and see her smile, just like a bunch of other guys in the area did. Young and old, all the guys liked to see her smile.

He'd heard the guy talk. Not locker room talk. But just a casual reference to how nice she was. That she was sweet, a good addition to town.

He knew, knew all those guys got that same kick just from looking into her eyes and seeing her smile.

Old or young, that sort of kick was a good thing to experience, no matter if you never hoped or expected anything to come of it.

Kinda like him now.

Those green eyes were emerald colored in the dark interior, glinting back a sparkle from the light coming through the window. Her hair caught a few penny colored highlights from the overhead light near the counter.

She was wearing a simple forest green cotton shirt that brought out the river color in her eyes and the red highlights in her brunette hair and a pair of worn jeans, her hair down around her shoulders. All in all, the girl next door.

If the girl next door was a cover model. Damn, his hormones kicked into full drive, called out of hiding by the estrogen the woman embodied.

That shirt fit her form as if it had been poured onto her, sliding over the curves that God and her mama gave her.

Yeah, it was gonna be hard. Damn hard.

"Hey," he said and turned toward the cooler.

"Hey yourself, Detective Luke."

He laughed and looked over his shoulder. "I thought I was Fisherman Luke."

"Used to be," she said with a tentative smile. "Now, you're Detective Luke."

He pulled out a bottle of cold water and took it to the counter. "And a bag of ice, please."

She nodded and rang it up. "Getting some fishing done?"

"Some. You?"

She smiled. "I don't have any gear."

An opening?

"I could loan you some. Till you get your own, of course. If you're gonna live round these parts, you'll want your own fishing gear."

"Of course," she said wryly, her face relaxing into a semblance of normal, the tension gone that had altered her face the first time she'd heard him called detective.

She met his eyes and said with a joking glint sparkling back from the green depths of her own eyes, "I'd make sure to get your gear back to you. A true fisherman has an affinity to his gear."

She was teasing. Teasing was good. She held up a hand and began counting off on her fingers.

"You have that rod and reel you fished with out in Montana." She tilted her head. "Hand carried it on the plane."

"Thank goodness I got an airport security check official who was a fisherman himself. Cause otherwise, I might have had to check the gear with my luggage and run the risk of them losing it." He crossed his arms and leaned back on his heels. "I do love that rod."

"I understand." She smiled and held up a second finger. "Then, there's the gear you used last month to catch that extra big fish." She wagged her head knowingly. "Not the really big one in the hole down by me." She shook her head. "But a big fish, never the less. Probably was your good luck rod and reel."

She tilted her head at him. "Yes?"

"It was."

She fanned her hand out in a *Price is Right* model's gesture as if all his gear was lined up on the counter. "Etc, etc, etc, to quote the king in *The King and I,* one of my Grampa's favorite movies."

"You told me," he said, grateful for any line of conversation that made this encounter easy.

She was making it easy.

"He used to get choked up at the end of *The King and I,*" he repeated what she'd told him. "Said he'd been forced to watch it so many times with your grandmother that he'd gotten to where he actually liked it."

She nodded and a dreamy, misty look came into her eyes. "He liked to watch it 'cause it reminded him of her. They were married for fifty years," she said with a catch in her throat.

"Yes, you mentioned that."

She always got that tone in her voice whenever she talked about her Grampa.

"They used to get up and dance around the living room every time the big dance number came on," she said.

He hadn't heard this part before.

She continued, with the same loving, distant look on her face, "He'd puff up his chest and act like Yul Brynner." She put her hands on her hips in imitation of the actor as the king.

Luke's mom had loved that movie too, so he knew what she meant.

"Grandma loved when he did that," Emmy continued. "Said it made her feel young and in love again."

She smiled, her eyes unfocused, as if seeing her grandparents dancing now.

"You gonna bring your Grampa up here?" Luke asked after a moment.

She met his eyes, then quickly dropped them to the register and rang up his order. "Maybe."

Non-committal.

Something clicked in his brain. "You still don't feel safe?" He cut straight to the heart of the matter.

To hell with beating around the bush on this subject. He was a former cop, maybe gonna be one again, and that was one thing cops knew, the fear that lurks long after the danger is gone.

That was the real heinousness of crimes against people, the way it took away their sense of security in the world, took away their feeling that the world was an okay place to live.

A fury seeped through his veins, that Carl had done this to her.

"He's still in jail down there, isn't he?" she asked.

He met her eyes. Saw the fear, the hesitancy, the misgivings.

"Yeah, Emmy. They're holding him on multiple counts of kidnapping, assault, breaking and entering, robbery, assaulting a police officer and other charges. That ought to hold him long enough for them to put together a case for murder."

She fiddled with the register keys, then moved her hand to the wood counter, tracing the patterns of the swirling knots.

The fear swirling off her sickened him.

He placed his hand over hers, wanting her to understand he would do anything to keep her safe.

She jumped, her gaze jerking to meet his.

But she didn't pull her hand away.

"You can call me anytime you feel afraid, Emmy."

She looked at him for a long moment, the connection holding, with the feeling there was something more between them than just used-to-be-lovers. It felt like a possibility of more.

Then, she simply nodded with a little smile.

"Do you kinda wish I'd killed him that day?"

Darkness slashed through her eyes, a homicidal black flash, but quickly she replaced it with a smirk that played along her lips. Played along her lips with an expression that made it almost impossible to look away from them.

But, he forced his eyes back up, away from those lips.

"Oh no," she said when their eyes met. "You are not gonna catch me saying something that horrible out loud."

Then, her smile faded. She leaned forward and met his eyes with an intensity. "What does he say about the day he killed Max? The Atlanta cops won't tell me anything, say they don't want to taint my testimony when this goes to trial."

He shrugged. His cousin talked to him about the case, the confusing evidence that didn't match up. "I shouldn't say too much. But, I can tell you stuff that's been said in open court. The defendant claims he's innocent of the murder, continues to say *you* killed his brother."

"They're using an insanity plea for the kidnapping and other charges connected to what happened up here. Said he was driven crazy by the fact that the woman who killed his brother skated free."

Her mouth twisted with anger and other darker emotions. Like homicidal impulses?

Absentmindedly, she turned her hand over so that their hands were palm to palm. His pulse leaped, along with the hope that they could recover from the circumstances surrounding their meeting.

"He better not get off." She chewed the words. "Saying he's crazy." Her eyes narrowed, fire and hatred in them. "I want him to pay for all the time he took away from me and my Grampa."

He threaded his fingers through hers, tightening his grip on her hand and she looked up to meet his gaze, her eyes widening, as if only then realizing they were holding hands. Still, she didn't pull away.

Instead, she cuddled her hand into his. "He won't get off by saying he's crazy, will he?" The plaintive tone in her voice cut into him, just how much it said about the pain of the last year and all it had cost her.

"He won't *get off,* Emmy. Not for murdering a cop, besides hardly anyone *gets off* that isn't truly crazy, and even then they usually get 'guilty but mentally insane'. Do the time for the crime but also get treatment and meds."

He laughed harshly. "Actually, I think all violent criminals are crazy. They'd have to be insane to act that way, hurting people."

He shrugged. "But that's just me talking."

She rubbed her thumb along the top of his hand. Blood coursed through him, as if it had been stored in his heart for the last month, waiting for her touch to release it.

"So, he's locked up tight?" she said. As if she weren't driving him crazy with just the contact between their hands, as if being near her wasn't driving him nearly insane.

"Yeah, he's locked up in the Fulton County Jail, a murderer who's that dangerous, killed one person, tried to kill you and said he was gonna kill the McClouds as well. They're not letting him walk free on bond."

She shivered and tightened her grasp on his hand.

It felt so right, as if it meant more than just her need for human contact and reassurance. But, that's all he had the right to interpret it as. He'd been a cop when he met her and he was still a cop. As the victim in this scenario, she had the right to view him as a resource, not a nuisance.

He was a cop and he had to act like one.

"Call me anytime, if you're afraid, Emmy, day or night."

Her gaze met his with an intensity.

With desire?

He felt the kick all the way through his body. Or was that just the stalker's slant, a self-serving interpretation of her expression?

She pulled her hand away, wiped off his bottled water with a paper towel, then handed it to him.

It was time to tell her his news.

"I might be a cop again."

A large smile flashed instantly across her face. "Good." She nodded. "Good."

"Good?"

"You're made to be a cop." Emerald intensity flashed in her eyes. "The way you sprang into action to protect me and the McClouds, how you rescued all of us." She shrugged. "Made to be a cop."

It felt good, hearing the words from her. He might never be a big city cop again, with all the ugliness that came with that. But a small town lawman? One of Grant's deputies? Yeah, it felt right.

"So, when do you go back to Atlanta?" she said, looking away toward the register, fiddling with the keys.

Was that a tinge of regret on her face, that he was leaving town?

"I'm not. I'm leaving the Atlanta force."

Her eyes widened. "Oh? So, where are you gonna be a cop?" She inhaled deeply.

Was it too much to hope for, that she wanted him to say here?

"Here, in Hawk's Peak."

She let out the air in a long shaky breath. Then, smiled. "Not Atlanta?"

He shook his head, unable to tear his gaze away from her face, with that beautiful smile, the way she'd looked before the incident. Before she knew about him being a cop.

Even if it pleased her, there was someone else who was disappointed by his decision.

"Forrester is really upset. Kept thinking I was coming back. We wanted to be cops together since we were kids." A deep sigh released from his gut. "I hate disappointing him."

Disappointment didn't even begin to describe how much he hated letting Forrester down. Would miss working with him.

She met his eyes with an understanding smile that brought him back from his thoughts of his cousin. "It's not in you anymore, Luke."

She always got him. Damn. This trying to be friends stuff was damned hard.

But, he wouldn't give her up. Whatever she was willing to offer him was enough.

Cause, the alternative? Not seeing her, being deprived of her entirely? That was totally unacceptable. Impossible to contemplate.

So, he sucked it up, pushed back the heat she sent through him with just a touch, just a glance, and acted *like a friend.*

"You're right. It's not in me anymore. I want a quieter life, less bad stuff, more good stuff."

He met her eyes and in their green depths saw reflected back an understanding. The same understanding that made him want to pull her to him and meld with all that was in her, all that they could have, a lifetime of living with a woman who got him, who didn't judge him for not wanting a competitive, aggressive lifestyle down in the big city.

A woman who didn't think he should be all about rising in the ranks, getting titles, etc.

He sucked in a deep breath, waiting for the oxygen to clear his head, as if that would ever be possible around her.

"What about you?" he asked. "You going back to Atlanta? You've been officially cleared. I hear the life insurance money has been released to you. You can go back to your old home, or buy a new one, bigger, fancier." He attempted a smile, but dread filled him as he waited for her answer, afraid she'd say yes, that she was going back.

Back to everything he'd left and didn't want anymore.

He held his breath, waiting to hear any revealing sound she made on the subject. Long seconds passed.

Then, she looked up. "No, I'm definitely not going back to that house. In fact, that house isn't mine anymore. The bank owns it. The cops went over there and had everything packed up and put into storage a long time ago."

She laughed. "I mean, they said they packed up everything. Afraid of losing a clue, something they might have realized later was important."

Her expression darkened. "I'm just gonna take over the storage payments once they release it officially. Don't know if I'm even up for going through it. Seeing Max's stuff, stuff we owned together."

She shuddered. "Carl hasn't shown y'all where the body is, has he?"

"No."

She stiffened and began rubbing at a spot on the counter that would never come off. It was part of the wood grain. But, she rubbed with her finger, worrying the spot.

"Carl's defense team will eventually hint they might be able to help *locate* the body," he offered. "Use it as a bargaining tool, to get a lighter sentence for him. Cause the DA could go after him with the death penalty even if there isn't a body, considering all he's done. Carl's lawyer will be doing everything he can to get life with no chance of parole, instead of the death sentence."

She nodded, letting out a shaky breath. "I'd feel better if they at least found Max's body, then I could put this whole thing to rest."

She looked away into the distance, river green shadows playing in her eyes, like the watery depths of the Chattahoochee River skirting along the banks of her sanity. "Finally," she almost whispered.

He studied her for a long moment. God, he wanted to pull her into a protective embrace, promise to defend her against any danger. "You still keep your gun with you?"

"Oh yeah." She laughed raggedly. "I look over my shoulder all the time, jump up in the middle of the night when I hear a noise."

Fury gripped him again, squeezing the life out of his self-control, at what this guy had done to her.

"You know," he said. "If you wanted to stay at my uncle's house…"

She arched an eyebrow and laughed slightly.

"I mean without me there. I could stay at your place. Maybe rebuild that ramp for you so you could bring your grandpa up here."

Her eyes turned soft at the mention of the ramp, a necessity if she were to get her grandfather up to Hawk's Peak. And Luke knew that desire was closest to her heart.

"At my uncle's cabin, you'd have the cameras and the entire security system. Just until you get over your skittishness."

She leaned onto her elbows on the counter, looking up at him through her eyelashes. Did they teach women to do that, some class in high school maybe?

Cause it had this come hither quality that made him want to lean down, tilt up her chin and place his lips onto hers.

She lowered her gaze to the counter, tracing the pattern again. "I'll think about it."

She straightened up, leaned back, and the moment was over. "Thanks," she added. "For everything. Thanks."

He just nodded. "No problem, ma'am," he said the way a cop should talk to a crime victim.

Just another day in a cop's life.

Then, he turned and walked out to get his ice.

Before he lost it. Lost it and grabbed her, pulled her to him, and took that mouth.

Damn it. Living in small towns had its own particular dangers. The danger of making a fool of himself over a woman who'd decided to move on.

The danger of doing anything that would make it impossible for him to be around her, to be friends with her, to be whatever she chose.

Cause he sure as hell wanted whatever she was willing to give. Even if it was friendship.

The memory of how she'd turned her hand into his, then gripped his hand tighter without even knowing it.

That was a stalker's no man's land, that little bit of middle ground of uncertainty where craziness lived. That bit of hope that they'd maybe have a future.

Was he approaching stalker crazy? Or did they have a chance once she'd gotten past the nightmare of the last year?

CHAPTER TWENTY-FOUR

Emmy hit the store's security system buttons, turned the lock on the front door, and walked to her car just as the streetlights clicked on. Dark so early?

Wind whirled a tornado of leaves around her. Chilly, fall air cut through her thin sweater.

She needed a coat. Maybe she'd actually go into a store and buy something new. What a luxury!

Maybe get herself a brand new shirt as well.

Not a thrift store bargain, but things no one else had worn except for her.

She got into her battered old Toyota and headed toward home.

Home.

First time she'd used that word in the last year. But finally, that's how Hawk's Peak felt.

Maybe tomorrow she'd go into a hardware store and start assembling what she needed to rebuild the wheelchair ramp.

Maybe take Luke up on his offer to help?

Maybe take him up on the other offer his eyes had extended when he looked at her?

A slow heat rose in her, spiraling quickly out of

control. She cranked down the car window and brisk, fresh air blew on her face.

Still the heat blazed through her. She had no immunity to the desire that swept through her veins every time she was near him. They should make a vaccination for that.

This heat for him begged her to phone him up, invite him over, change the sheets before he got there, and otherwise freshen up the bedroom.

Why was she still holding back? Why this reluctance toward probably the nicest and hottest guy she'd ever met?

She could finally start to live again, like a normal person. This year of hell was over. Max was dead and the man who'd been stalking her was in jail.

Then, at the thought of the two hellish men, a panicky snake slid along her nerve endings. From force of habit, she checked her rear and side view mirrors and glanced around as she drove, on the alert for cars tailing her. She whirled around for a quick full look behind her for anything she might have missed.

Her pulse accelerated, and she pushed down on the gas, speeding up, readying for a chase. To run from a monster.

Wait, what was she doing? No one was back there. Slowly, she let off the accelerator.

Sucking in a deep breath, she exhaled on a three count. And then did it again until the panic receded. And the tiredness took over, with an after the adrenalin rush letdown.

This was why she wasn't ready to start her new life. A life that could include a man like Luke.

Because it still felt like it wasn't over. Wasn't over with Max.

As long as she kept looking in the rearview mirror, afraid to see him, it wasn't over.

Sure, his crazy brother had appeared out of nowhere to torment her, sure a case could be made that she was free of all that had happened, all that had haunted her this past year.

So, why did she still double-check every window and door when she entered the house and before she went to bed?

Because of the body of her little dog lying in all that blood?

The body of her little Charlie haunted her still, thinking of his final moments of terror.

Carl might have killed him to shut him up, silence his barking so neighbors wouldn't look out their windows.

Still, killing Charlie felt like a signature move that had screamed of Max's evil mind.

Was she endangering anyone else she loved, making them a target for Max?

It was hard to accept that he was dead. That he was lying in a shallow, unmarked grave dug by his own brother.

Her cell phone rang and she jumped, her reaction to a simple everyday thing heightened. She looked at the phone ID. Callie.

She drew in a few calming breaths as she put on her ear bud and hit the connect button. "Hey, girl."

"Hey girl, you alone?" Callie's impish tone made her smile.

"We're all alone, everyone is alone," Emmy intoned in a mock doomsday voice.

"You don't have to be alone. Detective Luke's just a phone call away."

Emmy snorted her answer. No words needed.

"You going home to stalk through the house, with your gun drawn, checking behind doors and into closets?"

"You know me too well."

Callie had caught her doing that once when they'd gone to her house together after the Carl incident. Emmy had thought Callie was outside but she'd come up behind her, almost scaring both of them to death when Emmy twirled on her, the gun in her hands.

"Maybe what you need is a resident cop?" Callie's tone was only half-joking.

"The answer to life isn't to have a guy around for security."

She needed to feel safe on her own terms.

"The answer to life?" Callie guffawed. "I just meant the answer to tonight. *One night at a time*, is my motto since I've gotten divorced."

A little twist of sympathy turned in Emmy. Callie was going through her own stuff. It couldn't have been easy, having to encounter Big Mike's new girlfriend the day her kid disappeared. The way Big Mike had put his arm around the new girlfriend, comforting her instead of Callie.

"You were quite the lady, by the way, at the vet's when Little Mike went missing. You could have just reamed Mike's new..." She hesitated at the word.

"Girlfriend," Callie supplied. "His new girlfriend. I'm his ex-wife, his baby mama." She snorted. Callie's snorts conveyed a lot of meaning.

"And believe me, no one needed any Baby Mama Drama that day, on top of the real life issues of a missing child." She snorted again.

Callie snorted a lot when she was close to getting emotional.

Big Mike had spoken so sweetly to his new girlfriend. When Callie herself had needed comforting.

Anyway," Callie said in a flip tone. "This conversation is about you. And why you keep pushing the oh-so attractive Detective Luke away. Girl, you are crazy."

"You know," Callie continued. "I heard he's going to be a cop up here. If you call the police some night about a falling limb that's freaked you out, it might be Detective Luke showing up. Detective Luuuuke," she trilled with an underlying laugh.

"Well, that's just perfect, isn't it?" Emmy kept her tone light. But, that emphasized one of the main reasons she couldn't be with Luke. She couldn't base a relationship on the need for protection.

Until her past was put to bed, until she chose to be with a man for reasons other than protection, she wouldn't be getting into Luke's bed.

"I want a clean slate for me and Luke. Not one tainted by confusion and doubts about why we're together," she said.

Would that day ever come?

God, she hoped so.

Cause how could she look into Luke's eyes and not think of what they'd had before everything had unraveled.

"So, you just need time," Callie concluded. She emhummed a bit. "Just don't take too long cause Detective Luke is a very attractive guy. Other available women might be phoning the police on nights he's on call, scared about some noise he needs to check out, to maybe look under their beds."

Emmy laughed at Callie's tone. "Girl, you are too much."

"I'm just saying." Callie's grin came through the phone. "Gotta go. Want to free up the line so you can call Detective Luke."

Callie hung up just when Emmy wouldn't have minded her company on the phone, as she rolled down the dark driveway to her house.

"I really need some more security lights out here. Maybe even a camera system, too," she talked out loud, to comfort herself, to feel like she wasn't alone out here in the country.

She pulled her purse closer to her, taking the gun out to sit beside her. Would she ever be over this? A punch of fury at Max and his stupid brother hit her in the gut.

Yes, she would be over this, damn it! They would not hold her hostage forever.

She had Max's life insurance money. She could use it to install a good security system, which was ironic.

In fact, she could use Max's life insurance money to buy this place.

All that money was sitting in her bank account, released to her by the insurance company after the police had said she was no longer a person of interest in her husband's death.

But, it didn't feel like her money.

Insurance money from the death of a husband she hadn't loved for a long time.

"Oh, hell no," Callie had said when she'd said that to her. "You deserve that money, after all that man and his crazy brother put you through. You were his wife, so who else should get it?"

Callie had leaned closer. "Wife. That word says it all. It's your money."

Emmy had just shrugged. She didn't want to touch it yet, just wanted to let everything stay the same.

Letting everything stay the same was a huge luxury. Changeup had been all she'd known the last year, every few months bringing a new town, a new place to stay.

As she got out of her car, her phone rang again. Probably just Callie with another few smart remarks.

She stuck the key into the front door, turning it and getting inside and locking it safely behind her before she answered.

"Hello." She grabbed it on what was probably the last ring before it went to voice mail.

"Emmy? It's Forrester. Luke's cousin."

"Hey, Forrester." She gripped her gun tightly in one hand, then pushed the curtain back just a bit to peek out into the front yard.

"I've got some information we weaseled out of your ex brother-in-law."

Ex brother-in-law felt so much better, put some distance between them.

"Yeah?" she answered as she walked to the front closet to peer inside, then quickly behind the door. She always left the closet door open so she didn't have that terrifying moment when you had to open the door, and wonder would someone jump out at you.

"Found out how he was tracing you. Through that social security number you were using. Criminals stick together. Those guys you went to down in Atlanta to get your fake driver's license and social security card. He knew them."

"Of course he did," she said. "How stupid of me. He was probably the one who told Max about those guys. I was just desperate and went to the first place I could think of. Max had told me once about how people could get any sort of documents to stay in the country, said terrorists could get them, even."

"Pointed out the place once when we drove by." She drew in a deep breath. "I didn't think he was really in contact with them, talked to them. Just thought he knew about it by word of mouth. I guess it was his low life brother who'd told him about it in the first place. How stupid of me." She exhaled on the count of three.

"Emmy," Forrester said gently. "Don't ever call yourself stupid. You managed to evade this guy, this crazy murderous son of a…" He inhaled sharply.

"For more than a year you evaded Carl, depending on your intuition and instincts. You survived," he said firmly and clearly.

The words sent a little spurt of pride shooting through her.

"Thanks, it feels good hearing you put it that way."

She walked from window to window, checking that they were locked.

"Well, start saying that stuff to yourself." Forrester's tone was gruff, a big brotherly tone. "Not that other crap, sorry, stuff that you say to yourself about it being your fault, and how could you not have seen it all coming."

She listened, sucking it all in, the affirmation that she didn't seem able to give herself, instead always putting the blame on herself.

She needed to check the kitchen.

"I remember when you first started dating Max," Forrester said.

"You remember that?"

"Yeah, I do." He waited a second. "Don't think I'm a perv but I remember those cute little shorts you wore, those long legs." He laughed as if to dismiss it.

"That's okay. That's how guys describe girls, I think," she said.

He laughed in acknowledgement. "I was single. All the guys thought you were a catch. Max was really in love with you. Who wouldn't have been?"

She smiled. Who wouldn't have been in love with her?

"And he was acting normal," Forrester continued. "I don't know when he changed, when he got all weird and possessive and crazy about you."

"I remember." The memory of that first abusive night flooded back full force. "I can pinpoint it exactly. Like before and after photos. The Christmas party a year into the marriage. I got a bit drunk."

"Oh well, who the hell didn't at those parties?" Forrester laughed dismissively.

"Max didn't. He was stone cold sober when he dragged me out of that party. Said I was flirting."

"And even if you had been, it was a party, flirting a bit is normal."

"I wasn't though. Which is what hurt. I was tipsy and overly effusive." She drew in a deep breath. "I definitely didn't deserve the slap he gave me in the parking lot."

"Bastard," Forrester spit out.

"Thanks. You're the first person I've ever told about that. I was too embarrassed."

Forrester growled an unintelligible sound.

She should have started talking about it openly back then, because it felt good hearing an outside take on it. "That's definitely an improvement on my part. Starting to remove myself mentally from all that, the occasional slap or push I would dismiss the next day as him being drunk, thinking he'd never do it again."

"You were in love, wanted your marriage to work. You weren't an idiot," Forrester reassured, removing the blame from her. "Can't tell you how many wives have shown up in court when the husband has calmed down, wanting charges dropped. You're not alone in that reaction."

A rustling noise came from the back door and a sound almost like someone trying the doorknob. She jumped and sucked in a quick breath.

"What?" Forrester's voice took on an intensity she hadn't heard from him since the night he and Luke had busted into the mountain cabin.

"Nothing." Her pulse said otherwise. "It's a squirrel or possum or a branch or something." She tightened her grip on her gun, put her finger on the trigger and quietly walked toward the kitchen.

"Still jumpy?" he said.

She didn't answer, just padded into the dark kitchen. She approached quietly, then pushed back the pantry door so if someone had been hiding behind it, it would hit them. As the door flew back, she stepped away quickly.

The edge of the door hit the wall with a solid thud.

No one there. The quick pulsing of blood through her body said the house wasn't secure yet.

The back window and door still needed checking. Her pulse kicked into a higher gear. She walked to stand beside the window.

Sucking in a breath, trying to still her heart so she could hear any noise from outside the house, she waited.

Forrester waited, no sound coming through the ear bud tucked into her ear, as if sensing what she was doing. Cops were good about that type of thing.

No further sound came from outside the door. Finally, inhaling deeply, she prepared herself to move the curtain. Just half an inch, she told herself.

Fear of what might be on the other side of that thin sheet of glass raced through her body.

Carl and Max were still controlling her life, damn it. This wasn't right. Nobody should have to come home to this much fear.

Anger was good, anger was her friend. It had kept her from curling into a fetus and crying helplessly so many times.

She embraced the anger, felt it strengthen her to the point that she was prepared to shoot anyone on the other side of that curtain.

She would just move the curtain a tiny bit and peek outside, put an end to this fear.

With a last inhaled breath, she held the gun tightly, pointed it toward the window and moved the curtain aside.

Nothing. There was nothing there. She let her breath out in a whoosh. Then, she looked toward the wood line. Was someone out there, enjoying the fear he'd inflicted?

No. Carl was in jail. And Max was in the ground.

Where? She needed to know where.

The legal proceedings needed to hurry and reach the point where Carl was motivated to divulge where his brother's body lay.

She dropped the curtain and walked back to the living room, trying to regain her voice as she walked. Breathe in for three, out for three.

Then, she looked up the stairs. The upstairs could wait a minute.

"Hey, Forrester," she said, finally. "Sorry about that. It was nothing. I just had to check things out."

He didn't say anything for a long moment. Finally, he spoke. "We're going to keep him locked up for you, Emmy. This man will never get a chance to hurt you again, maximum security prisons and all that."

She nodded, wishing it felt true, felt that any prison could keep her safe from a monster like Carl. "Thanks," she said into the phone. "Thanks for the call."

"All right, if you're sure you're okay?"

"Yep."

"I'll keep you in the loop."

"I appreciate that."

"And Emmy?" His tone softened.

"Yes?"

"My cousin's a really good guy. He didn't come up there looking for you, to investigate you. More than anything, I think once he realized who you were, he wanted to clear you. So he could move forward with you with a clear conscience. Like he'd done his duty as a cop. And maybe clear you as a person of interest for your own well-being."

He waited a second.

She didn't say anything.

"My cousin's a man of honor, Emmy. If you don't want to see him, you won't see him. He's nothing like Max. Nothing."

Was that was the real reason for the call, to put in a pitch for his cousin?

"Thanks, Forrester," she finally said quietly, pushing the words past the lump in her throat. "Thank you for everything that you and Luke did."

"You're welcome, Emmy. If my cousin takes that job up there, I'll be happy for one reason, if no other."

He waited a beat. "Cause maybe the two of you could have a future. Once this gets put to bed."

"Thanks, Forrester. I'll talk to you later." She hung up before he could say anything else.

Once the case got put to bed, then, she could be back in bed with Luke?

The image of the two of them close, skin against skin invaded her mind constantly. With a blistering heat and desire that blasted through her when she remembered their time in bed.

Would she ever be able to see him as just another guy in town? Did she want that?

If she didn't allow herself a relationship because of her hellish time with Max, then Max would have won and be controlling the rest of her life.

The house seemed so much lonelier. Now that she'd spent time with Luke.

But, this was her space. She inhabited this space, this home.

Then she continued with her routine survey of the entire house, making sure everything was secure.

Maybe she'd get a dog. Another living thing in her house waiting for her when she got home.

She laughed. She was really starting to settle in if she was thinking of getting another dog.

The whole last year, having a dog would have been impossible, never knowing where she would stay next, if they would accept pets.

A dog to cuddle with would keep her mind off Luke and the warmth of his body, and his soul. A new dog wouldn't be Charlie. But, what dog couldn't weasel its way into your heart, become the pal you loved.

She set the front door's No-Kick-Ins device then went upstairs to finish her security check, then she'd run a bath, a poor substitute for the warmth she could find in Luke's bed.

Or even from a wiggly lovable pup, for that matter.

The image floated in front of her of a life with a loving man, a cute pup.

And eventually, maybe even a kid or two?

She should be so lucky as to have it all. Did anyone really have it all?

She started the water, picked up a towel and laid it on a chair beside the tub. Then, beside that towel, she set her gun.

Close at hand, ready, more reassuring than any phone call from Forrester saying she was safe.

CHAPTER TWENTY-FIVE

Luke cradled his phone against his shoulder, and cracked open a beer as he lifted the grill cover to check on his fish. "Hey, Forrester. I called about the Carl situation."

"Oh, hey, Cuz. Just got off the phone with our Emmy."

"She's ours now?" Luke laughed.

"You know the old saying, you save someone's life and you become responsible for them."

"Yeah." Luke took a gulp of beer and turned the fish. "How 'bout I take it from here."

"Soon as we get this Carl guy put away for life, she's all yours." Forrester laughed his old familiar laugh, the soundtrack to much of Luke's life. Forrester's voice was deeper than it'd been as a kid, but the laugh was the same—knowing, smartass.

"Then, let's speed this show up with Carl," Luke said.

"What'd you have in mind?" He'd bet money Forrester already knew what Luke was thinking.

"I'm still technically a cop for about another week or two," Luke said. "How about we go a little good cop, bad cop on Carl's ass?"

"Oh, let me guess." Forrester chuckled. "You want to be the bad cop."

"Don't think I can help be anything but bad cop with the jerk who did all this to Emmy."

"His lawyer will have to be there."

"No problem. Who is his lawyer?"

Forrester mentioned a name they were both very familiar with.

"That guy's okay. He's not a media whore, wanting to get on TV as much as possible, or use this case to get public notice. He once told me, 'I don't try to get my clients off. I just try to get them justice'."

"Yeah," Forrester agreed. "He's not a bad sort. He might not care if we bully his client a bit in the name of justice."

Luke snorted. "That's what I'm hoping. You think if you give him a call he might make his client available to us?"

"Stranger things have happened," Forrester said, the sound of a beer popping coming through the phone.

"You just get home?"

"Yeah," Forrester mumbled, as he slurped down some beer. "Called Emmy even before I got myself a beer." He waited a beat. "She's as jumpy as a bass at feeding time."

Luke grunted acknowledgement of the message, even as a fierce rage spiked up in his belly at the reminder of all Carl had put Emmy through. "Let's get this show on the road. Call our lawyer acquaintance and see if we can arrange to meet his client tomorrow."

"Yeah." Forrester took another long gulp of beer, then burped.

"Nice," Luke said.

245

"Yes, sireee."

Forrester had something else he wanted to talk about. It was in the tone of his voice, his words getting longer, like he was stalling on getting to the point.

He'd done that since he was a kid. If he only knew how easy he was to read by their inner circle of cop friends and close family. Everyone joked about it.

Forrester didn't say anything for a long moment, then cleared his throat. "I hear you might be taking a job up there."

"News travels fast."

"I got a call from the police chief of Hawk's Peak," Forrester said.

"What'd he say?"

Forrester laughed uncomfortably. "Wanted to know if you're still postal."

Luke threw back his head and laughed. "The things folks say about you when you're not listening."

"Yeah. He asked if you're ready to get back in the swing of the cop business. I said if you'd gotten interested in some young thing you might be trusted to take your gun out of the holster."

Luke chuckled. Then, it flashed on him just how far he'd come, to be able to joke and laugh, and not take it personal that people were worrying about him.

"Yeah, I'm gonna be just fine," he said. "But, actually Grant got to me first. I agreed to be an investigator with the sheriff's department.

"Will the circle be unbroken?" Forrester quipped. "Working with our old buddy. Seems right."

Then, he was quiet for a long moment before he said in a gruff tone. "If I can't have you working with me, I like that it's Grant you'll be working with. He's a good guy."

"Hmm," Luke agreed, then he growled, "Set up this jail thing with Carl for tomorrow?"

"I'll let you know," Forrester said.

"I'll see ya at the jail, Cuz."

Luke hung up and took the fish off the grill. He probably needed to brush up on his tough guy face.

It'd give him something to do after dinner rather than think about Emmy.

Emmy. Damn. Just a phone call and a short drive away.

Yeah, he needed to find Max's body, put that issue to bed.

His tough guy face wouldn't be hard to achieve. Just think how this jerk might be all that stood between him and Emmy.

And a bed?

He and Forrester needed to intimidate the smarmy bastard, get him to tell them where the body was. And then Emmy could feel like all the bad stuff was behind her.

Then maybe she'd only be an arm's length away.

Damn. A guy could dream.

He sucked down another long gulp of beer.

Luke sat beside Forrester in the jail's holding room, rage pulsing through him, looking for a release.

"You pissed off?" Forrester slanted a look at Luke, then began laughing like when they were kids.

"Don't distract me, being pissed off is my job today," Luke growled

"Oh yeah, it is." Forrester continued chuckling quietly.

Luke stood up and threw his chair across the room. The cheap, plastic chair bounced off the wall and hit the floor hard. He glared at his cousin and Forrester shut up his laughing, instantly.

"It's working for ya." Forrester stood and picked up the chair, set it upright, then pushed it further away from Luke before sitting in it. "I'm not sure if you're demonstrating or are really out of control."

Luke hit his fist into the palm of his other hand then pointed a finger at Forrester. "Your job is to pull me off him if I lose it completely and start really trying to kill the guy."

"Gotcha," Forrester said. He looked away, not making eye contact. If a gorilla charges you, don't look it in the eye. And for God's sake, don't run.

Just sit there and wait it out.

Luke would have laughed at how intimidated Forrester looked for once in his life.

He would have laughed if he weren't so filled with fury, like a beast ready for dinner. He was minutes away from facing down the man who'd made Emmy's life a living hell, had tried to kill her.

Voices sounded dimly through the locked door and the beast inside of Luke stood, ready to pounce. The door squeaked open and a guard walked in, followed by an inmate.

Who wasn't Carl.

Luke looked at the guy and waited for an explanation.

"Got your boy here, boss," the guard said, looking at Forrester. "And here comes his lawyer." He turned to walk out, holding the door open for the lawyer to walk in. "Knock on the door when you're done with him."

"Hey, hey, hey!" Forrester yelled at the guard, just before he let the door close. "You got the wrong guy here."

The guard stepped back into the doorway and shook his head. "Nope. They said to bring the guy who was in cell block C 49." He looked at them, blandly. "He was in cell block C 49."

"There's a mistake," Forrester ground out through tight jaws. "Get your supervisor. We're here for Carl Weber. White guy, early thirties, blondish brown hair…" His voice trailed off as all four of them looked at the inmate who actually fit that description but still wasn't Carl.

The lawyer looked confused. "This isn't my client."

"Get the sergeant," Forrester said. "Quick!" The guard sprinted out the door.

A smirk sneaked up the inmate's face.

"Oh, hell no." Luke jumped up, grabbing him by the collar, jerking it tight so the man almost squealed with alarm. "Get that look off your face. I've only got another week on the force. I got nothing to lose."

The blood drained out of the guy's face.

Luke twisted the material of the prisoner's jumpsuit tighter, reeling him in like a fish until their faces were inches apart. "What's going on?" Luke growled into the guy's face.

The inmate turned his head to the side, like Forrester had, not wanting to look an aggressive animal in the eye.

Luke jerked him again. "Talk. What's going on?

"I don't know what you're talking about, man." His voice was raspy and dry.

The heavy door opened, saving the prisoner an ass-kicking. Luke shoved him into a chair and turned toward the sergeant.

The sergeant looked down at the prisoner. "What's he doing in here?"

The inmate pulled an innocent face. "Don't know, man, they just dragged me down here."

Luke jumped forward half a step toward him, and the prisoner pulled backward as far as the plastic chair allowed.

"You'd better be careful or I'm gonna pull that stupid face right off you," Luke growled like the animal he felt inside of him pacing back and forth, wanting flesh, the pound of flesh Carl owed Emmy.

The prisoner slumped down, slinking as far into his orange jumpsuit as possible. As if that would protect him from Luke's rage.

The sergeant pointed at the prisoner dismissively. "I wasn't asking you." He looked at Luke and Forrester. "You guys. What's up?"

"By the way, congratulations on your retirement." The sergeant extended his hand to Luke and Luke shook it.

"Sorry about your wife, though. That must've been rough. She was a pretty lady, and sweet."

"No more niceties," Forrest interrupted. "No offense, Sarge, but we got ourselves a situation here. We're here to interview Carl Weber. And this ain't him." He jerked a thumb toward the inmate.

The sergeant looked down at the inmate. "Course that isn't him." He opened the door and yelled down the hall. "Get this guy out of here and bring down Carl Weber."

Another guard walked up. "The other guy went to check out the mix up."

A nervous feeling began crawling through Luke's gut. Something was going on here. There'd been nothing normal about this case since the very beginning.

Why should now be any different?

He looked over at Forrester and he had that look on his face too.

"You getting the same feeling I am?" Luke asked.

"It ain't a good one." Forrester's mouth turned down.

Luke pulled out his cell phone. "Damn, there's no reception in this place."

"It's like a bomb shelter in here." Forrester began to pace the small room.

"You ain't s'posed to have cell phones in here," the inmate said, forgetting his fear of Luke once he thought he *had* something on him.

"Shut up," the sergeant, Luke and Forrester all said in unison.

"I'm going outside. Come get me when they find him," Luke said. *If they find him.* He didn't want to say it, but his mind was going there. Something was fishy, on a case that had *fishy* written all over it from the start.

He nodded to the sergeant who hit the security code to unlock the door to the room. Then, Luke sprinted outside to the parking lot where he hit redial.

He had to get hold of Emmy. Now.

The phone rang and rang. "God, let her answer her phone." Long seconds of ringing, then voice mail. "Damn it." He waited through the message, which seemed to take forever. "Call me as soon as you get this, Emmy. Immediately. It's an emergency!"

He hung up and immediately dialed again.

Voice mail again.

He hung up and called The Corner Store.

"Corner Store, Callie."

"Callie, it's Luke Bradenton."

"Detective Luke," she sing-songed.

"Yeah, no time for fun. Is Emmy there?"

"Nooo," Callie stretched the word out.

"Do you know where she is?"

"No." Her voice tightened, all joking gone.

"Listen," he said. "I've got a real bad feeling. You need to be on the lookout in case Carl Weber shows up. I'm going to call the sheriff and the police chief right now. If you hear from Emmy, tell her to call me."

"I'm locking the back door right now," she said, her voice tight, obviously realizing the gravity of the situation. "You think Carl's out?"

"I'm thinking so. I'll let you know when I find out for sure." He heard the loud click of Callie locking the door. "Do you have a gun around, Callie?"

"Yes, I do," she said emphatically. "Don't usually keep it out 'cause nothing ever happens around here. Just keep it in case I get a case of the willies locking up at night. Sounds like it might be a good idea to get it out."

"Yeah, definitely. Listen, sorry to be such an alarmist. I'm sure the cops will keep a good eye out on the roads into town."

"But no harm in being overly cautious," she interrupted him.

"That's right. I'll call if I hear anything." He hung up and dialed the police chief, then his buddy Grant, the sheriff, filling both of them in, telling them he'd call if he heard anything different.

Experience told him that really scary dudes had walked out of the Fulton County Jail before. Not the first time a murderer got let out by mistake. Or on purpose.

He tried Emmy's phone again. He was leaving a message when Forrester came charging out of the door at a dead run.

"Get in!" he yelled needlessly cause Luke was already on the other side of the car, just waiting as Forrester hit the unlock button. Then, they jumped in.

"They let out the wrong guy, right?" Luke ground out.

"Yeah." Forrester screeched backward, turned the wheel and roared out of the parking lot, heading toward the Perimeter Highway, the quickest way to get around the city.

Highway 85 was the fastest route out of town to Hawk's Peak. But, it seemed like it was a state away as Forrester turned on his blue lights, getting in the fast lane.

"One guess where he's headed," Luke said through clenched teeth.

"We don't know that. Why would he head up there again? It wouldn't make sense."

"Yeah, well none of this makes any sense," Luke said. "I just don't want to take the chance that's where he's going. So, what's the story on him getting out?"

Forrester shook his head. "That inmate they brought in to us?" He raised an eyebrow.

"Tell me."

"He was wearing Carl's wristband."

Luke cursed loudly. "Someone had to have paid a lot of money for that to happen."

"I know. The guy said that was the wristband they put on him. Says he never even looked at it."

It wasn't possible.

"Sounds like Carl has some contacts at the Fulton County jail. I can't figure out where he's getting his money. Drugs maybe?" Forrester gripped the wheel as he wove in and out of traffic, swerving around vehicles that didn't get out of the way fast enough.

"That guy and Carl were actually cell mates," Forrester continued. "What's the odds of that? He said Carl kept saying he had some unfinished business to take care of. Said Carl seemed really ticked off about something."

"What's different about that from any other inmate?" Luke answered. "Most of them are pretty pissed off in general. Even before they go to jail."

Then, he cursed a long blue streak. "Good thing for that prisoner I wasn't standing across from him when he spurted that bullshit about not knowing anything was up."

Forrester laughed darkly. "I jerked him out of that chair and against the wall for you. Made the sarge and the asshole's lawyer pull me off him."

"Thanks. I'd have done it for you," Luke answered.

Luke began making calls to confirm to the police chief, the sheriff and Callie what he'd only suspected when he'd first talked to them.

"This is like some horror movie." Forrester shook his head in disbelief. "Where the monster keeps coming back again and again."

"Carl should have stayed in jail where he was safe." The acid in Luke's stomach churned. The rage inside him needed an outlet.

Carl had escaped and that was a legitimate excuse to kill him. Yeah, the guy should have stayed in jail. Cause now, he'd given himself the death penalty.

And Luke would be a willing executioner.

Forrester pressed down on the accelerator, racing toward a confrontation with a monster. Carl was worse than a horror film creation. He was a monster that had taken human form and thus was harder to detect as he crawled among normal people.

But not for much longer. His time was running out.

CHAPTER TWENTY-SIX

"I need my car," Luke spit out as they neared the exit where he'd parked his Jeep in order to ride with Forrester.

His cousin glanced at him but apparently realized he wasn't going to broach any opposing points of view.

Forrester accelerated off the expressway to the park and ride lot where they'd met. His blue lights on, he slowed at the intersection then went on through.

Seconds later, Luke jumped out. "I've still got my scanner, the mobile one, but it's not as good as yours so let me know if I miss anything."

He jumped in his car and followed Forrester and his blue lights as he roared back toward the freeway. Together, they barreled up Interstate 85 toward the mountains, Forrester putting his foot down heavy on the gas, Luke close on his tail.

Seconds later, Luke hit his blue tooth when Forrester dialed in. "Yeah?"

"They've spotted the car Carl was seen in when he left out of the jail. It's crossing the county line," he paused briefly, then continued, "heading toward your girl."

A fierce hurricane of fury unleashed inside of him,

the storm building in strength as it barreled toward the landmass of Carl's body.

"He's insane," Luke ground out.

"Tell me about it." Forrester bit off a blistering curse. "His insanity defense may hold up in court, after all."

"If he lives long enough to make it to court," Luke growled.

"Hey buddy, don't go off and ruin your exit from the department."

"Are you kidding me?"

"Let *me* kill the bastard, instead," Forrester said darkly. "I could use a little paid time off, a little administrative leave. Hope the guy gives me an excuse."

"Killed a cop, kidnapped three people, attempted to kill them, escaped jail. Plenty of excuses already." Luke steered behind Forrester as he changed lanes to pass a car in front of them that didn't move over.

"Wish I had time to ticket that guy," Forrester said.

"Yeah, waste your anger on that lady." Luke barked out a laugh. "Or just save it for someone who really needs it. Someone who needs killing."

"Gotcha, Cuz." Forrester's tone sounded like he could chew up bullets. "I'm gonna hang up and drive now. I want to be the first one who gets a bead on this guy."

Luke disconnected. Then, immediately hit redial for Emmy's number. "Damn it, Emmy, pick up your phone."

A cracking knock on her front door sounded as if

someone was trying to break it down. Emmy jumped, alarm rocketing through her body. Every muscle tensed and shockwaves shot through her nerve endings.

Then she remembered it was probably just the cop who'd been parked outside her house all morning. Still, it showed how on edge she was. She walked to the window to peek outside.

Just the cop.

She'd known it but still had freaked. The cop stood, waiting politely for her to open the door.

His K9 dog sniffed around the bushes, making use of them for the reason all dogs thought they were invented. Marking his territory.

She opened the door and smiled at the cop. "Hey."

"Emmy, they need my dog down at the county line. Got a big search going on. Carl's surrounded. They're going to send another patrol car out here but I figure you'll be fine since they've got him surrounded way down there. You feel okay out here alone, just till the other deputy gets here?"

Carl was out. And they had him surrounded. She could only hope he got what he deserved when they found him, for running, for killing Max, for all he'd put the McClouds through. The guy was begging to be killed in a big shootout with a bunch of ticked off cops.

Those cops deserved to go home to their families at the end of the day. Whereas, Carl deserved to go home to meet his maker.

"Go." She waved the deputy off. "Go get him. Don't let him get away."

He smiled and nodded, compassion written all over his face. Such a nice change from the way cops in

Atlanta used to look at her, as if they knew she was guilty and they just hadn't proved it yet.

"I've got my gun. I'm okay."

He nodded. "Come on, Jocko. Let's go get this son of a..." he trailed off, shooting her an abashed look. "Sorry."

She laughed darkly. "Any cuss word you can come up with wouldn't begin to describe what a sorry son of a...gun he is."

The deputy grinned at her. "Yes, ma'am." Then, he loaded his dog and sped out the driveway in a cloud of dust.

She walked back into the house, locked the door, fastened her No-Kick-Ins in place and un-muted the sound on the television. Then, she picked up her cell phone.

"Oh, man. Dead." The cell phone's battery was always running low. She really needed to get a new one. "And I can," she laughed out loud to herself.

What a luxury to have enough money that if she wanted to get a new phone, she could just do it. Didn't have to worry about every penny, knowing at any moment, she might have to run.

And the money she might have spent on a new phone might have been needed for a deposit on a room somewhere, or gas money.

"I'm buying me a new phone. A smart one this time." She plugged her phone in to charge and went to the fridge for a diet root beer.

"And I'm gonna get me a dog," she announced to the empty room. "Going out to the animal shelter and getting a dog."

She looked around the kitchen. "And some plants."

A nervous laugh bubbled up inside of her. She touched the pistol tucked into the waist of her jeans.

As if on automatic pilot, when the cop had shown up at her front door saying Carl had escaped somehow, she'd gone upstairs and changed into long pants, and put on her best tennis shoes, tying them tightly.

She'd found her purse, put extra bullets inside, and all her money.

She'd walked toward her car before the cop had stopped her, saying she was safer here than anywhere else cause cops and sheriff's deputies all over the county were watching for this guy.

He might have been right. She'd just reacted as she'd always done.

Get ready to run, get beyond his reach, live another day, her gut had yelled. Cause she didn't want to die today.

An intense urge to run filled her again, panic crying out for distance between her and Carl, yelling for her to get away from her last known location. From the place Carl might know about.

She paced the floor, looking at her phone, waiting for it to charge enough so she could power it up.

Then, the CNN newscaster began talking about the search for the escaped murderer. She spun and headed toward the TV.

Cable television was one luxury she'd already allowed herself, getting that the first week after Carl had been captured. It was paying off since she'd been following the coverage out of Atlanta all morning of *Search for a Cop Killer*, as they'd repeatedly called the event. A good catchy name always increased viewership.

Helicopter aerials showed cops swarming a heavily wooded area. It didn't seem like there was even enough room for a man to run between them, they were so closely spaced as they moved through the thick vegetation, large guns drawn, pointed inward toward the epicenter of the circle.

Nothing agitated the blood of cops like a cop killer.

"The escaped prisoner headed straight back toward the area where he is accused of taking three hostages only a month ago. It would seem as if he's determined to get the woman he says killed his brother." A beautiful blonde looked at her co-anchor, an African American male who had quickly become one of Emmy's favorites.

The blonde looked at him. "Could he be this...careless," she said. Emmy felt certain she'd wanted to say *stupid.*

"We like *careless* criminals," the male anchor answered seriously. "They're our best resource in the fight against crime."

If only Carl *was* stupid. He'd been smart enough to chase her from state to state, almost succeeding in killing her and the McClouds, making hers look like a suicide, and almost getting away with his own brother's murder for more than a year.

With her dead, all the life insurance money would have gone to him. He'd almost gotten away with it.

Coming back didn't make sense. After all, hadn't he escaped jail so he wouldn't have to pay for his crimes? He'd been so careful for an entire year. Still...

The slowly creeping fear she'd felt sneaking up on her all morning began to run—began to sprint straight to her brain, racing in alarm, and shrieking with panic.

This was not what it seemed. An idiotic lunatic determined to avenge the death of his brother?

No.

She bolted for the kitchen to grab her phone, then slung her purse across her body and ran to the window.

Peeking outside, all the feelings she'd lived with the last year and had sworn never to feel again swept through her. Desperation, terror, hopelessness.

It wasn't over.

Nausea boiled up inside of her and she went to the bathroom and threw up, heaved until she was empty. Empty—a feeling she recognized from the last year. It was usually accompanied by its friends—loneliness and social isolation.

She flushed the toilet, washed her mouth out, and then brushed her teeth, taking her time, removing the foul taste from her mouth.

She rinsed and spat, then looked at herself in the mirror and saw the anger in her eyes, the rage because this man thought he could destroy her peace of mind and take away the life she'd begun to build.

"Hell no," she said to her reflection. "Hell no. We're not running anymore."

Something had clicked inside of her. A fierce anger beat back the fear, anger at anyone thinking he could take everything from her. She'd already lost so much time spent with her Grampa, when it seemed there might be so little of it left.

She was done running. He'd found her before, he'd find her again. She might as well take her stand here. Pain shot through her jaw and she realized she was grinding her teeth.

Forcing herself to loosen her jaw, she took long slow

breaths, while visualizing herself wining against evil, having the life she wanted and deserved, here with people who cared about her.

She pictured herself walking a little dog along the riverbank, coming back to the house to make lunch for her and her Grampa. She could see it all. And, with every determined breath she took, she willed it to happen.

She wasn't running. This would end today.

She pulled her hair back into a ponytail and fastened it with an elastic band. Then, she walked to the hall closet and took a baseball cap and tucked it down tightly over her hair.

She took a small backpack out of the closet and dropped her purse into it, added extra bullets, and zipped it up tightly.

In the kitchen, she added a few granola yogurt bars, a bottle of water and a diet root beer. Tucking in some paper towels, she leaned under the sink and pulled out bug spray.

She sprayed the bottom of her jeans and shoes then tucked the canister into an outer compartment of the backpack, along with the pair of binoculars that had been sitting on the counter.

She was ready.

Ready to face down her stalker. Someone was going to end up dead. Preferably him. But either way, the fear was over.

Fight or flight?

She chose fight.

Chapter Twenty-Seven

Luke clicked his Bluetooth phone connection on. "Talk to me."

"They've found Carl," Forrester clipped off the words quickly. "Nowhere near Emmy. He was down on I-20 heading the other direction out of Atlanta," Forrester said, triumph in his voice. "We were right, he wouldn't head straight back to Emmy."

"So, who are the cops looking for at the county line then?" Luke said, pushing his foot down on the accelerator. He had to get to Emmy.

"I'll let you know when we catch him."

Something in Luke prayed it was Max, that the guy hadn't gotten off so easy for all he'd done to Emmy by just a bullet in the head.

That guy needed a lifetime of sitting in prison, with only his rage for company.

Let him sit in a cement holding pen, frothing about his inability to get his hands on her. Luke would make sure he'd be sent to a hardcore, maximum-security prison.

"Okay, I'm hanging up now," Luke said. "Cause I'm driving like a maniac, uh, I mean like a cop on a mission."

Forrester laughed. "Go take care of our girl. I can't believe they pulled that canine deputy from her house."

"They thought they were doing the right thing," Luke said begrudgingly. "Resources are limited up here. Thought they had a cop killer cornered. If they get the guy who was driving the car, they'll know who helped Carl get out."

Who had done that? A feeling roiled in his gut that had been growing all morning long.

"Damn it, why isn't Emmy answering her phone?" He let loose with a long string of curses.

"Yikes, my ears are bleeding." Forrester barked a dark laugh. "How close are you?" That question indicated the level of worry eating at Forrester.

"Less than ten miles." Another phone call tried to click in. "Hey, gotta go, that's Emmy."

"Thank God." Forrester clicked off.

"Hey, where are you?" Luke said before Emmy could say anything.

Her voice was low and quiet when she answered him. "I'm in the woods."

His heartbeat accelerated.

"I'm almost there. Where in the woods?"

"Don't come here," she whispered.

What the hell?

"Is someone there?"

"No, it's just me, so far. Listen." Her voice resonated with power and strength. She sounded like anything but a victim. "I'm in the woods across the road from the driveway into my house. Do not come here, you'll ruin everything. I'm going to get him myself when he comes in after me."

"They found Carl. He was all the way on the other side of Atlanta, hightailing it to Alabama."

"This is Max coming for me." The conviction in her voice was compelling. "This is so his style."

The image of her facing Max, alone, flooded through him like a spring thunderstorm, the kind that foreshadowed tornadoes, with winds that could rip houses apart, strewing bodies across the mountains.

"I will not leave you on your own with Max, if that's who this is. That's crazy, Emmy. I'm coming there."

"It *is* Max," she said resolutely. "And he'll see you and then he'll just wait for another time when I'm less prepared. He thinks he's caused enough distraction with everyone looking for Carl. I know him, Luke," she said, vehemence lacing every word.

"He will come today. He's built up to the exploding point. He sent Carl and that didn't work. Now, he's crazy to get me dead."

She sucked in a long breath. "I cannot live this way, running in fear. I want it over, one way or the other."

The image of *the other* flashed through his head. Emmy's body lifeless, all of that energy that flowed through her terminated, put into the ground. Damn if that would happen today.

"I know a back way in there, a trail that leads from the road over behind the woods across from your house. Forrester and I used to hike through there to get to the river."

She didn't say anything.

"Leave your phone on so I can find you," he said, encouraged she didn't argue with him. "I couldn't get hold of you this morning."

She sighed. "I can't. My phone is almost dead. I'll

turn it on in a bit to check for messages. Text me where you are when you get in here. I'll text you back."

He wouldn't try to talk her out of this anymore. The fear she'd lived with for so long was incomprehensible. Just this morning's drama and when she'd been taken hostage by Carl had been almost more than he could bear. And he wasn't even the intended target.

She'd been driven beyond the limits of human endurance. He'd seen it before in his cop career, people turning on the person who'd tormented them for so long.

It wasn't a pretty sight, the animal fierceness that overtook them when they finally decided to strike back.

No, change that. It was a beautiful thing, the strength of the human spirit. The will to survive.

He turned left, beginning the circuitous route that would take him to a spot on the other side of the woods across from her place. It would allow him to sneak in undetected.

Then, he was gonna hike in for all he was worth. All Emmy was worth. To save the person who'd made living worthwhile again for him.

She might decide he wasn't the man for her. But he'd be damned if anybody else would make that decision for her.

"I'll have my phone on. Give me a call if you need me," he said quietly, holding onto the phone tightly, not wanting to break the connection.

"Thanks," she said. "For not telling me what I have to do. Thanks for the help." Her voice quavered on the last word and, as if she didn't trust herself to speak anymore, she clicked off.

That silence, the lack of connection terrorized him,

with its empty space. An empty space that could so easily become permanent.

A person could just disappear from the planet. Like his wife had done. But that had been a force beyond the control of humans.

A human taking Emmy off the planet?

Damn that person to hell. He would not let that happen.

His phone buzzed again and he hit his Bluetooth. "Talk to me."

"Hey," Forrester said, darkness in his voice. "We got the guy in the woods. He's on probation, running drugs up north for *someone*, says he doesn't know who let Carl out. Said he was just told to pick him up. I think this guy was a decoy all along, to get all our resources over there."

A sinking feeling hit Luke hard.

"I think you're right. So does Emmy."

"I'll get everyone headed up there to her place right away."

"No, don't."

"Why not?"

"Emmy thinks Max is coming for her. She's determined to take him out."

Forrester cursed harshly. "Okay, so let's get everybody up there."

"Just listen. She's hiding in the woods across from her house."

"What the hell?"

"Says she's gonna take him out."

"Herself?"

"I know, I know, sounds crazy, but this has been going on for a year. Longer if you count the time she lived with him and was afraid to leave him. Can you really blame her for wanting to end it now."

"This does sound like him," Forrester said viciously. "I never told you about something that happened 'cause I didn't want to speak ill of the dead, to influence you not to believe in the search for his killer."

He sucked in a long, tormented breath. "But Max got a burr under his saddle about Roberto. Thought the guy had done something to him." He laughed harshly. "Then, me, Roberto, and Max all ended up working together on a standoff. We ended up having to go in before the SWAT team got there, 'cause a mother and child were in danger. I was behind Roberto and Max."

"The guy inside got a bead on Roberto. Max had his gun trained on the guy. I thought he would take him out. Before I could get my gun turned that way, the guy shot Roberto."

He waited a beat. "Max never took the shot. I would have but I didn't have the angle, was covering the other corner. Max never took the shot. Said later that he didn't have the angle. But, he did. He had the perfect angle."

He cursed. "I didn't report it, didn't write him up. Kept thinking I had to have been wrong. But I used to dream about it all happening again, night after night. One of the reasons I got off that task force. I couldn't get past the fact I was on a team with a guy who if he got a grudge against me, would just let someone shoot me."

He breathed deeply for a moment, a raspy chainsaw sound cutting through the phone line. "I should have done more to get him off the police force for good. But, I thought nobody would believe it. I didn't want to believe it. And, I was the one who saw it. The only one."

"Enough," Luke cut him off. "We're not gonna let that son of bitch make all of us think we're the bad guys. We're gonna take him out today, me and Emmy. He's done. After your story, I believe this guy would have the need to make her understand she can't do this to him."

"How can I help?"

He thought about it for a long moment. What would be the best, how not to alert this guy, how to have the assistance he might need but still be low key enough to get the job done once and for all?

"This is what we're gonna do," he said. And Forrester listened.

———

Emmy held her breath listening. A crackle of leaves over the hill could be the wind through the leaves, it could be a squirrel.

Or it could be Max.

Her pulse beat in her head so loud she wasn't sure which noises were imagined and which were real.

She listened intently and waited, her gun trained toward the sound, at the ready.

She'd chosen the highest spot she could find, and built herself a little hiding spot, branches she'd pulled together to camouflage herself.

Picking up her binoculars, she trained them on the spot where she'd heard the noise. Finally, she saw it.

A squirrel. He ran up over the hill, followed by another squirrel. Together, the two of them foraged through the leaves, looking for acorns to store for the winter.

It was going to be a hard winter, from all the acorns she'd seen on the ground. The squirrels were as intent to ensure their survival as she was. She felt a kinship with these little creatures with so much going against them. Predators on the ground throughout the woods, hawks circling above, yet they kept on plugging away, looking for nuts to take them through the winter.

She watched them for a moment, knowing their presence meant no one was sneaking up on her yet from that angle. The squirrels would be an early warning system for her. She hoped they stayed there for a long time.

How long had it been since she'd spoken to Luke? It was hard to keep track of time without her cell phone on.

Maybe thirty minutes. Could he have gotten here by now? She didn't want to end up shooting him or getting shot by him.

She hit the power button on her cell phone and waited for it to come up. She'd put it on silent before she'd left the house so she didn't have to worry about any beeping noises giving away her location.

There it was, a text from Luke. He was nearby. She looked around. Had she missed him? If so, what did that say about her detection skills?

Where are you? she texted and waited.

Three hills from overlooking your house. Where are you?

At the hill just before the turn into my driveway, she texted back. *Look for me. I'll wave when I see you.*

She waited, glancing back down the hill toward her

house, then back at the faint trail behind her that ghosted away through the trees. Then, again toward her house.

Movement across the river caught her eye, on a trail leading along the river, heading to her house. A male form moved slowly, slipping from hidden location to hidden location.

She trained her binoculars on the form, adjusting the focus, straining to see. Then, the form assumed an identifiable shape. She'd recognize him anywhere.

Adrenalin jolted through her. "Max. Damn you. I knew you were alive. Damn you to hell," she whispered, pushing the fear, panic and hatred out of her system with the words.

A faint noise behind her almost caused her to scream.

"It's me," Luke whispered. "It's me."

She jerked around, meeting his eyes, knowing by the expression in his that he read her alarm.

He crept the last few feet to her side, following the finger she pointed in the direction Max had been just a second before. But Max was gone. Putting the binoculars to her eyes, she traveled along the riverbank, searching for him.

"Found him," she whispered. She looked left and Luke had his own binoculars pointed where she'd indicated.

He pulled them back to meet her gaze, his expression disbelieving, shocked, all the emotions that ran through her. It was too hard to believe.

Even though she'd known it would be true.

"Stay here," he said, his hand fastened to her shoulder, reassuring but also keeping her in place. "I'm going down there."

"Oh, hell no." She shrugged his hand off her shoulder. "I'm not staying here, waiting and wondering if you're okay."

He shook his head.

She met that with a firm headshake of her own head. "I'm not letting him get away. This ends today. With him dead or going to prison. I don't care which. And we have a better chance of getting him if we go together."

"No," Luke said, with all the strength of his being. He had to convince her not to go down that mountain where Max could get his hands on her. "I'd like him in prison, or dead. But more than I want him dead, I want you alive."

He peered into her eyes, those beautiful river colored eyes and willed her to accept this. Damn the color of those eyes.

If anything happened to her, if he lost her, he'd never be able to look at that river again, without feeling the pain, the stabbing loss of all that might have been between them.

Because he knew without a doubt, that when this was behind her, as soon as she could breathe without doing that one two three count, there'd be a chance for something between them that might last a lifetime.

She smiled at him, and for just another moment, he wanted to relish her alive, wanted to connect with her. He leaned his forehead toward her and she followed suit, touching her forehead to his. He placed one hand in her hair, holding her there, holding her in his life.

Alive.

CHAPTER TWENTY-EIGHT

Together, they crept down the hill, keeping Max in sight as he snaked forward, slowly stalking the house, like some evil creature emerging from the woods.

But nothing existed in nature like him. He couldn't have been born that way. He had to have grown that way. What was his upbringing that he and Carl both would turn out so hateful and evil?

Luke stopped and texted something on his phone. She looked at him with raised eyebrows. "Forrester," he mouthed.

She nodded. Good, backup they could count on being subtle.

He waited for a second, reading a return text from Forrester. Then, he pointed toward the hill where they'd been.

She squinted up that way, but couldn't see anything. Max was well hidden.

Slowly, they descended the hill. At the bottom of the hill, they lost sight of Max. But, hopefully Forrester could still see him, maybe even get a bead on him.

Would it be legal to just take him out like that, without even giving him a chance to give himself up?

She knew, morally, it would be justifiable for all that he'd done, all that she knew he intended to do.

He'd kept himself hidden this whole last year and now was sneaking up on her home. For what reason would he come here? Except to finish the job his brother hadn't been able to do.

She motioned back toward the hill, then toward her eyes, then toward the direction of Max, raising her eyebrows in a question. Could Forrester see Max?

Luke shook his head.

Forrester didn't have a bead on Max.

She nodded in acknowledgement, then tilted her head toward the road. As they crossed the road, they'd be out in the open.

Luke held up three fingers, then did a countdown to one. At one, they both bolted from the cover of the woods and ran across the asphalt.

A bullet could take either of them out. They pounded through the open air as Emmy anticipated death taking either she or Luke out as quickly and surely as if a hawk dropped out of the sky onto a chipmunk or squirrel.

As she ran, she scanned the trees on the other side of the road.

Where was Max? Where was Max? Where was Max? The question beat in her head in time to her footsteps on the hard pavement.

Could Max hear their footsteps?

Finally, they slipped into the woods on the other side and stopped for a moment, listening for any telltale sign that Max had turned back toward them.

They took cover behind two trees and waited. Emmy held her breath and listened.

The wind whistled along the river, mingling with the watery sounds of the rushing river. She and Luke met eyes and nodded, then Luke pointed a finger toward the driveway that would cross the river and lead to Emmy's house.

Slowly, they made their way toward the driveway, scanning the trees and undergrowth that provided a hundred hiding places. Max could easily pop out at any moment and take one of them out with a practiced shot.

They were going up against a trained warrior, a SWAT officer that knew all the tricks of taking out someone while never being seen.

Luke put his hand on her shoulder, stopping her. He pointed toward his ear.

She held her breath, trying to make out any sound that didn't belong. The sound of footsteps in the leaves, crashing glass at the house.

The river rustled with the reassuring sounds that she loved falling asleep to at night. But now, it was a nuisance, covering up for Max, disguising noises that could give away his whereabouts.

At the same time, it would hide theirs too, and they knew he was out there, hopefully, he hadn't figured they were trailing him. He would be looking toward the house, away from them. She hoped.

Luke moved forward and she followed. They made a good team, communicating without words, understanding exactly what needed doing.

Finally, they reached the spot where they had to cross the bridge over the river. It would leave them exposed again as they ran across it.

Luke pointed at himself and held one finger up. Then he pointed at her and held up two fingers.

Him first, then her.

She nodded and positioned herself behind a tree with her gun extended, scanning the trees across the river, ready to shoot. Then, she held her breath, alert for anything.

Luke ran, exposing himself, taking the chance that had to be taken if they were to go after Max on the other side of the river.

He was halfway across, only about twenty more feet to go, when a shot rang out, skipping at his feet, throwing dirt into the air. Luke threw himself over the side of the bridge, with a huge splash into the river.

Max burst from the woods on the other side of the river and ran onto the bridge, his gun pointed toward the water.

Luke was easy pickings below the bridge. Probably still trying to get his bearings in the deep water, unable to get to his feet, his gun possibly disabled.

Emmy braced herself against the tree and began firing.

Shot after shot, she fired.

They pinged along the bridge, dirt and dust blowing up into the air.

Non-stop, she leveled bullets at Max. When the first several missed him, he stopped and glared at her as if to intimidate her. She hesitated.

Shooting a person wasn't second nature to her. She'd never shot any living thing before, only targets.

To kill someone? The ultimate act of violence? A powerful shudder rippled through her.

Max's eyes met hers and he smiled. "Emily," his deep voice boomed out, controlling, domineering, intimidating. The voice he'd always used to let her know she'd gone too far, that it was time for him to rein her in. Max still thought he had power over her.

That voice had always inspired terror in her. This time, it inspired courage.

She trained her gun on him, aiming for his chest.

"Emily!" he yelled again, as if to warn her that she would pay. Then, he looked away, dismissing her as a real threat, and stepped to the downstream side of the bridge, looking for Luke, to see if the current had taken him underneath the bridge.

All of this had to have taken only seconds because Luke hadn't reappeared yet.

Then, as if he'd seen him, Max leveled his gun toward the river.

And Emmy took her shot.

A killing shot, straight toward his torso.

Max's body seemed to explode as blood shot from his side. Whirling, Max looked at her, shocked and furious.

The rage on his face was familiar, saying she wouldn't dare do this, that she knew what he was capable of and knew that his reprisal would be fierce.

With an ugly twist to his mouth, he raised his gun toward her. Ignoring his controlling gaze, she fired again.

Her bullet struck him in the chest and his gun flew from his hand as he fell to his knees, still gazing at her. Disbelief covered his face.

As he fell sideways, the last expression on his face was comprehension, knowledge that his wife had taken him out, had finally stood up to him. He'd been killed by his wife, his disobedient, non-submissive wife.

That was his dying thought.

Something inside of her screamed out, "Yes. I won't be your victim. I won't."

Max collapsed and lay still, unmoving.

"Luke," she yelled and ran forward. "Are you okay? Where are you?"

Luke struggled up out of the water, on the other side of the river, his gun trained upward toward the bridge.

"I'm okay!" he yelled back. "Don't expose yourself. Stay under cover. He might not be dead."

She watched as Luke crawled up the riverbank, then toward Max's body, his gun trained toward him the entire way. She kept hers on the body as well.

Was it finally over?

She'd expected to feel a weight lifting from her soul when he died. Had expected it to feel like a punch almost hitting her in the stomach, then stopping at just the last second, with such relief, because she would know she was safe.

But, was it really over? Like this?

Luke reached Max, and kicked Max's gun further away, then he toed Max's body.

No movement. Luke leaned down to take a pulse.

And like a demon from hell, Max lunged up, one hand to Luke's throat, the other pushing Luke's gun away, then grabbing onto it, struggling for control of it.

Like a horror movie, he'd erupted to life, arose from the dead.

Emmy ran forward, crossing the bridge, trying to get there in time. The two men rolled, over and over, their bodies intertwined, making it impossible to shoot one without hitting the other.

Then, with superhuman strength, the type that is supplied by incredible hatred and evil, Max forced

Luke's gun upward, toward her, training it on her as she ran.

"Nooo!" Luke yelled, kneeing Max in the groin. Then, as Max crumpled in pain, Luke grabbed Max's gun hand with both of his. He wrenched Max's hand away from the gun and rolled free of him.

Emmy had the space she needed. She took aim.

And shot Max nearly pointblank, sending a killing shot into his chest, then another into his head.

This time, Max had no time to process what had happened to him, his face just went blank, anything that had been human in him vacating, leaving nothing but a body, a shell, with all of the evil gone, sucked from the earth in one powerful whoosh.

He fell limply to the ground, immobile. A long final breath wheezed slowly out of him, and as if it were her own, she counted silently, one, two, three, and felt all the fear, frustration, anger and despair of the last year evaporate into the air with his last breath.

Relief blew through her, lifting a weight from her chest. She could finally breathe freely, easily. She no longer needed the counting coping technique.

Because he was dead. He'd never bother her again, never hurt anyone she loved again.

She was free.

She turned slightly away, so she didn't have to see him, didn't have to look at his lifeless body. He was the past, and now she was looking toward the future, looking at Luke.

Luke sucked in several deep breaths, then put his hand to Max's throat.

"Nothing." He stood and turned his blue eyes on her.

True blue, the true blue of a good cop shone from his eyes. "He's really dead this time," Luke said.

Emmy closed the distance between them with one giant step, fell to her knees and threw her arms around him. She needed to feel him alive, to reassure herself that Max hadn't taken him away from her.

For a long moment, she pressed herself against his body, feeling his heart beat next to her own, felt his skin warm next to hers, his breath against her skin as he pushed his face into her neck, bringing her close against his body as he held her.

Then, she pulled back to look for blood on him. "Are you hurt?"

"Just wet," he said, pulling her tightly against him, again. "I rolled instinctively when he shot, knew it was my only hope." He pulled back to look in her eyes. "And you. I knew I could depend on you."

She smiled into his eyes. "That you can," she said, her voice husky, emotion closing her throat, making it hard to speak.

She pressed her face into his neck, breathing him in.

They were both alive and well.

The future was for them to decide.

CHAPTER TWENTY-NINE

Three days later, all of the reports had been filed with every type of police agency possible. The media coverage had died down.

Carl had been interviewed. And it was clear he'd truly believed that Max was dead by Emmy's hands.

He'd blurted out everything when he learned his brother hadn't been dead until now, stated he thought he was entitled to the insurance money since Emmy had killed his brother.

He'd acted out of anger, vengeance. And, yeah, greed.

Max had played him, used him as his tool, to pursue Emmy, torment her, hoping that finally she would commit suicide, leaving Carl as his only living benefactor.

Even in "death", Max had been playing them all. He'd wanted Emmy dead, wanted to show her who was boss. He'd been unable to accept a woman leaving him.

Later, with her dead, he'd probably believed he would have been able to remotely access Carl's accounts, counted on being able to outsmart his little brother and go on living well with the insurance money from his own death.

But it was all over now.

Emmy was determined to turn her back on her tormentor, her dead husband, and make him just a bad memory. She'd moved on.

"Are you sure you're ready for this?" Luke looked her up and down, as if she were getting ready to jump off a cliff. "Do you need to breathe in and out on a three count?"

She laughed and leaned into him, his arm circled around her back, pulling her close. "No, I'm done with that. I'm sure."

He kissed her softly. "This is what you want?"

"Definitely."

"It's a big commitment," he said, his tone cautionary, warning.

"It's what I want," she said, close to his mouth, watching his lips move.

"If you're sure."

"I am."

"You're sure you've found the one, the perfect one made just for you?" He looked into her eyes, with a warmth that enticed her closer. No one had ever drawn her to him with this perfect blend of attraction and friendship.

"How do you know you've found the right one?" he asked.

"In life, you'll meet ones that are lovable, that gaze at you lovingly, longingly, their eyes calling to you. And you could love them."

She drew in a deep breath.

"But when you find the one, that you can't help loving, the one you can't live without." She shrugged. "Well, you know it."

Luke pulled away, leaning down onto one knee. He looked up at Emmy, then turned and peered into the cage at the little knee-high mutt that looked soulfully at Emmy with huge, brown eyes, unfixed, unwavering, gazing only at her.

As if he knew she was his best hope.

They'd come to the Hawk's Peak Animal Shelter so that Emmy could pick out a dog. It was time.

"It's a lifetime commitment," Luke said, standing and pulling Emmy into him, his hand around her waist.

His eyes were saying this was more than just a conversation about a dog.

She looked down at the mutt. "He's not just a dog," she said lovingly. "He's the future. He's what I expect tomorrow to bring—good things, wonderful things. He needs me and I need him."

"I know how he feels." Luke laughed, low in his chest, transmitting through his skin into her body, the sound tickling down her spine.

"I know he'll never replace Charlie," she said, with just a brief flash of nostalgia for the little dog that had died at Max's hands. "But he and I can have something different, something equally special. This whole last year, I haven't been able to do normal things, like have a dog, have a boyfriend." She looked up into Luke's eyes.

"Boyfriend? Do I need to fill out an application for that position, give you references?"

She smiled up into his eyes. "You're pre-approved." His mouth moved toward hers, ever so slightly.

"The position is yours if you want it," she said, breathlessly, feeling like she needed to practice her three count breathing. But, she purposefully refrained, loving the thrills that ran through her, not wanting to control her feelings, wanting to fully experience this anticipation.

She felt out of control.

In a good way. Because within the safety of Luke's arms, the out-of-control feeling was a good thing, a spiral of emotions and passion that would bring only a wonderful outcome.

His mouth moved toward hers and she didn't want to move above herself to watch. She wanted the full, in-the-moment, physically-there experience of loving Luke.

The dog gave a little bark, demanding her attention. She looked down at him. "There's enough of me to go around, Roscoe. I can love you both."

"You can love us both?" Luke looked down at her, his eyes full of emotion as he inched closer to her lips.

"I can love you both," she confirmed. And knew her future would be wonderful and full of all that decent, good people have a right to expect.

A lifetime commitment?

Might not be a problem.

The End

Read Mick's story
Targeted to Kill
A Men of the Badge Novel

Romantic Suspense at its best, with a keep you up all night reading intensity. Sometimes redemption and second chances at love come with the worst circumstances. Guilt and grief were copartners in the death of Mick Hampton and Becca Jefferson's love. Now, FBi agent Mick Hampton must stop a horrific attack on American soil as well as save the woman he has loved for most of his life.

The undercover operation to stop the attack takes a dramatic left turn when Mick's former fiancé is kidnapped by the terrorists.

Is Becca Jefferson's kidnapping a matter of simple revenge? Or do the terrorists know more than Mick thinks they do?

The operation becomes a desperate attempt to survive for Mick and Becca, while still preventing the murder of countless innocent civilians.

Love is the prize if they survive.

Read Weston's story
Tempted to Kill
A Men of the Badge Novel

The chemistry between Alisa and Weston could be as deadly as the drugs that are readily available in the dark underworld of sex and drug trafficking in Atlanta.

An undercover cop, Weston's job is to "blend in with scum," and go after the big guy in the drug ring. Protecting Alisa as she searches for her missing teen sister could jeopardize the mission as well as his and Alisa's ability to keep breathing.

Read Grant's story

The Killer You Know

A Men of the Badge Novel

Someone is trying to kill Katie Taylor. Does she have information worth killing for? Amnesia after a car crash leaves her unable to remember a lot, like the fact that she is no longer engaged to Sheriff Grant Campbell.

Men of the Badge continues in Hawk's Peak, a small mountain town in North Georgia, where Grant Campbell, a former Atlanta cop, has returned after many years to be sheriff.

Katie Taylor is the love of his life – the woman he loved and lost years ago.

Grant must keep Katie alive long enough to remember the secrets worth killing for, even if it means she remembers she stopped loving him. Even if it costs him, once again, the love of his life.

Riley can be found at:
https://facebook.com/riley.mckissack
http://rileymckissack.com
https://twitter .com/RileyMckissack

JOIN THE RILEY MCKISSACK NEWSLETTER
http://www.rileymckissack.com/contact